A SECRET ES(_ I U
SUNSHINE ISLAND

GEORGINA TROY

Boldwood

First published in Great Britain in 2022 by Boldwood Books Ltd.

Copyright © Georgina Troy, 2022

Cover Design by Leah Jacobs-Gordon

Cover Photography: Shutterstock

The moral right of Georgina Troy to be identified as the author of this work has been asserted in accordance with the Copyright, Designs and Patents Act 1988.

This book is a work of fiction and, except in the case of historical fact, any resemblance to actual persons, living or dead, is purely coincidental.

Every effort has been made to obtain the necessary permissions with reference to copyright material, both illustrative and quoted. We apologise for any omissions in this respect and will be pleased to make the appropriate acknowledgements in any future edition.

A CIP catalogue record for this book is available from the British Library.

Paperback ISBN 978-1-80426-038-8

Large Print ISBN 978-1-80426-037-1

Hardback ISBN 978-1-80426-039-5

Ebook ISBN 978-1-80426-036-4

Kindle ISBN 978-1-80426-035-7

Audio CD ISBN 978-1-80426-044-9

MP3 CD ISBN 978-1-80426-043-2

Digital audio download ISBN 978-1-80426-040-1

Boldwood Books Ltd
23 Bowerdean Street
London SW6 3TN
www.boldwoodbooks.com

To my husband Rob, who loves this island as much as I do

1

Matteo stopped to breathe in the warm salty air before descending the steps from the private jet that had brought him across the English Channel to Jersey. They had flown over the pale golden sand and rolling waves of St Ouen's Bay just moments before and thanks to the cloudless blue sky his flight had been a smooth one. He had made this trip once before as a child, coming with his parents and brother for their summer holiday. Matteo had thought the place exciting and exotic then, and was surprised to find that he still felt the same excitement as his seven-year-old self had done.

Several minutes later he walked out of the private VIP terminal at Jersey Airport to be greeted by his best friend Alex. Matteo smiled at his friend and returned his wave. The pretty girl with the dark hair in a ponytail must be the local girl, Piper, who Alex had told him about during their most recent phone call. She was the first woman Matteo knew of who had completely captured Alex's heart. He noticed her tee shirt and black shorts and, suspecting she was as unimpressed as Alex by expensive fashion, instantly understood why the two of them were attracted to each other. Despite Alex's success, he had never changed and was still the chilled and friendly guy Matteo had always known. It was part of the reason why he had trusted him to find the perfect location for his next music video.

'You're here,' Alex shouted, reaching him and giving Matteo a brief hug and a pat on his back.

'I certainly am.' Matteo smiled, taking a long slow breath in and feeling his shoulders relax for the first time in weeks. 'I feel like I'm on holiday already.' He smiled at the girl standing quietly next to Alex. If he wasn't mistaken she seemed a little nervous. He was used to people not knowing what to expect from him and liked to think that he soon put everyone at their ease. Being a popstar was an odd life even for him. He had had several years to get used to the adulation, but it still seemed unwarranted. 'And I guess you must be Piper. I've heard a lot about you.'

'I am,' Piper said, reaching out her hand to shake his. 'I have to admit I've heard a little about you from Alex, but obviously I've read a lot about you in the media and listened to your music whenever it comes on the radio.'

He liked her and was relieved to note she wasn't a fan. Matteo knew from experience that it would make things easier for the three of them. Not that Alex had introduced him to a girlfriend for several years now. He presumed his friend spent most of his time working on his apps and, Matteo mused, more recently spending time on the island his grandfather seemed to have made his second home.

'You're looking very well, Alex,' he said, happy to see the obvious change in his best friend. 'More relaxed.' He turned to Piper. 'I imagine it must feel like being on a permanent holiday living here.'

Piper thought for a moment. 'I suppose it does in the summer months.' She glanced at Alex. 'Would you like to go straight to the location Alex has found for your video? It's not too far from here.'

He liked that idea. 'Good idea. I'll be relieved to know that we have a location sorted out.' He accompanied them to her Mini. 'I'm sorry for the rush to find somewhere,' he said. 'But when my management team decided to make the most of how well my records were selling and added several more dates to my tour it cut down any available time we had to record this video for my Christmas release.'

'It's fine,' Alex said, getting into the back seat of the car. 'I'm sure you'll be happy with the place we've found for you.'

Matteo relaxed in the car while Piper drove them down a hill with the most incredible view across the wide arc of the bay.

'I love this view,' she said as they went around the lower bend and Matteo was gifted with the most incredible view across St Ouen's Bay.

Surfers rode the rolling waves and a small Martello tower sat on an islet in the sea. He could see the long stretch of golden sand between the pine trees as they drove along the road and sand dunes made a surprise appearance to the right. 'I can see why you thought of this place,' Matteo said, seeing a small plane coming over the bay and landing to the right of them on the hill. 'Did I fly in over this beach earlier?'

'That's right,' Piper said. 'Sometimes the planes come in from over St Catherine's on the east of the island where I live. This is the west.' She pointed up to the right on top of the higher land where more majestic pines stood proudly shading the area. 'That's where we're going and where we suggest you record your video.'

Matteo liked what he had seen so far and was excited to reach the place.

Piper and Alex stood quietly to the side as Matteo took in the huge pine trees surrounding the partially enclosed grassland standing high above St Ouen's Bay. The scent from the pine trees, as their branches swayed gently in the breeze, gave a calming atmosphere to the area and when Matteo spotted the view between the trees down to the beach and out across the rolling waves he stared in silence. It was beautiful here, he decided, imagining it to be the perfect place to build a secluded home with one of the most awe-inspiring views he had ever seen.

'Well? What do you think?' Alex eventually asked, taking hold of Piper's hand. Matteo could see his friend was anxious to have pleased him and smiled.

'It's incredible. I love it.'

Alex's shoulders lowered and he exhaled sharply. 'That's a relief. When Jax suggested this place I wasn't sure if it would be right for what you wanted, but I agree that it's pretty spectacular.'

Piper turned to him, smiling. 'It's on private land too so the production shouldn't have any disturbances apart from the occasional plane taking off or landing over there. Even then, if the wind was in the right direction it wouldn't be a problem.'

'You've done very well.' Matteo was grateful to the pair for coming up with such a beautiful setting. 'I'm very thankful to you both and to—Sorry, who did you say suggested this place?'

'Jax,' Piper said. 'He's my cousin.'

'Now all we have to do is hope the weather stays this fine,' Piper said thoughtfully, looking a second later as if she had wished she'd kept her thoughts to herself. 'I'm sure it will do though. It is summer after all.'

'Bad weather?' The thought concerned Matteo. He didn't want to have to make alternative plans. 'Surely it's going to be fine at this time of year.'

'It should be,' she said, 'but it's not something we can rely on. The island is nestled in the Bay of St Malo, off the French coast, and it's drenched in sunshine for most of the year, but it's still open enough to suffer bad storms either coming up from Paris or down from the English mainland,' Piper explained. 'There aren't any storms forecast though,' she added before he had time to fret. 'So that's good. Probably our worst outcome would be to have fog descend over the island.'

'Fog?'

'Yes, or sea mist. It can settle for several days when it does come in.' She cringed and looked away.

Matteo didn't want to leave anything to chance. He had more than enough to deal with as it was with the filming and preparations for the tour. He saw Alex take his phone from his jeans pocket and begin searching for something.

'What are you looking for?' Piper asked.

'Checking the five-day forecast.' His friend frowned as he scrolled thoughtfully.

'Bad news?' Matteo asked, his mood dipping as he recognised his friend's worried reaction.

Alex shaded his phone from the sun with his hand and squinted at the screen. 'Hopefully not.' He held up his phone for them to see for themselves. 'It says here that there's a storm forecast to come up from Brittany in two or three days.'

'It might pass us by though,' Piper said, hope obvious in her voice.

'Let's hope it does,' Matteo said anxiously as he looked up through the pine needles to the cloudless azure sky.

'Shall we go and find somewhere to buy a cool drink?' Piper suggested. 'I'm parched.'

Matteo assumed she was trying to distract him and was happy for her to do so. He was tired, having set his alarm to wake him at five that morning for his driver to take him to the airport.

'He's not at all like the press make him out to be, is he?' Alex gave Matteo a wink, tipping him off that he was joining Piper in distracting him while they tried to think of a Plan B. 'In fact, growing up he was the shyer one out of the two of us. Isn't that right, mate?'

Matteo nodded. 'Hard to believe now, I imagine.'

'It is.' Piper stared at him as if trying to imagine him being that way.

'I still can't believe he's seen as this cocky, confident superstar,' Alex laughed, slapping Matteo on his back.

Matteo pulled Alex to him, an arm loosely around his friend's neck. 'Are you saying I pretend to be cocky?' He saw the surprise on Piper's face.

Alex laughed. 'No, I'm saying you pretend to be confident.'

Matteo knew Alex wasn't being mean, it was the banter they had with each other. He smiled at Piper. 'It's true. People automatically see the two of us and presume I'm the confident one and Alex is the shy, retiring type.'

Piper listened to him thoughtfully before glancing at Alex. 'I have to admit to thinking the same thing. Although...' She looked unsure whether to continue.

'Go on,' Matteo said, encouraging her to voice her opinion. 'You won't upset me: I've got a thick skin nowadays.'

'I was actually thinking of Alex when I first met him,' she said thoughtfully. 'He seemed fairly quiet and kept himself to himself.'

'I think designing apps probably doesn't help my inner introvert.' Alex laughed.

'You could be right. And my standing up in front of thousands of fans and singing has done a lot for my shyness.'

'I can't imagine many people have the guts to sing in front of all those people,' Piper said. 'I've only ever been persuaded to do karaoke once and I've never even thought of myself as shy.'

Matteo shrugged. 'I suppose if you want something enough,

as I wanted people to hear my songs, then you can do much more than you ever imagined.'

'You write as well as sing them then?'

She really wasn't a fan, Matteo thought, amused. Then again, he reasoned, he had discovered early in his career that some people didn't like him to think they were fans in case he thought they had an ulterior motive for befriending him. 'I do.'

Alex slipped his arm around Piper's waist. 'He initially wrote them hoping to sell them on to other artists, isn't that right?'

Matteo thought back to writing songs as a teenager in his box room at the family home. 'It is. But no one seemed interested in recording them, so I recorded one myself hoping to tout it to the record companies. Then, when that also failed to work, I auditioned to go on *The Biggest Star*.' He laughed. 'And surprised everyone, most of all myself, by winning. I was offered representation and that was how it all began.' He calculated how long ago it was. 'It's hard to believe that was seven years ago.'

'Wow.' Piper shook her head. 'I never knew that.'

'You don't watch *The Biggest Star*? I thought everyone watched that on a Saturday night.' He was only half teasing. It was the biggest-rated talent-finding show on British television. Matteo only ever recorded the shows he had been in to see how he had done, hoping to improve his performance for the following week.

'Sorry, no. I don't like those sorts of programmes,' she said. 'I'm more into period romance, or geographical documentaries.'

'I understand the documentaries,' Matteo said. 'Not so much the period romances.'

Piper sighed. 'Now, why doesn't that surprise me?'

He liked this girlfriend of Alex's. She was funny, smart and clearly had a mind of her own, unlike some of the women he had dated since becoming famous. He pushed away the thought of the last few women he had been out with, all extremely beautiful, but they seemed to act more like show ponies than interesting people. He needed to step off the celebrity merry-go-round and spend more time with real people, he decided.

They got back into Piper's car and she drove them through the narrow lanes. Matteo allowed his mind to clear as they reached a long straight road with a row of colourful hydrangeas running down each side.

'This is beautiful,' he said, admiring the blue, pink and white blooms as they passed.

'It's known locally as Hydrangea Avenue,' Piper explained. 'It's not the correct name, I think that's Route des Marettes, or something. Various parishioners look after groups of the bushes to keep them this perfect.'

'They do a brilliant job.'

'I agree,' she said. 'I love it in the summer when the cushion-like flower heads are in full bloom, as they are now.'

'I can see why.' Matteo leaned back against the headrest and watched the colourful display pass them. It felt good to take a couple of hours away from the constant intensity of his upcoming tour. Soon they were gliding back down the hill towards the open expanse of St Ouen's Bay.

'Alex told me that your presence on the island has to remain as secret as possible.'

'That's right,' Matteo replied. 'If people realise I'm here then they'll want to know why and the filming could be disrupted. Although I don't like to hide from my fans, the plain truth of it is that I don't have time for any delays right now.'

'I understand,' she said. 'You don't have to worry about me. I haven't told anyone.'

Matteo could sense her disappointment. He wished secrecy didn't have to be kept so tight and that she could tell her friends. He wouldn't mind meeting them, especially as they would be people Alex must spend time with now that he and Piper were so close. It had been weeks now since Alex had come to visit his grandfather and stayed at the Blue Haven Guest House in Gorey, where Piper worked and lived with her mother.

'Although,' she added, 'locals here are used to famous people coming over to the island...' Her voice trailed off. 'Hmm, I do think that you're rather more famous than most people we get here though and a lot younger, too. So maybe you are right to keep your visit quiet.' She turned to him briefly and smiled. 'I promise not to tell a soul.'

2

Piper told them she would take the scenic route along the south coast. He didn't recall being taken this way when he was smaller, but then his memories of childhood holidays with his parents and paternal grandparents were mostly of building sandcastles on one of the beaches, eating picnics his mother had made and sitting on a sandy towel.

'How's your grandad doing, Alex?' Matteo had heard how difficult Mr Cooper had found life since his wife had died, and had been relieved when Alex told him that his grandfather had come to Jersey and seemed to love it here.

'He's staying at a friend's house,' Alex said. 'He seems to have settled well into island life and I can't see him returning to the mainland any time soon.'

Matteo wasn't sure whether to ask about the other situation that had arisen soon after Mr Cooper's initial arrival on the island, but then decided that Alex would have tipped him off if there was a reason not to bring it up in front of Piper. 'Wasn't there some issue with your gran, Piper?'

Piper nodded. 'Yes, there was a bit of a drama, but Gran and Alex's grandad have become friendly since then.' He was relieved to hear it. 'In fact, the four of us went out to dinner last week.'

'Yes,' Alex said. 'I'm not too sure how pleased Grandad's friend, Vivienne, was about it.'

'Who's Vivienne?' Matteo wondered.

Piper smiled at him in the rear view mirror. 'She's the lady who's invited him to stay at her home in the spare room. She clearly likes him, but I think he's happy to remain friends.'

'At least everyone seems to be getting along now though.'

'I agree,' Piper said. 'It's certainly a relief for us two.'

'It is,' Alex said, smiling.

They reached the private cottage where he was staying about half an hour later.

'I'll leave you both here,' Piper said. 'Call me if you need anything dropped off and I'll come as soon as I can.' She glanced at the clock on her dashboard. 'I'm a bit late for work so need to hurry to The Cabbage Patch.'

'Cabbage Patch?' Matteo asked, trying to picture what that place might be.

'Yes, it's a large barn where artisan stallholders sell their wares.'

He was intrigued. 'What do you sell there?'

She smiled. 'I have a stall selling bits and bobs that I upcycle. Old mirrors, jugs, picture frames, that sort of thing, mosaicking using sea glass I've collected from the beach.'

'I'd love to see it sometime,' he said, regretting his need to remain incognito.

'Hopefully we can sort something out,' Alex said, clearly guessing what he had been thinking.

'I'd like that.'

He thanked Piper again as he and Alex got out of the car. They watched Piper drive under the granite arch they had entered through and turned to look at the impressive country house hotel.

'I'm staying in a cottage around the back somewhere, right?' he asked Alex.

'That's right,' Alex said, walking next to him. 'It was Piper's mum, Helen, who came up with the idea of you staying here and I gave your manager Martha the details so she could book it for you. It's not too far from the Blue Haven where Piper lives, and I'm staying, and this place has a world-class restaurant and private dining rooms if you or Martha need somewhere to entertain.'

'It was good of you to do all this for me,' Matteo said gratefully. 'I must remember to thank Helen when I meet her.'

They turned a corner and Matteo spotted a smart property further down. It had its own small driveway and was surrounded by immaculate grounds. 'It's more of a house than a cottage,' he joked. 'I love it. And you say it has a swimming pool out the back?'

'It does.'

Matteo nodded. 'It's perfect, Alex. I love it.'

'I'm relieved you're happy to stay here.'

'I'll probably not want to leave.'

An hour later, changed into shorts and a tee shirt, Matteo leaned back in the sun chair, fingers linked, his hands behind his head. He closed his eyes, relishing the coolness of the huge sunshade after the heat of the morning. 'You've done good, Alex mate.'

'I'm glad you approve.'

'I do,' he said opening his eyes and gazing at the neat lawns with heavily planted flower borders, giving the area added privacy. 'I'm surprised the swimming pool is as big as it is too.' He pointed towards it. 'Why don't you take a pair of my trunks and we'll cool down in there in a bit when we've digested this lot,' he suggested before eating another mouthful of the perfectly cooked fillet steak that had recently been served to them from the hotel restaurant.

'Good idea,' Alex said.

Matteo looked up and noticed Alex watching him thoughtfully. 'What?'

He saw his friend's face redden slightly. 'Piper's great, don't you think?'

Ah, so that was it, Matteo thought. His friend must be serious about this girl to ask him. 'She's very lovely,' he said honestly. 'Sincere, too and...' He tried to find the right words to describe the fresh-faced, genuine girl he had met earlier. 'Perfect for you.'

Alex's face brightened and his mouth drew back into a wide smile. 'I'm glad you like her. She's great. I like her a lot more than I ever expected to like any one.'

Matteo smiled. He had suspected as much. 'I'm glad. I was watching you both earlier at that location in St Ouen and it was clear you're as infatuated with her as she is with you.'

'You really think so?' Alex asked, his fork half raised to his mouth. 'Really?'

'Yes.' Matteo laughed. 'I wouldn't lie to you.'

Alex nodded sagely. 'No, you wouldn't.' He ate the piece of steak and sighed. 'I'm glad you like her. I'm hoping we all see more of each other once your tour is over and done with. If you like Jersey enough to keep coming back, that is.'

'I'm certainly enjoying it so far,' Matteo said, liking the idea of spending down time somewhere so close to home but with a holiday vibe that seemed to relax him as soon as he had landed. He closed his eyes, relishing having a few minutes to chill, when his phone vibrated on the table. He groaned and picked it up, wishing he could ignore whoever was interrupting time with his friend. Noticing his manager's name on the screen, he turned to Alex. 'It's Martha. I have to get this.'

He knew his manager would only contact him if necessary. She was busier than he was, always planning some event for him or one of her other clients. She was constantly making phone calls or networking and Matteo knew he wouldn't have nearly the audience reach he had now without her working hard behind the scenes to get his name out there.

He answered the call. 'Hi, Martha. How are you doing? I'm here with Alex and have you on loud speaker. We're chilling by the pool at this place you booked for me.' He gave Alex a wink, aware that Martha had only booked it because Alex had made the suggestion, but knew Martha liked to know her hard work was appreciated.

'Never mind that, sweetie,' she said, a harshness in her voice that could only spell one thing. Matteo's smile vanished and his stomach contracted. Something was wrong. 'Go on,' he said, dreading what was about to come.

'It's a bloody disaster. I thought you assured me that no one would find out about you being on the island.'

Alex scowled. *Hell, he had only been here for an hour.* 'Well, I didn't tell anyone,' he said. 'And I know Piper and Alex haven't either.'

Matteo raised his hand to try and reassure his friend. 'I know neither of you will have said anything. Martha,' he said, 'what exactly has happened?'

'I've been contacted by the local press for a quote,' she

snapped. 'I gather someone saw the three of you up at some place called Grantez?'

Matteo cringed and shot a disappointed look at Alex. 'Ah, that's not good?'

Alex frowned. 'No, I imagine it's not.'

Matteo shook his head. 'I presume that means we'll need to find somewhere else to film now, doesn't it?' he asked as Alex took out his phone and tapped away. 'No one knows where I'm staying, so that's something.'

'Damn,' Alex said.

Matteo's good mood dipped. 'What is it?'

'Piper can't immediately think of anywhere else that might be private enough and suitable for your recording.'

'Please thank her for me anyway.'

'Did I hear correctly?' Martha shrieked down the phone.

Matteo took a steadying breath and closed his eyes for a few seconds. 'You did.' He knew his voice was weary and any enthusiasm he had felt dispersed. Here he was hoping that the storm in France wouldn't hit the island. The storm was irrelevant now that the setting for the recording had been discovered. 'What the hell are we going to do?'

'I've no idea,' Martha snapped, her voice harsher than before. 'I have enough to be getting on with now we've agreed the extra dates. We can't change those now.' There was a momentary silence which troubled Matteo even more than her anger. 'You'll just have to speak to Alex's new girlfriend again. Maybe she knows someone who might come up with an alternative. And be quick about it. We need to record in three days' time. Let me know how it goes.'

Matteo went to answer her but Martha had already ended the call. 'And here I was naively thinking I was going to have a relatively calm few days before filming.' He leaned forward and rested his elbows on the table before sinking down to lower his head in his hands. 'What the hell am I going to do now?'

'Don't panic,' Alex said, his voice quiet but controlled. 'We'll sort this out somehow.'

Matteo wasn't sure how confident his friend was but appreciated his reassurance. 'Thanks, Alex.'

'You stay there and take it easy. I'll go and give Piper a quick call to let her know exactly what's happened. Maybe she'll know someone who could help us find an alternative suggestion for the filming.'

Matteo nodded. 'That would be great. Thanks.'

Alex took his phone and began walking towards the cottage.

'Are you serious?' Matteo heard Piper exclaim a moment later. 'But it's the height of the summer, Alex. There's not going to be anything available now. That's why I suggested an outdoor place.' He cringed, wishing he wasn't causing his best friend and Piper so much concern. He heard Alex's voice as he mumbled something soothing to her. 'I understand, but everything else for big events is booked up at least eighteen months in advance for the summer months.'

Alex ended the call and walked out of the living room to join him again. 'Piper's going to come round to see us as soon as she can get away from work,' Alex said. 'And she's going to speak to a couple of people to try and get some ideas.'

'That's fine,' Matteo said, past caring who she told now. 'If the press already know I'm here then the rest of the island will find out soon, no doubt.'

They sat for a few minutes each lost in their own thoughts. Matteo's phone vibrated again. He picked it up, looked at the screen and grimaced. 'Martha again.'

'I wonder what's gone wrong now?' Alex asked.

Matteo closed his eyes and shook his head before answering

the call. Martha was a brilliant, determined manager but her tempers were legendary. 'Martha?'

'I knew we shouldn't have tried to fit this filming in to three or four days,' she growled.

'What's happened now?' he asked not really wanting to find out.

'The actor? The one playing your love interest in the video? The ridiculous girl only went skydiving and broke her damn ankle. Who the hell goes skydiving?'

'Lots of people enjoy it, or so I'm told,' Matteo said before realising that he would be antagonising Martha. 'What do you need me to do?' he asked knowing that being proactive was the best way to keep her sweet.

'You need to find a replacement for her.'

'What?' *Was she mad?* 'As well as finding a new location with hardly any notice?' He didn't even try to keep the panic out of his voice. 'Martha, you're the clever one who does this sort of thing,' he reminded her. 'Not the other way around. Where would I start a search for an actor?'

He heard Martha give a snort of fury. 'You've been out with enough in your time, Matteo. Don't you have a couple who might do you a favour?'

He struggled to think of even one that he might want back in his life again.

'Matteo, think. Surely you can come up with someone?' He heard her groan impatiently. 'Damn, I have another call coming through. Phone me later when you have news.'

Relieved she had ended the call, he placed his phone back on the table. 'I don't suppose you have any idea where we can find a female actor at short notice?' he asked Alex sarcastically.

Alex shook his head and frowned. 'Nope.'

'Then it looks like I'm not going to have a video to go with this new Christmas record I'm releasing,' he said miserably. 'What a bloody disaster.'

Alex rose to his feet. 'Right, we're going for a swim.'

'Why? Is there a mermaid at the bottom of the pool who might be available for a gothic themed video?'

Alex laughed. 'No, but it'll cool us both down and give us something to do while we wait for Piper to arrive.'

3

Casey handed her customer the carrier bag containing the carefully wrapped scented cathedral candles. 'I'd put one hand under the base of the bag while you carry it,' she suggested. 'I'd hate for the handles to break under the weight and for them to be damaged.' She had offered two bags but the customer had assured her she didn't need them.

She tidied away the leftover tissue paper, placing it into a drawer beneath her stall counter and noticed Piper frowning and staring at her phone.

'Are you going to tell me what's been bothering you today? Or am I going to have to force it out of you?' Casey asked, acting as if either of them might think for a second that she was tough as she balled her hands into fists and rested them on her slim hips. 'Don't try to tell me it's nothing, because I know you too well to believe that's the case.'

Piper sighed. 'I'd love to tell you.'

Then why wasn't she? 'You do know you can confide in me about anything, don't you?'

Piper looked away from her phone and nodded. 'I do.'

'Then why can't you tell me what's the matter. You know Tara and I will do anything to help you if you need us to. At least I hope you do.'

'Yes, we would,' Tara agreed, walking up to join them. 'But first I need to go and speak to Perry.'

Casey watched her cousin walk away to chat to the potter she'd had a crush on since the day he set up a stall at The Cabbage Patch.

She turned back to Piper. 'Well? What's it to be?' When Piper gave her a questioning look, she shook her head. 'You have two seconds to confide in me before I confiscate your chocolate snacks from the back of the cupboard under your stall.'

Piper stared at her for a moment before shaking her head. 'I'll tell you but only because I need your help.'

'Thanks, I'm sure,' Casey said, nervous suddenly about what it might be.

Piper winced. 'I don't mean it that way. It's just that I've promised Alex's friend I'd keep it a secret.'

'It's fine, I'm only winding you up,' Casey said, not wishing to put any more pressure on her friend's troubled shoulders. 'You don't have to tell me if you'd rather not. I really should have just asked if there was anything I can do.'

'I think you might be able to help though,' Piper said thoughtfully.

'Help with what?' Tara asked joining them.

'I thought you were going to speak to Perry about something?' Casey asked, looking over Tara's shoulder but unable to see him anywhere.

'I had hoped to, but he was leaving to go and meet with a client.'

'Was it important?' Piper asked, giving Tara a concerned look.

Tara shook her head. 'No. I just really wanted to talk to him about anything.'

Casey could see Tara was disappointed. 'Never mind,' she said. 'Hopefully he'll be back soon and you can go and chat to him then.'

'I suppose so.'

Casey and Piper swapped sympathetic glances as Tara folded her arms across her chest sulkily, before gasping and gazing at Piper.

'What is it?' Piper asked looking confused.

'I heard you say Casey might be able to help with something. Can I help with whatever it is too?'

'I don't know what it is either yet,' Casey said. 'So let's not be too hasty offering our services.' She gave Piper a wink to show she was teasing.

Piper frowned. 'The problem is I shouldn't be telling anyone about this, but I can't see how I can help him if I don't confide in you two.'

'Him?' Tara narrowed her eyes.

Now Casey really was confused. 'Why don't you tell us then and let's see if I can do something.'

'If *we* can do something,' Tara insisted.

Piper breathed in deeply through her nose. 'Fine. Here goes.'

When Piper had finished explaining the situation she looked from Casey to Tara and added, 'I know it's a lot to take in, but like I said, he's Alex's closest friend and he needs our help.'

Casey struggled to process what she had just been told. She glanced around to check no one was in hearing distance and lowering her voice, asked, 'You're telling me that Matteo Stanford is Alex's friend?'

'And he's here? On this island?' Tara gasped, pointing down at the ground. 'Now?'

Piper nodded. 'I am telling you that and yes, he is.'

Casey stepped to the side to let Tara move in closer to the pair of them. She swapped glances with her cousin. 'Keep your voice down.'

Tara shook her head. 'I'm still struggling to take in what Piper's just told us. I think I must be having an out-of-body experience. I've dreamt of something like this happening hundreds of times,' she said in a faraway dreamy voice.

'You dreamt I asked you for help with...' Piper mouthed Matteo's name.

'No.' Tara laughed. 'I dreamt that he needed my help and I gave it to him.'

Casey groaned. 'I think we should leave your dreams out of this.' She stared at Piper for a few seconds. 'If he needs our help then we're more than happy to give it to him,' Casey said, aware Tara would be only too willing to help. 'Aren't we, Tara?'

'Hell, yes. Just tell us what you need and we'll do it for you.'

Piper pulled a face. 'I wouldn't go offering too much too readily,' she teased.

'Will we get to meet him?' Tara asked.

'I'll make sure that you do and that he knows how helpful you've been.'

Casey couldn't believe how their day was going. This was surreal and very exciting. She nudged her cousin and pointed at Piper. 'Haven't I always said how Piper was my favourite person in the whole world?'

'No.'

'Well, she is now.' Casey still couldn't believe it. Matteo Stanford, the biggest and most successful British popstar in the world right now, had secretly come to the island to record his Christmas video. 'He's actually in Jersey.'

Tara did an excitable dance that made her look a little crazy and made Casey giggle at her cousin's antics.

Piper shushed Tara. 'Quiet,' she said. 'I'm trying to keep this as secret as possible. Although now the press have got hold of the news it's not going to stay a secret for long.'

Tara grimaced. 'Sorry, I didn't think,' she whispered. 'I promise I'll keep my voice down and I won't tell a soul.' She thought for a moment. 'You haven't actually told us what help you need from us yet.'

Piper waved them even closer and Casey listened with her cousin as Piper explained what the issue was. 'Jax suggested he record the video to go with his Christmas release up at Grantez.'

'It's stunning up there,' Casey said quietly. She'd been to a couple of outdoor concerts there a few summers before and knew how beautiful it was. 'Great suggestion.'

'Didn't he like the idea?' Tara asked.

'He loved it, but someone spotted us when we were showing the area to him earlier today. Now the press know and his hope of secretly recording the video in three days is in tatters.'

'Three days?' Casey asked, shocked that he expected to do such a thing so soon. She had no idea how long these things took to arrange but had assumed it would be months, not days.

'Yes, he's got a big tour starting soon so it has to be now.'

'Why leave the planning so late though?' Tara asked.

'Because they've just decided to add a few more dates to his tour.' Piper shook her head. 'I'm not sure of all the ins and outs of it but there's no other time he can film it. He needs a new venue, and fast.'

'Gorey Castle,' Casey said almost without needing to think. She had always loved the magnificent castle standing high above Gorey Pier, behind Piper's mum's guest house. 'Surely he can be certain of privacy behind the battlements.'

Piper's mouth dropped open for a second before she beamed at Casey. 'You are a genius, do you know that?'

Casey was thrilled to have come up with a suitable solution so quickly. 'I'm glad to be of help,' she said giving a curtsy, delighted to have helped her friend out so easily. Then it occurred to her that the idea might be a good one, but none of them knew whether the right room at the castle would be available at such short notice. 'Hold on a sec. We still have to check whether the place is available.'

'I'll give them a call,' Piper said, grabbing her phone from the top of her stall.

Casey reached out to stop her. 'Let me. My Uncle Bill works there. He might be able to help us. We don't want to contact them and be given a flat no, do we?'

'Good point,' Tara said. 'If we're going to help my future husband sort out his recording problem then we need to get this right.'

'I thought you were in love with Perry the Potter?' Casey teased.

'I was. I am. But I'm sure even he would understand if my affections were diverted to a hot superstar like Matteo.'

Casey doubted it but didn't say so. Anyway, she mused, did Perry even realise how much Tara liked him? Probably not.

'I think the first thing we need to do before we go speaking to people is to find out whether or not Matteo likes the idea of the castle as a venue.' It seemed odd to her to be saying the name of a world famous superstar as if she knew him personally.

'Good point. We do need to do that,' Piper said. 'Right, let's pack up here and I'll take you to him. I have a feeling he won't mind us turning up if we have a solution to his problem.'

Casey hoped Piper was right. She didn't relish upsetting this man. It wasn't the best way to be introduced to someone and she doubted Tara would ever forgive her if she embarrassed her in front of her idol.

4

The closer they got to where Matteo Stanford was staying, the more anxious Casey began to feel. Why had she been so willing to get involved in something she had no experience of dealing with? She reminded herself that she was doing this to help her friend and that Piper had always been there for her and Tara whenever they needed her to be.

'Tell me again why you're the one trying to sort this out, Piper?' she asked, needing to know how her friend had become involved in the first place.

'He's Alex's best friend and asked him to come to the island to find a perfect location. If Jax and I hadn't come up with Grantez he might not be in this mess now and I'd hate for there to be any ill feeling between two best friends on my account.'

'I can see how that would be horrible,' Casey said, determined to do all she could to help her friend out of the pickle she had found herself in.

As soon as the car was parked, the cousins followed Piper around the side of a pretty granite cottage at the back of the smart hotel where she had always dreamt of going for a meal. Casey wondered if she might even get to see inside the wood-panelled restaurant she had heard so much about but doubted it would happen unless she sold a hell of a lot more candles.

'Hi guys,' she heard Piper say as she rounded the corner to the back of the building.

Casey glanced at Tara and was about to admit how nervous she was to meet this over-confident superstar when Tara gave a little squeal and rushed forward. Casey took a deep breath to brace herself for what was about to happen. She could hear Tara telling Matteo how much of a fan she was and presumed he was loving every second of the adoration. 'Urgh.' This really wasn't her scene at all.

'I hope you don't mind but I brought my friends Casey and Tara with me.' Piper explained. 'They have a stall next to mine at The Cabbage Patch.'

'Yes,' Tara said enthusiastically. 'We make candles and use acid to etch old mirrors. We source them from various places and upcycle them to sell them on.'

Casey stepped forward, hoping to calm her cousin's enthusiasm slightly. She could hear the excitement in her voice and didn't want Tara to feel awkward later on about how she had reacted to Matteo. And the last thing Casey wanted was for him to say anything that might upset her friend.

'Sounds interesting,' she heard him say. It wasn't the best response but at least he wasn't being stand-offish with Tara.

'I thought it best if they came with me to explain their suggestion to you,' Piper added. 'I hope you don't mind. They know not to tell anyone else and I trust both of them with my life.'

Casey saw Matteo's shoulders lower and presumed he was happy with Piper's reassurances. He seemed to sense her standing there and turned to her with a smile on his face that for some reason became strangely fixed when he locked eyes with her. Casey's breath caught in her throat. He was gorgeous. She had seen his videos sometimes on television and his picture was in magazines everywhere you looked, or so it seemed. She had always thought him handsome, but it was only now that she was seeing him in the flesh that her entire body seemed to be reacting to him. How could he be more beautiful in real life? she wondered.

She didn't mind his music but hadn't really ever taken much notice of him. Probably, she mused, because Tara went on endlessly about him, replaying his latest hit so often that Casey thought she might scream. But now she was standing in front of him, staring at him like a deer caught in headlights, she could completely understand why her cousin was transfixed by this man.

Someone coughed and Casey snapped out of her dreamlike state at the same time that Matteo became more animated. Alex stepped forward, placed a hand on Matteo's shoulder and reached out the other towards Casey. 'Matteo this is Casey, Piper's friend and Tara's cousin.'

'Er, I'm pleased to meet you, Casey,' he said like some sort of robot.

What was wrong with him? She stared at him. *In fact, what was wrong with her?* She forced a smile. 'Nice to meet you too, Matteo,' she said. 'We're hoping we might have a solution for you.'

'Come over here and take a seat,' he said. 'Drinks anyone?'

Casey waited for him to make the three of them cool drinks and tapped her foot nervously hoping she did have a solution for him, because if she didn't there was no Plan B in her mind.

He sat down and she studied his neatly cut, almost-black hair. He had a mischievous glint in his green eyes that she suspected had floored many girls just as it had done her moments before. Although, she mused, he hadn't smiled at her, merely stared.

Strange. He wasn't quite as tall or as broad as Alex but he was certainly charismatic and she could understand why his fans adored him so much.

He finished serving their drinks and sat opposite her. Casey was happy that he couldn't see the way her foot was tapping on the paving under the table. She forced herself to speak. 'Piper confided in us about your urgent need for a location.'

'It's crucial that I find something quickly,' he said, looking anxious.

'We thought you might try Mont Orgueil.'

He looked baffled and frowned. 'Mont Orgueil?'

'Where?' Alex asked. 'Do you mean...?'

'Gorey Castle,' Casey said, giving the name the locals used. 'My uncle works there. We haven't asked about the availability yet because we thought it best to clear it with you before making any queries. There's no point in bothering him if you're not interested,' she added, feeling a bit more comfortable talking to him.

'Let me have a look.' Matteo picked up his phone and searched for the castle. 'It's stunning. I see they do weddings there.' He scrolled for a little longer. 'They have a room that would be perfect.' He peered closely at the screen. 'The Medieval Great Hall looks as if it would fit perfectly with the sort of feel I was hoping for with this video. I need something with a gothic vibe.'

'Great,' Casey said. 'Then that's what I'll get Uncle Bill to ask about. Leave it with me.'

'Thank you,' Matteo said. 'I also need to find out how we request permission for the room.'

'I'll make a quick call and see what he can do.' She could feel Matteo's eyes on her back as she walked away from the group to make her call. She sensed his concern but tried to focus on what she needed to ask her uncle. Moments later, she ended her call and returned to sit with the others, unable to miss Matteo's anticipation about what she was going to tell him.

'Uncle Bill said he would happily let us use the room.'

Before she had a chance to finish there was a loud cheer from everyone else at the table. Casey hated to spoil their celebration but had no choice. She raised a hand and shook her head. 'Sorry, that's not all, I'm afraid.'

Matteo's smile vanished. 'No?'

Her heart ached for him, but he had to know. 'I'm afraid he also told me there's already a wedding taking place in that room that same afternoon.'

'There's no way a wedding can be postponed, not three days before it takes place,' Tara said, immediately standing up for Casey.

Casey gave her cousin an appreciative smile.

'A wedding?' Matteo asked looking as if she had just slapped him. 'Well, that's that then. Damn and it looked perfect too.'

'I know,' Casey agreed. 'If it was anything else we could maybe use the room and then set it up for the wedding when you're finished filming. But the wedding is being held in the early evening and there won't be time.'

'Are you completely sure about that?' Piper asked, a look on her face that told Casey she was contemplating some idea. 'Please call your uncle back and tell him that we might still manage to use the room.'

'Are you sure?' Casey asked doubtfully.

Piper shrugged. 'I'm not, but this is too important to Matteo for us to give up at the first hurdle.'

Alex sighed. 'I think this was probably the second hurdle.'

Casey could see Piper wasn't finished yet. 'Can you ask your uncle who's getting married there? Maybe we know them and can work something out.'

'I doubt he'll be able to find out that information. Not without breaking data protection, or whatever it's called.' When Piper didn't react Casey knew she had little choice but to at least ask her uncle. 'No harm in trying, I suppose. I'll call him now.'

'Brilliant,' Piper said. 'Please thank your uncle and thank you too, Casey.'

'It's no problem at all. I'm happy to help.' She realised she was also quite enjoying the excitement of dealing with something this unusual. She picked up her phone, found her uncle's number and gave him another call.

Five minutes later Casey ended the call. 'Well, that was interesting,' she said noticing that a barman and waiter had arrived from the hotel and Matteo had ordered them all beers.

'What was?' Matteo said.

'What did he say?' Piper asked leaning forward, her elbows resting on the table. 'Would he tell you whose wedding it is? Do we know them?'

Casey thought for a moment. She hated to divulge someone else's secret but in this case decided she had no choice. 'Look, my uncle shouldn't have told me anything but I promised him no one would find out that I discovered whose wedding it was through him.' Everyone knew everyone else around the village and thankfully this person was someone she knew well enough to be able to get away with contacting them.

'Whose is it?' Tara asked tapping the table with the tips of her fingernails.

'He didn't give me a name and I think he thought he was being vague, but, well, he told me that she was a florist in Gorey. There's only one florist that I can think of there and we all know Nancy is already married, so...'

'Vicki?' Piper asked.

'Who's Vicki?' Alex asked.

'Dan's fiancée,' Piper explained. 'Dan is the guy who took us all out on his RIB with Jax a few weeks ago. He and Vicki got engaged a couple of years ago but he's always insisted they save for a deposit on a cottage, believing that's more worthwhile than spending money on a fancy wedding.'

'Maybe he's changed his mind,' Tara said doubtfully. 'Or maybe it's not them after all.'

'There's only one way to find out.' Casey tried to recall if she had heard about Vicki and Dan getting married. 'I'm sure I would have known if that was happening. Don't you think we all would have heard something?'

'I would have thought so. But if it's not Vicki, then who can it be?' Tara asked. 'Dare we ask her, do you think?'

'Who out of us knows her best?' Piper asked looking from Tara to Casey. 'I'm happy to speak to her if you like?'

Casey realised that although she and Tara had known Vicki for the same length of time, she had become closer to Vicki over the years. 'No, it's all right I'll do it but first I need to have some clue about the plan I'll be proposing.'

'What do you mean?' Alex asked.

'Well, what do we want her to do? Put off her wedding until later that evening? Bring it forward? Will she be able to use the setting Matteo has set up in the room?' She turned to Matteo. 'Is the design something that can also be used for a wedding back-drop either before or afterwards?'

He shrugged. 'I've no idea. Do you want to know what the record is about?' Matteo asked when they all sat at the table with their ice cold beers. 'I can play it to you, if that helps.'

'Oh wow!' Tara cried. 'I can't believe I'm getting to hear a song that isn't even out yet.'

'I hope you like it,' he said.

Casey listened intently to the words trying to picture how the medieval room could be set up for the video so it might also complement the wedding. 'It's a very romantic song,' she said relieved.

'Yes. Do you like it?'

Going by the way goosebumps rose along the length of her arms, Casey sensed that this song would be his next number one hit. 'I love it, actually.'

He beamed at her. 'Great. I always worry how new releases will be received.'

'Even now? After so many of them?'

He seemed surprised at her question. 'Yes, I think most musicians are the same. You're only as good as your last record.'

'That's so sad,' Tara said voicing the same thoughts as Casey was having.

'Why?'

'Because yours have all done so well. Shouldn't that be enough?'

'For whom? Me, or my record company?'

'Both, I suppose.'

He took a long drink from his bottle. 'The castle sounds, and from the pictures online, looks very atmospheric.'

Casey agreed. 'I think it would be far more atmospheric there even than at the Grantez site.'

'All that history and you wouldn't have to worry about privacy and the press being able to sneak in and take photos. Those walls have never been breached in hundreds of years,' Casey said. 'At least, I don't think they have.'

'Neither do I,' Tara agreed. 'But what about the set?'

'I have a feeling Casey has a plan for that too,' Alex said smiling. 'Don't you?'

'I do,' she admitted a little shyly. *Why was she taking such an interest in this situation? It wasn't as if she really knew Matteo, or Alex, that well.* She caught Matteo watching her and could feel her cheeks heating. Damn it, she thought. She liked him. Really liked him.

'Why are you putting yourself out this much to help me?' he asked as if he could sense what she was thinking.

She shifted in her seat embarrassed by his scrutiny. 'I'd do it for anyone who I thought might benefit from my brilliance,' she said trying to make light of her thoughts. 'But also, I've had an idea that might benefit you, Tara and me. Maybe. I'll need to speak to Vicki first, we'd need her to be willing to adapt her wedding.' She reminded herself that they didn't know for certain that it was Vicki's wedding they wanted to change. 'If it even *is* her wedding.'

Tara gasped and clapped her hands together. 'I know exactly what you have in mind, you clever thing,' she said, nudging Casey in the ribs.

'Ouch, that hurt.'

'Sorry. I'm a little over-excited.'

Piper laughed. 'I think we can all see that. So, go on then, Casey, what's your idea?'

Casey frowned and tilted her head towards her cousin. 'Tara's so clever she can tell you.' She didn't doubt for a second that Tara had worked out what was in her mind. They might be cousins but they had always been very close and the best of friends as well as business partners. Tara knew her better than anyone. 'Go on, Tara, tell them.'

Tara grinned. 'Casey and I earn our living making and selling homemade candles. They're not just any old candle but beautiful vintage looking ones with aromatic scents and character that wouldn't look out of place in a gothic period film.' She smiled at Casey and raised her eyebrows in question. 'Am I on the right track?'

Casey laughed, delighted. 'You know you are. Carry on.'

'Yes, please do,' Matteo said. 'I'm liking the sound of where this is going. Aren't you, Alex?'

'I certainly am.' Casey saw Alex give Piper a wink, as if in approval of her friends' ideas.

Tara took a sip of her beer and, placing the bottle back onto the table, leaned back in her chair and folded her arms with a satisfied look on her face. 'We already mentioned that we acid-etch mirrors, making them look antique.'

Casey watched Matteo lean forward focusing all his attention on her cousin. This was exciting, although rather daunting.

'I'm sure we'd both be willing to help dress the Medieval Great Hall using as much stock as we have available,' Tara continued, glancing at Casey. 'We would, wouldn't we?'

'We would.' It was the busiest time of the year for most of the stallholders at The Cabbage Patch. Although for her and Tara their business picked up mostly in autumn and winter, for Halloween and Christmas, and the colder winter months when people were looking for ways to brighten their evenings. 'Your record might be intended for Christmas but you said it has a gothic feel. The candles and mirrors from Smoke and Mirrors – that's the name of our business – could give the room an edge and be perfect for your video and for Vicki's wedding.'

'What do you think?' Alex asked, holding his bottle between both hands.

Piper took a nervous sip of her drink and Casey could see how anxious her friend was that Matteo would like this suggestion. She suspected Piper wanted everything to go perfectly since Alex had originally been the one tasked with finding the setting.

Another thought occurred to Casey. 'I'm sure we could source fabrics and antique furniture from friends and family to add to the set. If you need them, that is.'

Matteo took another mouthful of his beer. He glanced at her and then at Alex, who gave him an encouraging nod. 'Go on then. It sounds great to me.'

Casey gave Tara a triumphant smile.

'We just need to speak to Vicki and agree things with her,' Piper said, reminding Casey that they still had a long way to go. 'I know she and Dan are struggling for money.'

Casey listened to her friend and wondered where she was going with this. 'I was thinking that if you were to allow them to use the set for their wedding, Matteo,' she said, hoping Piper didn't mind her interrupting, 'and offer to cover the cost of the room, then hopefully she will have more of an incentive to agree to let you film on that day either before or after her wedding.'

'You think this will work?' Matteo asked, his face a mask of concern.

'I think there's a good chance it might,' Alex said.

Matteo thought for a moment and then smiled at Tara and rested his gaze on Casey causing her stomach to do a little flip. 'You've got very clever and very persuasive friends, Piper.'

Alex laughed and leaned to his side to give Piper a kiss on the cheek. 'You're not kidding.'

'I've always known Casey and Tara were brilliant,' Piper said, smiling.

Casey wanted to get everything sorted as soon as possible. If she and Tara were going to help with this idea then they would have to source as many candles from their stock as possible.

'The room won't be available to set up for another two days but I thought we could spend that time getting organised,' she said.

Matteo grinned. 'I'll leave you to get approval from the bride and groom and then as soon as you let me know they're happy with everything, I'll get on with whatever you need me to do.

Charge everything to me. I'll call my manager and let her know what's happened so she can fill in the production team.'

'Great,' Casey said wondering what it must feel like to have the sort of money where you didn't need to come up with a budget. 'I'd better go and speak with Vicki and Dan and hope I can persuade them to share their wedding venue. We won't be able to do much without their say-so.'

Instead of Matteo looking happier that they at least had a plan, he rubbed his chin and frowned.

'We have another problem,' he said quietly. 'It's not for you guys to worry about, but it is something that's worrying me.'

'What is it?' Alex asked looking concerned for his friend.

Casey could see how troubled he was and, hating to see anyone looking so forlorn, shook her head. 'Tell us. We're your friends now,' she said wondering if that was too silly to say to a superstar she had only known for a little over an hour. 'Who knows, maybe we can help with this problem too.'

He shook his head and smiled at her. 'I doubt it, but thank you. You've all been incredibly helpful already and I can't impose another thing on you.'

He reached across the table and took Casey's hand in his. The touch of his hand on hers sent shivers through her entire body. She looked up directly into his eyes and saw an intensity that delighted and scared her at the same time.

Casey suspected that Matteo Stanford had the power to break her heart. The thought frightened her; she had no intention of letting that happen.

5

'Casey. What brings you in here today,' Nancy asked, shooting a glance at her assistant, Vicki. 'You've not come to collect flowers, have you?'

'No, nothing like that.' Casey noticed a bunch of pretty pink peonies. It was her mum's birthday that week and although she had bought her a small gift from the selection of ideas her mum had given her she knew she would love these blousy blooms despite no doubt moaning about how much Casey would have spent on them. 'Although now I've seen those I think I'll have to treat Mum to a bunch.'

'Rowena does love peonies,' Nancy said. The bell jangled above the door, alerting her to a customer. 'Get those wrapped prettily for Casey, will you, Vicki love?'

Casey watched Vicki choose the best bunch from the aluminium bucket and shake off the worst of the water. 'These do you?'

She nodded, trying to quell her anxiety about what she was intending to ask her friend. 'They're gorgeous.'

Vicki's free arm went around Casey's waist in a welcoming

hug and Casey felt a few drops of water from the stems dripping down the side of her leg.

'Ooh, sorry about that,' Vicki said. 'I hadn't meant to get you wet.'

'It's fine,' Casey assured her, laughing and following her friend to the counter. She waited as Vicki expertly wrapped the flowers in a couple of sheets of magenta tissue and then a thicker paper, and deftly tied a piece of string around the middle before adding a delicate pale pink ribbon. 'There. What do you think?'

'Perfect, thank you.' Casey sighed, picking them up and gazing happily at them. 'Vicki, could I ask you something? It's a little private.'

Vicki rang up the flowers and held out the card machine for Casey to tap her debit card. 'Of course.' She handed her the receipt. 'What's it about?'

Casey made sure to keep her voice low. She presumed Nancy would know about any wedding plans Vicki might have but wasn't certain and it wasn't her place to share a secret that wasn't hers. 'I have a dilemma and also a plan I need to put to you.'

Vicki grinned and leaned against the counter. 'Now I am intrigued. Go on.'

She decided to act more certain than she really was and took a deep breath. 'I've discovered that you're getting married in three days' time at the castle.'

Vicki's mouth dropped open. 'How on earth do you know that?'

Casey forced herself to continue. 'I promise it'll all become clear as I explain the favour I'd like to ask of you.'

'Go on, I'm listening.' Vicki picked at one of her fingernails.

Casey hoped she wasn't about to lose a good friend. She would have loved not to need to broach the subject but it was the only way she could help Matteo out of his situation. 'I know someone who needs to use the Medieval Great Hall at the castle on the same day as your wedding.' She concentrated on keeping her voice down. 'I gather you aren't needing it until early evening. Is that right?'

Vicki nodded slowly, frowning.

'Um, they were hoping that if you didn't mind, they might have use of the room before your wedding is due to take place. The room would be decorated beautifully with lots of candles, mirrors and greenery. Naturally they'll ensure the room is exactly as you wish it to be in good time for your wedding.' She hesitated and when Vicki didn't speak, added, 'Obviously the person will pay for setting up of the hall and for any staff or supplies required to have it ready for you. What do you think?'

Vicki seemed lost in thought. Casey noticed the customer leave and Nancy giving Vicki and her an inquisitive glance, but was relieved when another customer entered the florist's almost immediately and kept the manager busy.

'Vicki?' she whispered, wishing her friend would give her some sort of answer.

'Um, I don't know what to say.'

'Yes, maybe?' Casey suggested, aware she was pushing her luck.

Vicki gritted her teeth and looked troubled. 'It's not exactly as I think you're imagining,' she said at last.

Casey held back a groan. *What now?* She had been banking on persuading Vicki to let Matteo's team have the room for the few hours prior to the wedding but it was clear that there was something else bothering her friend.

'Would you be against them using the room that day?'

Vicki shook her head. 'No, not if it fits in with what I need the hall for.'

Relieved to have a glimmer of hope restored, Casey relaxed

slightly. 'Why don't you tell me what's worrying you and we can see if there's a way around it?'

Vicki looked past her. 'Look, Nancy will be wondering what we're chatting about.' She glanced at the clock on the wall. 'I'm due a half an hour break in a few minutes. Why don't I pop round to your place and we can talk further then?'

Casey liked the thought of being able to confide properly in Vicki. After all, if her friend was going to be kind enough to allow Matteo to take over her wedding venue then she deserved to know exactly what it was for.

'No problem at all. I'll take these back to Mum and see you there when you're ready.'

She left the shop, giving Nancy a brief wave before stepping out of the door. The heat of the day hit her and it occurred to her that it would be much easier filming in the cool of the Medieval Hall if the weather was going to be this hot in a few days' time. As Casey strolled along the pier, she stopped to chat to Piper's gran and her friend Dilys, who were sitting on the bench in front of the Blue Haven Guest House. She noticed they had rolled towels between them.

'Going swimming in the sea today?'

'Yes,' Dilys said. 'We go most days if we can.'

Piper's gran, Margery, mumbled something under her breath.

'I'm sorry,' Casey said. 'I didn't hear what you said.'

'I was grumbling about Colin Cooper,' she explained. 'He was supposed to be here to meet us ten minutes ago and we're having to wait for him.'

'He swims with you and your friends now?' He really was settling in well to the island, Casey mused.

'He does sometimes.'

Dilys smiled at Casey. 'Colin is probably chatting with Alex somewhere,' she said, obviously trying to make excuses for the man.

'Yes, well if he doesn't get here soon we'll go without him,' Margery said, frowning.

'They get along well really,' Dilys said, looking amused. She pointed at a coach full of holidaymakers. 'The shops along here are going to be busy for the next half an hour or so.'

They chatted a little longer before Casey left the two ladies reminiscing about the island in the 'good old days', when the tourists flooded the place looking for duty-free cigarettes, perfumes and alcohol for themselves, and jewellery and other treats for family and friends back home.

Casey hurried to Gorey Village, a few minutes' walk away from the pier, and was relieved to enter the cool hallway of the house where she lived with her parents and sister.

'Mum?' When her mother didn't answer she walked down the hallway, through the kitchen and out to their small garden.

Her mother looked up from where she was lying on a sunlounger under the apple tree reading her book. 'What have you got there?' Rowena asked, trying to peer around Casey to see what she was holding behind her back.

'Ta-dah,' she said, bringing the huge bunch of blooms in front of her with a flourish and a little difficulty. It wouldn't do to damage the beautiful flower heads this close to handing them to her mother. 'For you.'

'But it's not my birthday yet,' she said beaming at them.

'No, but I saw them and had to buy them for you. Like them?'

Rowena held out her hands. 'How could I not love them?' She took the flowers and breathed in the fresh scent Casey had relished while carrying them. She had moved out to a flat in her late teens but soon realised that living in the island's capital, St

Helier, lovely as it was, didn't make sense, especially when she and Tara had wanted to start their own business.

'It makes far more sense to move back home,' her mother had suggested. 'You can still pay towards your keep but you're going to need all the money you have to get this business of yours and Tara's up and running and we all know how you love living in Gorey Village.'

It was true, she did. Casey was sure that most of her friends might prefer the busy town with its nearby bars and nightclubs but the novelty of living in town had soon worn off for her and she had been secretly relieved to move back to live in her parents' dormer bungalow across the road from the sea.

'How thoughtful of you, Casey,' her mother said, bringing her mind back to the present. 'I think these are Pillow Talk. They're gorgeous. My favourites.'

'I thought they were the ones you liked best.'

Rowena stood and pulled Casey into a hug. 'Thank you, sweetheart, this was very thoughtful of you.'

Casey heard footsteps in the kitchen and they both turned to see Vicki appear at the back door. 'That was quick.'

'Hello, Mrs Norman,' Vicki said. 'I hope you don't mind me interrupting your afternoon.'

Rowena stepped forward. 'When will you stop calling me that?' Rowena smiled. 'I'm Rowena. Now, I suspect you put these glorious flowers together for me. I can tell they're from Harbour Blooms.' She held up the bouquet. 'You wrapped them so beautifully.'

Vicki's cheeks reddened and she smiled. 'I did. I'm glad you like them.'

'I love them. Now, I sense the two of you are hoping for a bit of privacy to chat about something, so why don't I go and put these in water and bring you a cool drink.'

'That would be lovely. Iced water would be perfect for me thank you,' Vicki said taking the seat Rowena had just vacated.

'I'll have the same, please, Mum.'

As soon as her mother had left them, Casey sat on the foot of the same sunlounger where Vicki sat tapping her chin.

'Thanks for coming. I'm sorry to do this to you but it's rather important and I don't really have much choice.'

'It's fine,' Vicki said, smiling past her as Rowena brought out two tall glasses of water, cubes of ice clanking against the sides and a slice of lemon perched over the top on one side. 'Thanks,' Vicki said, taking a glass and a long sip of the cool drink. She placed her glass down on the table next to them and waited for Rowena to return to the house before continuing. 'I should be completely honest with you about the wedding before we go any further though.'

'You don't have to tell me anything,' Casey said, embarrassed to have made her friend feel like she had something to explain. 'It's none of mine or anyone else's business what you've arranged.'

Vicki shook her head. 'Maybe not, but I think I should explain a bit about it.' Casey nodded and Vicki gave a deep sigh. 'The truth of it is that a few months back I heard of a cancellation for that day. As you know Dan proposed years ago, but was dragging his feet about setting a date for our wedding. I thought that if I booked a venue he would have little choice but to commit, but he said that there was no rush and that we should wait until next year at the earliest to give us time to save enough for the flipping cottage he's so desperate to buy for us.'

Casey was a little confused why Vicki had booked the venue knowing her fiancé had no intention of being married then. 'But, then why—?'

'I know what you're going to say,' Vicki interrupted, frowning. 'And you'll think I'm mad if I tell you what I did.'

'No, I won't,' Casey promised.

Vicki took a deep breath. 'No one knows about this, well not until now that is.' She took a sip of her drink and, having put the glass back onto the table, clasped her hands together. 'The thing is that when I suggested we book the room at the castle I failed to mention to Dan that I'd paid a deposit.'

Casey gasped. Everyone knew how careful Dan had been with money since he and Vicki became serious. 'He doesn't know?'

Vicki shook her head slowly. 'He has no idea. He'd be horrified if he knew what I've done and how much I've taken from my savings to do it.'

Casey couldn't believe her friend had chosen to go behind his back with something she knew would antagonise him. 'So you're not getting married in three days then?'

Vicki sighed. 'No.' She narrowed her eyes. 'Now, who's this friend of yours and why does she need the hall?'

Here goes, thought Casey. 'This might sound a bit far-fetched but I promise you it isn't. There's this popstar...'

Vicki leaned forward, resting her elbows on her knees. 'I love this already.'

'He's Alex's best friend. You know, the guy Piper's been seeing for the past few weeks?'

Vicki nodded. 'And?'

'This guy has come to the island especially to record a music video. It was supposed to be at Grantez overlooking the bay.' As she spoke she watched Vicki's expression change from one of confusion to disbelief.

'Sorry, what?'

Casey repeated what she had just said.

'And it's not happening now?'

Casey shook her head. 'Someone saw them at Grantez and told the press. He wants the recording to be kept hush-hush until he's ready to release the video just before Christmas.' She watched Vicki's eyes getting bigger with every second she spoke and hoped she wouldn't pop when she discovered who the singer was.

Casey pulled a face. She explained requesting to hire a room at the castle and then discovering that a wedding was being held there but refrained from mentioning her uncle's name, not wishing to land him in any trouble. 'I wasn't told it was you but I put two and two together and thankfully hit the jackpot.'

'Wow.' Vicki looked entranced and Casey wondered if she was actually taking everything in.

'The thing is, this singer can't delay the shoot for various reasons and needs to record it in the next three days, which ties in with your wedding day. He needs to set up the room for the recording and is happy either for you to use the setting afterwards, or bring in a team to clear it and set the room up ready for your event.'

'But there's no need because, as I said, there isn't going to be a wedding,' Vicki said her eyes welling with tears. Casey slipped her arm around Vicki's slim shoulders. 'He's welcome to use the room for the entire day and evening if he needs to.'

Casey swallowed her own tears. She hated to see her friend so humiliated and disappointed by Dan's choices and then her own.

'That's so kind of you, Vicki.' Recalling that Dan's reluctance to get married was due to money worries, Casey wondered if maybe she might find a way to solve not only Matteo's problem but Vicki's too. 'I wonder...'

'What?'

'Sorry?' she asked unsure what her friend had just said.

'You just said, "I wonder" and I asked about what.'

Casey's breath shortened as the excitement rose in her. 'Look,

I've no idea if this will work,' she said, trying to quell her rising excitement. 'But bear with me.'

'I'm bearing,' Vicki groaned. 'Spit it out then.'

'I haven't had a chance to think this through, but as Matteo is willing to pay for the room and setting, and all that. How about we, or you,' she added remembering this was Vicki's big day and not really anything to do with her, 'secretly invite all the people you would like to come to the wedding.'

'Seriously?' A mixture of emotions crossed Vicki's face. 'But I told you it can't go ahead.'

'Why not? Look, Vicki, you've had the guts to come this far. Matteo is willing to pay for it, and Tara and I are going to dress the room. You don't need to worry about the deposit.' She wasn't sure how Vicki might explain booking the hall to Dan, but that was irrelevant right now. 'Why not go the whole way and at least try to get Dan there?'

'You really think we can do this?' Vicki bit her lower lip, her eyes wide.

'We can give it a try.' Casey reached out and took her friend's arm.

Vicki's mouth gaped open for a few seconds. 'I'm not sure I should but if this works then I'll be the happiest newlywed in the world.'

'We'll have to make sure it works, or at least give it our best shot,' Casey said, nudging her and laughing with her. 'We'll have to tell Jax, of course,' Casey said almost to herself. 'He can be in charge of making sure Dan gets to the venue on time.' Her mind raced. 'Do you think Dan will be too horrified if we do this to him?'

Vicki thought for a moment. 'It's the cost of the venue he minds, not us getting married, or at least that's what he's always led me to believe. I'm sure he won't mind, once he's over the shock.'

Casey hoped her friend was right. 'You'll need to sort whatever licence is required.'

'I already did that,' Vicki said in a quiet, embarrassed voice. When Casey gave her a questioning look, she added, 'I know what you're thinking. Why get a licence if I don't think I'll be getting married? I think it was because I wanted to enjoy as much of the experience as I could. It probably sounds daft.'

'It doesn't,' Casey said honestly. 'That's good then. You'll just need to invite everyone.'

'What about the video.'

'What about it?'

'You said you were setting up the room for it. I was wondering what it was like and if it might work well as the backdrop for the wedding.'

How could she have forgotten to mention something this important? Casey couldn't miss the expectant look on her friend's face. 'I think it'll be perfect.' She explained about the candles, mirrors and floaty material. 'It's a gothic theme, which I think will be perfect for the Medieval Great Hall, don't you?'

'Oh, yes.'

'Right, so if you can find a dress that works with that theme then all the better.'

Vicki laughed. 'You don't have to worry about a dress. I already have one hidden in the wardrobe in Mum's spare room.'

'Great,' Casey cheered leaping to her feet. 'Matteo will be delighted when I tell him you don't mind him using the venue, and Alex and Piper will be massively relieved.'

'Sorry? You keep saying "Matteo"?' Vicki asked aghast. 'Not *the* Matteo?'

Casey cringed. She wasn't intending to tell Vicki who the singer was until after the event. 'Blast. It was supposed to be a secret. But, yes, *the* Matteo. But you must keep that bit to yourself. Promise?'

'I'll promise anything you like,' Vicki laughed, tears coursing down her face, which Casey realised a few seconds later were a mixture of delight and hysteria at the unexpected turnabout.

6

Casey saw Vicki out and then immediately phoned Piper and asked her to pass on the good news to Matteo.

'You're incredible, do you know that?' Piper said. Casey was glad her friend thought so, aware she might not have been successful. 'I'm with them now. Do you want me to hand my phone over to Matteo so you can break the good news yourself?'

'I'll leave that to you, thanks,' she said, overcome by an attack of shyness. 'I need to go and speak to Tara now. If we can't supply enough candles and mirrors then we'll have to think of another idea. We also need to see if we can come up with somewhere I can source material and any other useful bits.'

'All right then. Good luck, Casey, and thank you so much. We're all enormously grateful to you for doing this.'

'It's fine,' she said, happy to be able to help Matteo and Vicki resolve their problems. 'Bye then.'

She sat quietly in the garden for a minute trying to take in all that had happened. So much for the ordinary day she had expected it to be when she woke that morning. Her phone rang but she didn't recognise the number. Concerned that it might be someone from The Cabbage Patch, she answered the call. 'Hello?'

'Casey, it's Matteo,' he said, his deep voice making her nerves tingle.

She cleared her throat to try and reply. 'Er, hi.'

'I wanted to thank you myself,' he said. 'Would you be free to come to dinner with me tonight?' *He wanted to take her out to dinner? Matteo Stanford?* When she didn't reply, he spoke again. 'I know it's short notice but as we have so little time to sort everything I thought we could talk through a few more details. Would that be all right?'

Casey thought she picked up hope in his voice and as awkward as she felt agreeing to something like this she knew she would kick herself if she turned down his invitation. And she smiled, knowing that if she turned him down Tara would be only too happy to do that kicking for her. Maybe it wouldn't be so bad.

'I'd like that very much,' she said, expecting him to assume she would be thrilled by his invitation.

'I'm glad. I'll send a taxi for you at seven tonight, if that's all right? We can eat here at the cottage or go somewhere else if you'd rather do that?'

She couldn't think of anywhere that might be private enough for him. 'No, the hotel is fine, thanks.'

'Great. I'll see you later then, Casey.'

'See you later, Matteo.' She ended the call and stared at the screen for a few seconds. She had just agreed to go to dinner with Matteo Stanford. What on earth was she going to talk to him about? She shook her head and reminded herself that he wanted to discuss the setting for his video. There would be more than enough for her to focus on so that she didn't get all tongue-tied and make a fool out of herself. Now all she had to think about was what to wear. That and to get back to work to see Tara.

* * *

'You're what?' Tara whispered. 'You are the luckiest girl I know and if I didn't love you like I do I'd be massively envious.'

'I still need to think what to wear though,' Casey said trying to picture all the clothes in her pathetically minimal wardrobe. 'I can't think of anything suitable.'

Tara tapped her chin as she thought. 'Hmm. What about asking your mum? She's the same size as you and she has some pretty decent things.'

They didn't really have the same sense of style though, Casey mused. Her mum was very much a flowery dress sort of person whereas she preferred anything that went with her trusty Doc Martens boots. 'I don't know. We're eating at the hotel and I'm sure it's rather posh. My DMs won't really go with anything she has.'

'Then you'll have to borrow her shoes too.'

Casey groaned. 'Really?'

Tara glared at her, hands firmly on her hips. 'Do you want to go out with Mr Gorgeous Superstar tonight or are you going to quibble about some flowers on a dress?'

Her cousin had a point. She was being ridiculous. 'When you put it like that I suppose I need to stop whinging and speak to Mum.'

'Right answer,' Tara said, looking satisfied. She slapped her hands together. 'Now, what do we need to think about for this...' She glanced around at the other stallholders and customers and lowered her voice. 'We'll call it The Event.'

'Whatever you like.'

'The first thing we need to do is work out how many candles we have in stock.'

Casey frowned. 'How many do you think we'll need?'

Tara frowned. 'I've no idea. Maybe we should pay a visit to the castle and see for ourselves exactly how big the room is so that we can work that out. There's no time to waste, so if you could call your uncle and arrange for us to go there in the next hour then we can make proper plans.'

'Good idea. I'll do that now while you go and ask Vivienne or one of the others if they can keep an eye on our stall until Piper gets here.'

Having looked at the location online, Casey began to make a list on her notepad.

Can use biodegradable confetti only
   Two nooks in walls for candles and ivy/eucalyptus
   Dark oak table with two cushioned chairs for bride and groom
   Beaten-earth floor
   High white-painted, vaulted roof and arched windows
   Large open fireplace
   Civil ceremony in there

* * *

Casey was glad the weather wasn't as hot as it could have been as they crossed the castle green, although the usually lush grass was now brown and dried from a run of so many hot sunny days. She stopped to look up at the battlements with the Jersey flag, Union flag and pennant representing the Parish of St Martin, where Gorey was situated, flying in the strong breeze. She stopped to take a photo of the azure blue of the sea in Gorey Harbour and the wide bay of Grouville below them before walking to the first granite archway taking them into the imposing castle.

They made their way along the stone pathway with the walls

high either side of them, stopping occasionally to look into the tiny archways leading up worn stone steps to other sections of the fortification. Through another arch they came across a pretty café, where families sat chatting and taking photos and then stopped for a few minutes to listen to a lady dressed in medieval clothes who was holding up different herbs and explaining to a group of people how they were used medicinally and the recipe for cooking a chicken for lepers in an effort to help them.

Casey nudged Tara. 'We'd better get a move on,' she whispered. 'Otherwise we're going to be here all day and we have too much to do.'

They began making their way up the many stairs, past a pretty manicured garden where Casey presumed the medicinal herbs had been grown among the immaculate box hedging and squares of rose bushes on their left, to an area where an enormous metal statue of a horse with a knight in full regalia stood in a grassy area. Two children dressed up as knaves were play-fighting with their father using wooden swords.

'This is amazing,' Tara said. 'I can't believe it's been years since I last thought to come here.'

'Me neither,' Casey agreed, enjoying seeing everyone having such a fun time. 'Come along, we'd better keep going before I run out of energy. We've still got loads more steps to climb.'

They passed a deep wishing well, from where water had been hoisted when the castle was lived in, and each threw down a few pence and made a silent wish. Casey wished for the venue to be perfect for the video. There was so much to do in such a short time and agreeing to a location for the filming would be a massive relief.

They finally reached the top of the wide granite steps and turned left onto the grassy area, where they saw a tower with a large bell and a cannon. Casey went to stand between a gap in the crenellated wall and took a few photos of the beach far below the rear of the castle.

'Where's the hall, then?' Tara asked. 'I have a feeling we should have turned right at the top of the stairs rather than left.'

'Let's go back that way then,' Casey suggested. They reached the top of the stairs and straight ahead was an arched doorway. 'Oh no, not more steps,' she groaned, concerned to think how exhausting it was going to be to carry boxes of candles and various mirrors up so many stairs. She could see several doorways at the top and decided that if it was the way to the Medieval Hall then they could decorate the way up to it somehow.

'Yes, this is it,' she said, reaching the top and taking the first door on her left. 'It's bigger than I thought.'

'Wow.'

They walked in and Casey stood next to her cousin in the middle of the white-walled room, gazing at the pretty nooks in the walls, with their arched leaded windows and their deep window ledges, which could each hold several candles, she supposed. At one end of the room an oak table and two regal-looking chairs sat in front of a white fireplace. She turned to face the opposite end of the room and was fascinated by an enormous metal statue that looked like a tree but with heads attached to each branch. Three complete figures were standing by the trunk of the tree.

'Look at that, Tara.' *What on earth was it?* She walked over and read the notice on a stand nearby. 'It's called The Tree of Succession,' she explained, reading all about it. 'Each of those heads depicts a member of the medieval monarchy from here.'

As she crossed the beaten-earth floor to peer out of one of the leaded windows at the sea far below, Casey looked up at the high, white, vaulted roof. She imagined that it was a perfect place to hold a wedding ceremony.

'It's incredible. We could do so much with this and it's going to be perfect for Matteo's video.'

Tara turned slowly, gazing up at the ceiling. 'Wow.'

It occurred to Casey that Vicki hadn't mentioned a wedding reception. She doubted that her friend would be able to afford hiring a marquee, especially in these grounds, or anywhere else for that matter. She shared her concerns with Tara.

'I can't imagine she has anything booked,' Tara said. 'Not if she wasn't expecting the wedding to actually go ahead.'

'And there's hardly any time to arrange anything now,' Casey mused. 'It would be sad if she had to have a wedding without one,' she said. 'I feel a little responsible now that I've persuaded her to invite guests along and ignited her wedding dreams again.' *Why hadn't she thought things through?*

'It's not your fault.' Tara frowned. 'You've helped her out of a deep hole and I don't think the reception is something you should feel badly about. It's not as if you have time to arrange things even if you wanted to.'

'I think I should at least try to help her arrange a wedding reception.' Her stomach churned in anxiety. *What had she got herself into?*

'Don't let's panic about that,' Tara said. 'We need to focus on this place first. I've been trying to picture how many candles we'll need and how they can be displayed for this shoot. The crew will have to set up their cameras and lighting.' She tapped her nose when Casey gave her a surprised look. 'I watched a documentary recently about the making of an advert. I know it's not exactly the same thing, but they'll need similar equipment to record it I would think.' Her voice trailed off.

'I suppose so.' Casey could see Tara had thought of something that worried her. 'What is it?'

Tara sighed heavily. 'Even if we use all the candles we have in stock I don't think we'll have enough to do this place justice.'

'What! We have to.' Casey tried not to panic. She tried to picture all their stock. 'We can't let Matteo down now, not since we've assured him we'll help make this work.'

'Did we do that?'

Casey realised she had been the one to make assurances rather than the pair of them. Her mind raced; she was starting to panic.

Tara shook her head slowly. 'It takes us seven to ten days to cure one of our candles, at the very least.'

Casey groaned inwardly. Tara was right. 'If only we had three days we could make them out of paraffin,' she said. 'But we only have two.' She struggled to find a quick solution. 'We'll simply have to find another source and buy more. We need to wrack our brains for any contacts we can speak to for help.'

'We have contacts on the mainland,' Tara said, 'but I doubt we can guarantee that anything they send us will get here in time.'

'Summer is such a busy time for most sellers,' Casey grumbled. 'I doubt anyone will be able to spare their stock anyway.'

'I agree,' Tara said. 'They won't want to risk letting down their regulars or holidaymakers by not having stock to sell. How would that look?'

'We need to think of something though,' Casey grumbled, trying to quell her rising panic.

'We do have one friend who might help,' Tara said thoughtfully. 'I'll give her a call.'

Casey didn't ask who; she was too busy trying her best to steady herself. 'OK, we need to calm down. By that, I mean that I need to do so. We're helping Matteo out here, so whatever we achieve is better than nothing, right?'

'Absolutely,' Tara agreed. 'We'll do what we can with what we have and hope that's enough.'

Casey agreed with more enthusiasm than she actually felt.

They took one last look around the room and after Casey had taken photos from every angle on her phone the two of them left the room, each lost in their own thoughts.

'We should ask Paddy if he has a couple of candle holders he can either lend us or make for us,' Tara suggested.

Casey liked the idea and hoped he wouldn't be too busy with his own metal sculpture commissions. 'Maybe a couple of cascading ones,' she added. 'One for each of the corners at the far end of the room either side of that amazing fireplace.' She pictured the scene and hoped that what she was imagining would meet with Matteo's expectations. 'It would give the candle displays better height. If he can't make them then maybe he has something he can sell to us. Matteo did say he was happy to pay for whatever we needed.'

'True. I'm sure Paddy'll help in any way he can,' Tara said as they walked down the wide stone steps past the battlements. 'He was saying only the other day how he's desperate for a couple of commissions.'

Casey slipped her phone into her jeans pocket. 'I can show Matteo the photos I've taken here this afternoon and go through everything with him. It'll give me something else to talk about with him over dinner.' She liked the idea and felt a little more confident about meeting with him now that she had an idea of things to discuss.

7

Matteo flicked through the photos on Casey's phone later that evening as they sat in the private dining room of his cottage. Two waiting staff and a chef who Martha's assistant, Louise, had arranged to come from the hotel were busily working. He could hear the chef chopping vegetables and placing pans on to the cooker while the waiting staff were putting the final touches to the dining room.

He was feeling uncharacteristically nervous for the evening and hoped that would pass soon. Casey's suggestion to use the castle had been an excellent one going by the photos he was looking at. The place looked incredible. He glanced up at Casey and caught her giving him a strange look.

'Is something the matter?' he asked without thinking.

Her eyes widened as if she had been caught doing something she shouldn't. 'No, I was, er, just thinking.'

She seemed a little uneasy. Maybe she had picked up on his unease and had thought something amiss. Irritated with himself for making her uncomfortable, Matteo pointed at her phone screen.

'The medieval room looks even better in these photos of yours,' he said, going back to study the previous picture hoping to put Casey at ease. 'Very atmospheric and with your candles and creative eye the room should look perfect for the recording.' He smiled at her and she seemed happy with his comment and, encouraged, Matteo added, 'I really can't thank you and your cousin enough for helping me in this way.'

'We don't mind,' she said. 'Tara and I are grateful to you for the opportunity of becoming involved in something so exciting.'

'I'm the one who is indebted to the pair of you.' He realised they hadn't discussed money and wanted to reassure Casey that he had no intention of leaving her and Tara out of pocket. 'I realise that I'll need to use a lot of your stock for the shoot.'

She laughed and it occurred to him that maybe they didn't have as much stock as he had supposed.

'Whatever we do use, you must make sure to let me or Martha know the cost so that you're not out of pocket. We need to cover your time too, of course.'

Casey seemed to relax slightly and he realised he should have spoken to her about paying for their services and stock sooner. She seemed to be considering something. 'Is there anything you wish to ask me, Casey?'

'What do you mean?'

Wanting to be certain that Casey did make sure he paid for all expenses, he said, 'You seem thoughtful and I want you to let me know of any difficulties you might have so that we can find a solution.' He smiled at her. 'Just like you've done for me with the castle and your offer to decorate it with Tara. That is, if there's any way I can help you both, I hope you would let me know.'

He watched as she gave his comment some thought. Then, when he was about to suggest he speak to Martha in case she could think of anything he might not have considered, Casey's mouth dropped open and she smiled.

'You've thought of something?'

She shook her head. 'No, it's fine.'

Wanting Casey to know how much he appreciated all she was doing, Matteo stared at her for a moment while he gathered his thoughts. 'I know I'm asking a lot of you all.' He handed her mobile back to her. 'But I'll recompense any of your or anyone else's costs fully. I'm relieved the shoot will be able to go ahead after all, and it's only thanks to you and your friends that it's able to.'

The waiting staff served their food. Matteo watched Casey eat a few mouthfuls. She really was very pretty, and so kind to offer so much of her time to his recording.

'Mmm, I don't think I've ever tasted anything as delicious as this asparagus and truffle risotto,' she said almost to herself.

Matteo tried the food. She was right, it was incredibly tasty.

Casey looked up from her food and saw him watching her as he swallowed his mouthful. Both stilled and he wished he could think of something amusing to say. Or wished she would speak again.

'Are you sure there's not something worrying you, Casey?' he asked. 'Please ask me anything you like. If we're working together, which we are, I need to know that I've done all I can to assist you and Tara.'

Casey stared at him thoughtfully again.

He gave her what he hoped was a reassuring smile. 'What is it?'

'I'm embarrassed to ask, but I know that if I didn't and then told Tara she would tell me I was foolish for not at least broaching the subject.'

'Then you must.' He was intrigued. He rested his fork on the side of his plate and waited for her to speak again.

'I understand there's a lot of secrecy about the shoot,' she said her voice low. She glanced towards the dining room door.

He suspected she didn't want the waiting staff to overhear what she was about to say. She looked down at her plate of risotto and after a few seconds ate another mouthful.

Had she changed her mind about asking him? he wondered. 'Go on,' he said, desperate for her to share whatever it was with him. 'Tell me.'

Swallowing, she placed her cutlery neatly on her plate. 'We're going to have to use up our entire stock for the shoot,' she explained. 'And will have to spend the few weeks afterwards building up stock again for our stall, so we'll be unable to sell any for a little while afterwards.'

'I see,' he said realising for the first time that theirs was probably only a fledgling business with little stock. 'I'm happy to cover any costs you incur from lack of sales over those weeks.'

'Thank you,' she said. 'But I think you've misunderstood where I'm going with this.'

'Right.' He couldn't work out what she might be getting at.

'It's not just our lack of sales,' she said. 'We're also concerned about using all our stock and losing some of the goodwill we've built up with our customers since we started our business.'

'Ah, I see,' he said giving her a reassuring smile.

'What I'm trying to say, badly—' she laughed '—is that it occurred to me that if you agree, we would love to take some photos before and after the shoot that we could use for promotion for our business.'

He stared at her as he gave her question some thought. It was an excellent idea and he wanted to agree immediately but was aware there needed to be conditions for Martha to accept the proposal.

'Obviously we wouldn't post any of the photos until after the release of the record and video,' she said as if reading his mind. 'I'm aware that confidentiality until then is paramount. But do you think we could do that?'

Relieved to see she understood the delicacy of her and Tara using photos of the shoot, he nodded. 'If you agree to wait until, say, the New Year, in case the release date is delayed slightly, then yes, I can't see why not. In fact,' he said, wanting to help her as much as possible, especially now he understood how much pressure her and Tara helping him had put on their business, 'I'll make sure you have photos of you two on set so that you have proof you were there.'

She beamed at him, clearly delighted with his reaction. 'And could we have a photo or two standing next to you?'

He laughed, happy to agree to her request. 'I don't see why not.'

'That's so kind of you.'

'Not at all. It'll be my pleasure, Casey.' He smiled at her and for a moment neither of them spoke. He was glad he had invited her to the cottage for dinner. Despite the initial awkwardness between them he was really starting to enjoy himself and he thought she might be too.

Casey tilted her head to one side thoughtfully. 'You said there was another problem you needed to sort out. Do you want to tell me what it is?'

His mood dropping slightly, he studied her face and then shook his head. 'No, I can't.'

'Why not? I'd like to help if I can.'

He sighed heavily. 'You've already done far too much for me already.'

'Rubbish. If you tell me, maybe I can find an easy solution to whatever it is,' she said smiling.

'Fine, but it's not something I want you to concern yourself with. You have enough to do.'

'Go on,' she said. 'I'm intrigued now.'

'I need to find a female actor.'

He didn't miss the startled look on her face, but she covered it quickly. 'An actor?' she asked, looking as if he had shared a strange request.

'Nothing, um, odd,' he said hurriedly, not wishing her to think him weird in any way. 'For the video.' He grimaced. 'Sorry, I should have been a little clearer.'

Casey exhaled sharply. 'Oh, right. You had me worried there for a moment.'

Unable to help seeing the funny side of what had just happened, Matteo struggled to remain serious.

He noticed Casey's eyes shining in amusement and within seconds they were both laughing hysterically. Casey wiped underneath her eyes with the backs of her fingers. 'That was hilarious.'

'It was eventually,' he laughed, relieved she had seen the funny side. Then, recovering his composure, he recalled his urgent need to find an actor.

'I'm sorry,' she said. 'Can I ask what happened to your other actor?'

'I gather she broke her ankle.'

'And you can't find another one anywhere?' She frowned as she ate the last couple of mouthfuls of her meal. 'I would have thought there must be queues of young actors desperate to take the place of the incapacitated one.'

'I suppose I could find one at this late stage but we would need to arrange to fly her here and I'd rather meet in person first.

There needs to be some sort of chemistry between us on screen.' He sighed. 'I know it probably sounds odd but I like to get a real sense of the person.' He tore a piece off the roll on his side plate, placed some butter on it and popped it into his mouth and chewed thoughtfully. 'I know Martha will be looking for the right woman as we speak. I'll give her a call later this evening.'

He saw Casey staring at him. 'Go on,' he said wondering what was on her mind. 'I can tell you've thought of something.'

'My sister,' she said, taking him by surprise.

'Your sister?' He hoped this wasn't going to be one of those difficult situations. He didn't want to upset her because she was not only unselfish and helpful to him, but she really was lovely.

'I know what you're thinking,' she said.

He hoped not. 'You do?'

'Yes, you're worried about why I would suggest Jordi.'

What was there to lose? he thought, pushing away the thought of all the work Casey had offered to do for the shoot. 'Tell me more.'

'She's an aspiring actress and has taken part in local productions for years.' Casey shrugged. 'Look, I know she's talented but I'm also aware that she hasn't ever been in a music video before. I've no idea if she's self-assured enough, but knowing how we're setting up the room for the shoot, I know she certainly looks perfect for the part.' She sighed. 'Is there any harm in seeing her?'

Was there any harm? 'As long as you, or she,' he added nervously, 'understand that she would only be accepted for the part if she was absolutely the right fit.'

'Of course.'

'And you think she would look perfect?'

'Yes. She has big blue eyes and long, wavy blonde locks that would be the perfect contrast to your dark, Italian movie-star looks.'

Taken aback by how she described him, Matteo was briefly lost for words. Did she describe him that way because she liked his looks, or was she simply being businesslike? He hoped it was the former. He noticed she was biting the side of her thumbnail absent-mindedly. 'Is something the matter?'

'I'm worried that if she's, well, not good enough, then I will have let her down.' She straightened her fork on her plate. 'And wasted your time.'

They sat in silence while the staff cleared their plates. 'Would you like dessert now or wait for a bit?' he asked, suspecting she wasn't in the mood for more food at that moment.

'I'd rather let my risotto digest, if that's all right?'

Once he had spoken to the waiting staff and they were away from the table, Matteo asked, 'Do you have a photo of, sorry, what did you say your sister's name was?'

'Jordi.'

'Of Jordi.'

Casey nodded and clicked into the gallery of her phone. She brought up a photo. 'I love this one of her,' she said, holding up the phone for him to see clearly.

He studied the beautiful girl on the screen. She was wearing a floaty white-and-pink summer dress with her glorious hair shiny and loose down her back and she was laughing at something. Matteo gasped. 'She's stunning.'

'She is. There's a sort of sparkle about her. She lights up a room and—' she smiled affectionately '—I'm probably a little biased but I do think she would be perfect.'

'And she's an actress.' He looked at Casey and then back down to the photo. 'You're quite different to each other, aren't you?'

'We have similar noses and...' She went quiet. 'People are always surprised to see that two girls who look so different are sisters.' She laughed. 'We don't even have the same eye colour. My hair is dark—'

'Almost chestnut,' Matteo said without thinking.

Casey gave him a look he couldn't read. 'Yes, it is. It's very different to Jordi's. I'm also shorter than my sister. I suppose that's about it. She's taller, fairer and certainly more outgoing than me.'

'You're both beautiful and I'm sure very lovely in your own ways,' he said, smiling at her. 'Do you think she'll consider doing the recording?'

'Would she?' Casey laughed. 'I'm sure she'd be delighted to.'

He couldn't help being relieved. 'Great. Can you send me this photo and I'll forward it to Martha. Then maybe you can ask Jordi to come here and we could meet.'

Remembering she had his number from his earlier call, Casey said, 'I'll send this to you right now.'

The photo sent, Casey added, 'Phone Martha now if you like.'

'You don't mind?' She shook her head. 'It's rather rude of me to invite you here then end up making a call to my manager.'

'It's fine.'

He supposed Casey wanted to know as soon as possible what Martha thought of her idea and he couldn't blame her. He called his manager and explained about their conversation before forwarding Jordi's photo.

'She does look perfect,' Martha said. 'The most important thing the actress needs to have is self-assurance and as much experience of shoots as possible. We don't want to waste time dealing with a terrified newbie or, worse, one of your hysterical fans. We don't have enough time for theatrics, Matteo.'

He sensed Casey's irritation, aware that Martha's voice would be loud enough for Casey to hear everything she said.

'Jordi might be inexperienced for what you're looking for,' Casey said as Matteo held the phone closer to her, 'but I can assure you she is always professional, and I'm sure she'll give it her best shot, otherwise I would never have suggested her to Matteo.'

Martha groaned. 'Fine. I'll keep looking and you give your sister a call, Casey. Matteo, you meet her, see how she is with you and whether you have any chemistry at all with her. I'm on my way to your cottage now with some of the crew and will arrange for Carl to film her and we can see how she does. We'll be there in about half an hour.' Martha ended the call. Clearly she had said her piece.

'Half an hour?' Casey asked. 'You want me to call my sister now?'

Matteo cringed. 'If you wouldn't mind. Do you think she'll come?'

'I imagine so. If she's at home and can get here. I think I'd better text her in case she's out somewhere noisy.'

She held up her phone so he could see the text.

I need you to come to meet me and a friend who might have an acting role for you. It's top secret. There will be a camera coming to record you, so be aware of that. Also please have your hair down and probably wear that white floaty dress I took the photo of you in at Mum's party last summer. Come as soon as you can. Here's the address... X

Happy with what she had typed, he nodded.

He watched Casey press Send. 'There, it's done,' she said. 'Now I've just got to hope that Jordi sees my message straight away.'

8

Jordi arrived forty minutes later. Casey had been listening out for footsteps and sat up straighter when she heard them. She stood and hurried over to greet her sister as she walked around the side of the cottage, her long, wavy, blonde hair so different to her own dark hair. They might be very different in looks and personalities but they had always got along well. Casey stood and waved her over, relieved to see Jordi looking calm and composed. Then again, she reminded herself, her sister was an actor and probably was hiding her true feelings. She hadn't been to that many auditions as far as Casey was aware and to have a mystery audition must surely be terrifying. Casey hoped to prepare her if only a little bit.

'Hi there,' she said, glad that Matteo had gone inside the cottage several minutes before with Martha when she had arrived. 'Well done for getting here so soon.'

'What's going on? Is everything all right?' Jordi asked, looking around. 'Your text sounded important and very mysterious.'

'I need you to keep calm. This might not be something you're asked to do but I thought you'd at least want to try.'

Jordi looked baffled and Casey realised she wasn't being very clear. 'I'll just spit it out.' She took a deep breath and took her sister's hands in hers. 'You're here to film an audition for the music video for Matteo Stanford's next record.'

Jordi stared at her for a few seconds. 'What?' Casey went to repeat what she had said but Jordi raised her hand to stop her. 'No, don't. I heard the first time and hearing you saying it again will make me panic.' She took in a deep breath and Casey immediately covered her sister's mouth with her hand, desperate to stop her from shrieking out Matteo's name, which she guessed she was about to do.

'Shush. This could be your big break, but you need to keep calm. They know you're fairly inexperienced but I've promised him and his manager you'll be professional at all times. You must make sure you are. They actually want a more experienced actor but agreed to see you because your appearance fits what they're looking for. Now you just need to prove to them that you are the perfect choice to play the part. OK?'

Jordi, still clearly in shock, nodded. 'Yes, right,' she whispered. She gave a gasp of delight. 'Oh my word, here he comes.'

'Jordi, I presume,' Matteo asked, striding over to them with his hand outstretched.

'Yes, here I am, just like you asked,' Jordi said giving him a beaming, confident smile as if she hadn't a few seconds ago looked as if she were about to faint with shock.

'It's very good of you to come here at such short notice.'

'It is,' Martha said in her husky seventy-cigarette-a-day voice as she followed him outside. 'We're very grateful to you.'

'It's my pleasure,' she said after a second's hesitation as she took his hand in hers. 'I just hope I'm able to give you what you need.'

'You certainly do look the part,' Martha replied, studying Jordi from head to toe. 'Let's hope you can act as well as you look and we'll all be very happy.' She turned her attention to Matteo. 'Shall we go and find out?'

'Would that be all right with you, Jordi?' he asked.

'Lead the way.' She smiled.

He looked at Casey. 'Are you joining us?'

Casey didn't want to put her sister off and gave her a questioning look as she answered him. 'I think I'll wait out here for you all. It's a beautiful evening and I'm happy to sit in the garden.'

She saw relief in Jordi's eyes and gave her a quick smile. 'Go knock 'em dead, sis,' Casey whispered as her sister walked past her and quickly gave Casey's hand a quick squeeze.

Casey watched Jordi accompany Matteo into the cottage, closely followed by Martha and two men. One of whom she presumed would be filming and the other covering the sound.

She hoped her sister's nerves didn't get the better of her. She exhaled sharply and willed Jordi to do well. For her own sake if not for Matteo's.

'Don't look so worried,' Alex said quietly. 'They'll be fine.'

Casey was surprised to see him there and then noticed Piper right behind him. 'When did you get here? I hadn't realised you were coming,' she said, happy to see them both. 'Did Matteo call you?'

Alex sat opposite her at the terrace table. 'He did, about quarter of an hour ago. He thought it might be a good idea for you to have someone you knew here to chat to while they were filming.'

'That was thoughtful of him.' She smiled at Piper as they both took a seat. 'I'm rather more anxious about my sister than I had anticipated.'

'We both know she's a really good actor,' Piper soothed. 'You did the right thing suggesting her, and if anyone stands a good chance of getting the part, she's certainly up there. You'd never put Jordi in a position to make a fool of herself.'

Alex touched Piper's forearm. 'Piper's right. And even if it turns out that your sister isn't quite right for the part, Matteo will let her down gently. He understands rejection and is very kind.'

She felt better hearing Alex's reassurances. She didn't know Matteo well but she also sensed that he would be gentle with her sister and that was what mattered most. 'By the look on Matteo's face he wants my sister to succeed nearly as much as I do.'

'I was thinking the same thing,' Alex said. 'I think my friend rather likes you.'

'What?' Casey hadn't expected him to say such a thing. 'He barely knows me,' she said, aware that knowing someone had little to do with chemistry. She had been attracted to him from the first moment they locked eyes, so why shouldn't he feel the same way?

Piper grinned. 'I agree.' She opened her mouth to add something more when someone shouted from the front of the cottage. 'I wonder what's going on?'

'Someone doesn't sound too happy,' Casey said, her heart racing. 'Maybe I should check if Jordi's all right.'

Alex shook his head as he stood up. 'No, the voices came from outside, not inside. I'll go and check and let you know.'

Casey and Piper watched him go around the side of the house followed by two other men wearing black tee shirts and charcoal chinos. She hadn't noticed them before but now realised they must be security. Before Casey had time to think anything further, two men marched to the back garden elbowing their way forward. One of the men with Alex stopped in front of the newcomers and said something Casey couldn't hear. The larger of the two men went to push him away and a scuffle broke out before Alex managed to grab hold of one of them.

'Hey, that's enough,' he said, his voice firm. 'This is a private area and I know for a fact that you haven't been invited here. Why don't you leave before someone calls the police?'

'Who the hell are you anyway?' said the larger of the two.

'I'm with the management,' Alex replied. 'You're not likely to get any photos because he's busy elsewhere. Don't waste your time waiting for him to come back.'

The men scowled at Alex before one of them scanned the garden and, unable to find Matteo, nudged his companion in the side. 'He's right. I can't see him. Let's go.'

Casey realised she had been holding her breath but relaxed as the men turned and left, disappearing back around the side of the building. Alex thanked the security guards, waited a few seconds and then returned to their table.

'Sorry about that.' He sat down next to Piper again.

'Who were they?' she asked. 'What did they want?'

'Paps wanting photos of Matteo.'

She realised one of them had been holding a camera. 'But how did you know?'

He shrugged. 'I recognised one of them. When you spend time with Matteo you get used to seeing the regulars.'

Casey finished the drink that had been served to her earlier and put her empty glass onto the table. 'But they will have had to book plane tickets to come here. Isn't that going to be expensive?'

'I suppose they get their travel costs refunded from whoever employs them,' Piper suggested thoughtfully.

'Photos of Matteo sell for a lot of money these days, so it's worth it for them to take a chance. Some pay off. Others, like just now, don't.' Alex sighed. 'The money they'll charge for a good photo of Matteo, especially one with a girlfriend, is worth a lot to them. Much more than the cost of a flight and hotel room for a few days.'

Piper was astounded.

'Really? I had no idea.'

'Yes, I suppose it's part of what Matteo does, unfortunately for him.' He smiled at a waiter who came over to their table. 'Can I fetch any drinks for you all?'

'A Pimm's for me, please,' Piper said.

Casey eyed her empty glass. 'That would be lovely. Same for me, thanks.'

Piper leaned forward. 'It's a whole new world this celebrity one, isn't it?'

'It is,' Casey agreed, wondering if she was opening herself up for a lot of heartache even acknowledging that she liked Matteo. She had no experience of this sort of lifestyle, and, if he did end up liking her, had no idea how well she would cope with it. She had been single for a while now and had been happy doing exactly what she wanted when she wanted.

'You're looking very serious,' Alex said, glancing at her.

Not wishing to admit her true thoughts, Casey said the first thing that came into her head. 'I was thinking how disruptive those paps were barging into the garden like they did.'

The waiter served their drinks and left them to return to the cottage. Alex took a sip from his beer.

'Don't worry about it. I wouldn't give them a second thought if I were you. They won't come back now. Not here anyway, though poor Matteo might find them turning up somewhere else over the next few days.'

She hoped not. 'It can't be easy for him when that happens.'

Alex shook his head. 'It isn't but it comes with the territory. He usually plans every outing meticulously before he goes somewhere. Or Martha does. She's very protective of him.' He laughed. 'Most of the paps are terrified of her.'

'Maybe we should have told Martha about taking Matteo to Grantez before going there,' Piper said thoughtfully.

Casey thought about what Piper had said. 'I'm not sure what Martha could have done to shield Matteo from whoever had seen him there though. You can hardly keep people from going there if they want to.'

'I suppose you're right,' Piper agreed.

'It's not your fault, Piper,' Alex said. I should have been more careful if anyone is to blame. I've at least spent time with Matteo and witnessed some of what he has to deal with.'

'That makes me feel a bit better,' Piper said.

Casey breathed in the evening air, which was fragrant with a mixture of roses and lavender warmed by the long sunny day. She was enjoying herself, she realised. She thought of how her meal with Matteo had been cut short so that Jordi could audition, and although she probably should have minded a little, she didn't. This was such an important event for both her sister and Matteo, and here she was sitting on a pretty terrace with Piper and Alex while her sister made the most of the biggest opportunity she had been given so far in her life. Casey smiled contentedly.

'I think they're coming back outside,' Alex said sometime later, peering towards the open doors to the living room. 'I can hear voices.'

Casey's stomach twisted anxiously. She clasped her hands together, willing Matteo to bring the news they wanted to hear. But before he could walk outside the two men who had gone with Alex to confront the paparazzi went inside and began speaking in low voices to him and Martha.

After a second or two Jordi stepped outside and Casey couldn't miss the excitement on her sister's face. She must have been offered the job. It dawned on Casey how tense she had been since watching Jordi go inside.

'It went well,' Jordi said, bending down to kiss Casey on the cheek. 'I was terrified but he's so kind.' She put her hand up at the side of her mouth and her voice quietened to a whisper. 'And drop-dead gorgeous. He helped me relax by talking me through everything he wanted me to do first.'

'I'm so relieved for you,' Casey said, patting the seat on one side of her for her sister to sit. 'I knew you could do it.' She picked up her Pimm's, taking a long slow drink from the glass.

'Well done, Jordi,' Piper said, grinning widely at her.

'Yes, well done.' Alex gave her a thumbs-up. 'Matteo will be delighted to have found you.'

'One half of me is glad that's over,' Jordi said eventually. 'The other half loved every second. I'm going to treasure that memory forever.' She smiled at Casey. 'Matteo said he was very impressed with me.' She gave an excited squeal. 'He also said how grateful he is to you for suggesting me.'

'Did he?' Casey asked, relieved to hear her sister say as much. Jordi nodded.

'What happens now then?' Piper asked.

'I'm meeting with Martha in the morning,' Jordi said. 'I need a fitting for some sort of floaty dress. I'm massively excited.' She sighed noisily and Casey thought she had never seen her sister happier. 'This is like a dream. I'm a little stunned and I can't quite take it in just yet. I'm determined to enjoy every second though.'

'That's the way to go,' Piper said.

'Congratulations,' Alex said. 'That's most things fixed now then, isn't it?'

Casey didn't like to ruin the mood but she also knew everyone needed to be realistic and told them about her concern about not having enough candles for the room at the castle.

'Ahh, right.' He frowned. 'Any idea how we'll sort this problem out?'

'Not yet,' she said honestly. 'I've emailed a couple of people who sell similar stock to us and phoned several others but none of them have any extra stock they can let us have.' She sighed. 'If I could tell them that it was for Matteo's video it might change their answers, but, as you know, I can't do that.'

'How about mentioning we need them for a wedding?'

'I tried that with a few but it made no difference.'

'We'll have to think of something, and quickly,' Piper said.

Alex slipped his arm around Piper's shoulders. 'Don't look so worried.' He pulled her gently towards him and kissed her on the cheek. Casey couldn't help wishing that Matteo would do the same to her. She wouldn't mind someone kissing her and telling her everything would be fine right now.

'We'll sort this out,' Alex continued. 'I don't want you two to feel like this is your problem because it isn't. We'll work everything out between us all.' He picked up Piper's drink and put it into her hands. 'Right now, though, I want you both to forget everything apart from relaxing and having fun tonight. Agreed?'

Why did she always feel like she needed to sort out everyone's problems? Alex was right. She looked over to where Matteo was talking to Martha in the living room near the open French doors. He seemed calm enough and she should try to do the same.

'Agreed.' She would worry about the candles again in the morning. It wasn't like she could do anything about them tonight anyway.

9

The following morning Casey woke to brilliant sunshine pouring through her thin bedroom curtains. She winced and covered her head with her summer duvet. Her head pounded and her mouth was dry. She must have had more Pimm's than she had realised.

She lay still, thinking back to all that had happened. Her sister's audition and getting the part in the music video. Casey grinned, content with how things had panned out and wondering how her sister felt this morning. Nervous, probably; excited, certainly.

She sat up slowly and rubbed her eyes. She couldn't wait to speak to her. She threw back her duvet cover and swung her legs out of the bed, slipping her feet into her slippers.

She walked over to her dressing table mirror and, bending slightly, gazed at her dishevelled reflection. 'Eugh,' she groaned, picking up her brush and dragging it through her messy hair. 'Thank heavens Matteo can't see me now.' She pulled a face at herself and then left her room.

She went to knock on her sister's bedroom door.

'She's gone, love,' her mum said. 'Left about an hour ago.

Some woman called for her. Gone for a fitting for that job you got her.'

Casey could hear excitement in her mother's voice despite her apparent coolness.

Rowena grabbed her and gave her a hug and pressed a kiss onto her cheek. 'You're a good girl thinking of Jordi like you did yesterday,' she said. 'I'm very proud of my two girls. Do you know that?'

'I do, Mum,' she said grinning.

'So, what have you got planned for today?'

Casey thought for a moment. 'I have to find candles.'

Her mother laughed. 'Don't you already have enough of those?'

Casey explained about the shoot and the issue with needing more cathedral candles like theirs. 'Or similar,' she said. 'But they must be cream rather than white for the right effect.'

'Surely you could buy some from the garden centre up the road? I know they won't be the same but they'll add to those that you have and can be hidden at the back behind the more authentic ones and will bulk up your stock a bit.'

'That's a good idea, Mum, I'll do that.'

'Good. I'll give some thought about locating more of the ones you do need,' Rowena said. 'Let you know if I come up with anything useful.'

'Thanks, Mum.'

'What else?'

She realised she still had to speak to Jax about Dan. She knew Piper would be very happy to sort out Dan, but didn't want to take up any time that her friend and Alex might have to spend together. 'I need to speak to Jax about something. I'd better get a move on if I'm to do everything I need to today.' She hurried to the bathroom to shower.

'Will you have a chance to take Ralph out for a walk sometime?' her mother asked.

Casey knew that she would probably have a bit of a walk on her hands if she was to go and find Jax. 'Sure. He can come with me this morning.'

She had tried to call Jax on his mobile but he hadn't answered, not that she ever really expected him to. He rarely bothered to take his mobile with him and even when he did it was mostly on silent so as not to disturb him when he was out foraging with clients. Deciding to start her search on Grouville beach, Casey attached their rescue dog's lead to his pink collar and led him out of the house, through the back lane and across the road onto the slipway and down onto the beach.

Ralph pulled against the lead, wanting to be let free. She checked her watch, and, seeing it was only just after eight-thirty, bent to unclip the lead.

'Go on then.' She watched him run off down the beach to the water's edge and followed slowly, looking either side of her, scanning the beach to see if she could spot Jax. Or, if not him, then Piper. Piper usually managed to find him, or had some idea where he might be.

She and Ralph weren't the only ones on the beach, she noticed. Others had already set up their own small areas, lying on towels, some with large sunshades and one or two individuals dozing, reading or listening to whatever music was playing on their mobiles. It was a glorious day and if she hadn't been running around trying to tick off some of the jobs on her mental list, or working at The Cabbage Patch, she would probably be down here too, making the most of the glorious early sunshine before it got too hot and the beach too busy with families and children.

'Out for a walk, too?' someone asked.

Casey turned to see Alex to her right and, seconds later, Ralph, no doubt sensing someone who might make a fuss of him, bounded up to him. He jumped up and down on his back legs before resting his front paws on Alex's left leg.

'Sorry. He's really friendly but thinks that everyone adores him,' Casey said, reaching to take Ralph's collar and pull him gently away.

'It's fine. He won't bother me.' Alex grinned, bending to stroke Ralph's brown-and-white head. 'He's a lively little guy. Is he yours?'

'No, my sister's.'

'What is he? A Yorkshire terrier? Something like that?' Alex asked, stroking the dog's ears.

'No idea. We think he has Yorkie in there somewhere, but no one has been able to decide for certain.'

'Where's Jordi now?' Alex asked. 'She must be very excited. I know Matteo was delighted with her audition.'

A thrill coursed through her to think that Matteo was so happy to have signed her sister for the video. 'I'm so proud of her,' Casey said. 'I'm sure I would have panicked if someone had called me and asked me to audition with no warning, especially for someone as famous as him.'

'Me, too,' Alex agreed. 'She'll go far with that courage.'

'I hope so. She's wanted to act ever since I can remember and this is an incredible addition to her CV.'

'It really is.'

Casey realised she hadn't answered his question about where Jordi was now. 'Martha collected her earlier, Mum said. She's taken Jordi off for a fitting, which is why I'm here with this little guy.' She saw Ralph starting to head back to the water's edge. 'He loves the water, so I'd better get after him before he swims too far out.'

Alex laughed and brushed his hands against his jeans to rid them of the damp sand clinging to them. 'I can see that.' He was about to say something else when he was distracted. Pulling his phone from his back pocket, he answered it.

'Matteo? On the beach with Casey, why?'

She watched as Alex glanced at her. 'Hang on a second, mate, I'll ask her.' He lowered the phone. 'Matteo wants to know if we'll join him for a barbecue at the cottage?' Casey couldn't hide her delight. She went to answer but he added, 'If you could let Tara and Jordi know they're more than welcome too.'

'I'd be happy to, although I have quite a lot to do first and need to drop Ralph off at some point.'

Alex said, 'I think he owes you all a decent meal after all you're doing for him.' He grinned at her cheekily. 'Although I'm not sure one of his barbecues will fit the bill all that well.' He raised his phone to his ear, listened for a few seconds and laughed. 'I did not.' Then, shaking his head, he grinned at Casey and added, 'OK, I might have forgotten you were still on the phone.'

She laughed. She loved that Alex was so relaxed with Matteo. It made Matteo seem more human and less of a superstar and she liked to think of him that way.

Alex ended the call. 'He suggested we get to the cottage for six-thirty. Will that be all right for you all?' She nodded her agreement. 'Great. I'd better go and meet Piper. She should have finished helping her mum by now and I promised to go with her to The Cabbage Patch to help her and Tara pack up whatever candles you still have on your stall.'

'Oh? I had no idea,' Casey said. He looked concerned. 'No, it's fine. I've been so busy with Jordi and now looking for Jax that Tara must have decided to get on with other things while I'm not there. It's all good. We have so much to organise in such a short time.'

'Let me know if there's anything else I can do, won't you?'

Casey spotted Jax in the distance. 'Will do. But right now I'd better get to him before he wanders off somewhere,' she said pointing to where Jax was throwing a ball for Ralph and his own dog, Seamus, throwing his head back and laughing loudly as the two little dogs raced each other to get to it first.

'The dog or Jax?' Alex laughed.

'Both,' Casey said. 'See you later.' She gave him a wave and ran down to speak to Jax.

He bent and patted his hands on his knees as both little dogs ran back to him, Seamus carrying the battered tennis ball and Ralph running next to the slightly bigger dog and bashing into him in annoyance that he had lost the ball to him. Jax noticed her coming towards him and indicated the two competing dogs. 'Ralph isn't happy to have lost out to my boy.' He laughed.

'That's because he thinks that every ball on this beach must be his.'

He took the ball from Seamus' mouth and threw it again, but this time in the opposite direction, giving Ralph a head start. 'I wondered who this little chap was with. Jordi not with you?'

'Not today.' She walked next to him as he began following the two running dogs. 'I'm glad I found you, Jax. There's something I need to ask you.'

He stopped walking and gave her a questioning look. 'Sounds interesting.'

She pulled a face. 'It is rather.'

'Go on.'

She explained all about a secret wedding and her involvement.

'Right,' he said dragging out the word. 'I can't see what I can do to help with any of this though?'

'I haven't got to the bit that involves you yet.' She watched his eyes widen and could almost hear his brain cells trying to fathom out who was getting married. 'Wedding? Not Piper?'

'What? No, of course not. She's only known Alex for a few weeks.'

He looked around and then, still confused, shrugged. 'Then who?'

'Vicki and Dan.' She waited for him to react.

'Dan's getting married? He never said anything.' Ralph raced past him, skidding to a halt, letting Jax take the ball to throw it again.

She waited until she had Jax's attention once more, aware that she was about to give him a shock. 'That's because he doesn't know yet.'

Jax stared at her. 'Seriously?'

Casey explained about Vicki booking the venue and paying several hundred pounds in deposit. 'So, you see, if all that was keeping Dan from getting married was the cost of the wedding, now the cost of the venue is being covered...'

'How?'

'There's no need for you, or Dan to worry about that. The most important thing is that Vicki won't lose a deposit she can't really afford.'

Jax shook his head. 'Why do you women make things so complicated all the time?'

She glowered at him. 'Rubbish. We just go for what we want and try to make things happen. If Vicki was to wait for your pedantic friend to decide it was the right time for them to get married, she'd probably be in her forties. He loves her enough to get engaged and ask her to marry him. All this plan does is take away his fears and any cost. If he's been honest about them,' she added, aware but not caring that she was now ranting, 'he'll be happy for this to happen and move them to the next step in their relationship. It makes perfect sense to me.'

Jax laughed. 'I'm sure it does. I just hope Dan sees it the same way you do.' He turned to face the sea, arms folded, clearly stunned by what he had just learned. Casey waited. 'Hang on a second,' he said turning back to face her. 'What's my part in all this?'

And there it was, she thought, amused. 'You're going to make sure he's dressed appropriately and is up at the venue in time for his wedding.'

He spun round to face her. 'The wedding he knows nothing about, you mean?' he asked sarcastically.

'That's the one.' This was going better than she had imagined, Casey mused.

'No.' He shook his head and started marching up the steps towards the pier.

'What do you mean, *No*?'

Casey called Ralph and, when he reached her, clipped his lead onto his collar. Seamus followed Jax up the steps and Casey ran after them, aware she couldn't shout and chance disturbing nearby residents or holidaymakers. 'Jax,' she hissed, reaching out to grab his arm. She missed, so grabbed the waistband of his shorts and held on tightly. His shorts began to come down and, remembering she was on a lower step than him, Casey reluctantly let go.

He grabbed hold of his shorts before they fell too low and dragged them back to where they should be and spun round to her. 'What do you think you're doing?'

She bit her lower lip, embarrassed. 'Sorry. I didn't mean to do that.'

'What did you mean to do then? For pity's sake, Casey, I know you're trying to help your friends out but this is absurd.' He looked around him and lowered his voice. 'Dan will never go for it. You know that as well as I do.'

'Why ever not?'

He thought for a moment. 'Because it's a wedding we're talking about here, not a surprise lunch, or...' He struggled to come up with an alternative. 'Or a... a surprise ice-cream.'

Casey giggled. 'Surprise ice-cream?'

'It's not funny.' He glared at her for a second before his face relaxed and his mouth broke into a grin. 'You're such an annoying person sometimes, do you know that?'

'I'm not,' she argued, knowing full well he was probably right.

He took her hands in his. 'Look, I know you're only trying to help everyone and I think that's a kind thing to do, but what if Dan is only making excuses about the cost of the wedding?'

She hadn't seriously considered that before and she was shocked. Jax knew Dan far better than she did. 'Then he's a complete moron.' She glared at him. 'Do you think that's what he's done?'

Jax shrugged and let go of her hands. 'I've no idea, but it's possible.'

The thought of Dan misleading Vicki in such a way infuriated her. 'But that's so underhand. I thought Dan had more courage than that.'

'I'm not saying it's what he has done,' Jax said hurriedly. 'But I do think you should be careful about this. He might not want to get married just yet and could be using the cost as an excuse not to hurt Vicki's feelings.'

Casey had had enough. 'Then he shouldn't have led her on. As far as Vicki's concerned money was his only concern. Look,

Jax, she's gone this far now and I'm certain she's going through with these wedding plans.'

'But...'

'But nothing. Vicki will be there. Her family and the friends she let into the secret will be there. I will be there. So will your mum, I imagine.'

'Mum knows?'

Casey shook her head. 'I don't think so, but knowing Sheila she will want to help in some way.'

'True.'

'Piper will be there, and her mum and gran. Nancy will be doing the flowers.' She wasn't sure that Nancy even knew about the wedding plans yet, but Casey knew without any doubt that Vicki's boss would be delighted to help make her day the best it could be. 'All you have to do is get him there. Wearing his best suit.'

Jax shook his head. 'And how do you expect me to do that?'

'I've no idea.'

'This is ridiculous. I can't just say, "Hey, mate, let's dress up in suits and wander up to the castle for a bit." He'd think I was ridiculous.'

'Hmm.' He had a point. She wrapped her arms around herself, desperately trying to come up with a plausible plan for Jax. Then it dawned on her. 'You thought Piper was getting married to Alex.'

'And?'

'If you thought that was plausible then why don't you tell Dan that's what's happening?'

'But he barely knows Alex. He wouldn't expect to be invited to the wedding,' Jax said.

'Vicki is Piper's friend and you and Dan took her and Alex out on the RIB, so he does know him.' Casey groaned in frustration.

'Look I've got a massive To Do list to get through today and this is only one of those jobs. Please stop looking for problems and tell Dan that Piper and Alex are getting married in secret.' She thought quickly. 'You can say it's a secret because they only want a few select people to know and that she's asked you to bring him along to make up the numbers on Alex's side, as he doesn't have many friends on the island. Do you think you can do that?'

Jax pulled a pained expression. 'At this moment I'll agree to any damn thing if you'll leave me to get on with my morning.'

Casey realised she had been far too bossy. She gave him a sympathetic smile, and, standing on tiptoes, kissed his unshaven cheek. 'You know we'll all love you forever for doing this, don't you?'

'I'm past caring about that too,' he said, his mouth pulling back in a lopsided grin.

'Thanks, Jax, you're a sweetheart.'

'If you say so.'

She hurried past him, stopping when he called to her.

'What is it?'

She hoped he hadn't thought of another reason not to go through with her plan.

'Put in a good word with Alex's sister for me when you next see her, will you?'

'Fliss?'

'Yes.'

From what Piper had told her, Alex's sister wasn't the nicest of people. Casey couldn't understand why someone as natural and friendly as Jax might like someone as spoilt and rude as Fliss. It wasn't her business, though, she reminded herself.

'Of course I will,' she said, breaking into a run with Ralph. 'We have to get you home if I'm going to sort out more stock,' she said as they made their way back to the village and her home.

* * *

Casey followed her mother into the kitchen, where Rowena was sewing the hem of one of her father's favourite pair of chinos. 'I'm tired of trying to keep these trousers going for him,' she grumbled. 'I keep threatening to chuck them away, but your father won't part with them, more's the pity.'

'Want a cuppa, Mum?' Casey asked, knowing her mother rarely turned down a fresh cup of tea. She flicked the switch of the kettle on and reached up to take down two cups. Then bending down and opening the cupboard nearby, she took out Ralph's treat tin and picked up a gravy bone. She waited for him to sit before giving it to him. 'Good boy, now off you go to eat it.'

'Thanks, love.' Rowena opened the fridge and took out one of her nail varnishes that she kept on a small tray in the fridge door. 'Did you find Jax?'

Casey realised she hadn't confided in her mother about Vicki's dramas yet. 'Let me make these first and I'll tell you.' Casey finished making their drinks and picked them up. 'Garden?'

'Good idea.'

She followed her mother and when they were outside placed both cups of tea down on the small plastic table between the two sunloungers. She confirmed that she had found and spoken to Jax.

'At least that's done now,' she said. 'I know Jax wasn't pleased to be dragged into this but I'm sure he'll do all he can to get him to the castle when he's supposed to be there. And we only have another two days to sort everything out.'

Her mother looked perplexed. 'Sorry, what are you talking about?'

'Um, the room was already rented by someone for a wedding.'

'Room?' Rowena immediately stopped what she was doing and looked up. 'Whose wedding? I haven't heard about a wedding taking place there in the next couple of days.'

Casey laughed. 'Probably because it's not one of your friends, Mum. Also, it's a secret.'

'I don't know them then?'

Casey grinned. 'You do.'

'Well, then tell me who it is.' She picked up her cup, blew on the steaming drink then lowered it again to the table. 'Too hot. Hurry up, Casey. I'm dying to know what's been going on.'

'It's... Vicki.'

Rowena's eyebrows lowered. 'From the florist?'

'Yes. Do we know another one?'

She continued sewing, her deft fingers making quick work of the hem. 'Surely we'd have heard if she was getting married though?'

Casey could see her mother was hurt not to have been invited and explained what had happened. 'She booked it without telling anyone, even Dan has no idea.'

'What? But why would she do that?'

Casey pulled a face. 'I'm not sure but I think she's hoping he will be too worried about upsetting her to refuse to go through with it. I've just had to persuade Jax to find a way to make sure Dan is up at the castle after the shoot ends so he can get married.'

Rowena stared at her aghast. 'You think he'll do that?'

'Who, Jax, or Dan?'

Rowena continued sewing. 'I know Jax will do as you asked, but what if Dan gets there and refuses to go through with the ceremony? The poor girl will have got dressed up for nothing.'

Casey thought of Vicki being embarrassed in front of her close friends and family and then pictured Dan. 'He did propose, so I don't know why he would do that to her. He's always insisted the reason he hadn't got round to marrying her was because he wanted them to save for a deposit for their own home. So he'll probably be relieved that issue has been resolved for them.'

'We'll have to hope that he is.' Rowena sighed deeply. 'For poor Vicki's sake.' She looked up. 'Am I invited do you think?'

'Yes, everyone on the pier and friends from the village are welcome.'

'That's good of her.'

'I think she'll need all of us there for moral support if nothing else.' Casey wondered what she should wear. 'I'm not going to have much time after the shoot to run down the hill, shower and change, and then hurry back up to the wedding.' The thought of the next few days and what it would entail made her feel drained. She wasn't so sure she still felt like attending Matteo's barbecue with all that she still had to plan.

10

Casey saw Piper and Alex cross the road towards her home and grabbed her car keys from the hallstand. She picked up the blue cardigan she had chosen to wear with her favourite pale-blue cotton dress and, seeing that Piper was wearing something in a similar style, was relieved to note that at least if they were under-dressed then they would be so together.

She would have liked Jordi to join them but she had made prior arrangements to meet a couple of friends in town for a meal and hadn't wanted to let them down.

Tara ran out behind Casey, calling her goodbyes to her Aunt Rowena and holding a thin cotton sweater in one hand. She was wearing a pair of floaty trousers and a smart tee shirt and had taken time with her make-up, something she rarely bothered to do.

'I'm so excited,' Tara shouted as she ran over to Casey's car and waited for Alex and Piper to get into the back seat. 'I can't believe we're actually going to see him again.'

Piper gave Alex a sideways glance. 'He's very pleasant, I thought, and not at all like a superstar. Very ordinary really.'

Alex laughed. 'Don't let him hear you saying things like that.' He smiled. 'Matteo is a great bloke but he'd hate to be thought of as ordinary.'

Tara turned in the passenger seat to face Alex. 'Don't worry, Alex. I can't imagine for one second that either of us will ever think that of him, not really. You'll probably have a bigger problem with us not trying to act like hysterical fans.'

'Speak for yourself,' Casey said quietly as she turned on the ignition.

'Yes,' she heard Tara reply. 'I forgot that you're not that into his music.'

Casey hoped her cousin wouldn't say as much to Matteo. It wasn't that she didn't like his music, she did, but she wasn't crazy about his songs to the extent that her cousin was, playing the latest release over and over again until it nearly drove her mad. In fact, she thought, maybe it was because of Tara constantly playing his songs that had slightly put her off them.

After a short drive they reached the hotel. Casey waited for several cars to pass before one stopped and flashed his lights, allowing her to turn into the granite archway. She gave a wave of thanks and carefully drove through. 'Good timing,' she said as a car was pulling out of one of the more shaded parking spaces.

Parked, they got out of the car. Casey's stomach gave a noisy rumble and she realised that she hadn't eaten anything since her single slice of toast and bramble jam that morning.

'Someone's hungry,' Tara teased. 'I have to admit that I'm a little peckish, too.'

Casey closed the car door nearest to her and pressed her fob to lock it. 'Let's get to the cottage then.'

She hoped Matteo had put out a couple of bowls of nibbles so she might fight off the worst of her hunger by eating a snack.

'Lead the way, you two,' Casey said, embarrassed to go first.

She didn't want to act too familiar despite Matteo's friendliness towards them all.

'It's kind of him to invite us all,' Tara said.

Casey smelt the tempting aroma of cooking as they walked around the outside of the cottage towards the terrace. She looked up at Alex. 'I'm sure he would rather spend the time with you catching up.'

Alex shook his head. 'Not at all. Matteo is a sociable bloke and loves any excuse for a party, be it a quiet barbecue for five, or a large, noisy party.'

They turned the corner to the walkway leading to the front door of the cottage and Casey couldn't miss the laughter coming from the back garden. 'It doesn't sound as if it's only us four he's invited tonight.' She wasn't sure if she was relieved or disappointed.

'It doesn't, does it?' Alex said thoughtfully. 'Maybe he's invited his production team. I'm not sure he knows many other people in Jersey.'

'We'll soon find out,' Piper said.

'You're here,' Matteo cheered, stepping away from a group of people Casey didn't recognise as being local. He marched over to greet them. Putting his arm around Alex, he caught Casey's eye and unless she imagined it his smile widened slightly before he led them back to his guests. Casey reckoned there must have been over twenty of them gathered on and around the terrace, drinks in hand and chatting and laughing with each other. So much for a quiet get-together.

'I thought we were just having a quiet barbecue,' she heard Alex whisper. 'Not one of your noisy parties.'

'Stop moaning and come and enjoy yourself. It'll do you good to relax.'

Casey wasn't sure why. As far as she was concerned Alex

seemed to be relaxed most of the time since his grandfather's leg had all but healed.

'Good to see you again, Casey,' Matteo said, kissing her cheek before holding her gaze for a little longer than she expected. Not that she minded. In fact, she rather liked to think that he might be attracted to her. Alex cleared his throat and Matteo glanced at him before leaning towards Piper and then Tara and giving them both a friendly kiss on their cheeks. Casey watched Tara's eyes widen at her over Matteo's shoulder and she couldn't miss how excited she was for him to be so friendly towards her.

'Shall we go over?' Matteo asked before leading them to a bar area that had been set up a few feet away from where someone was turning chicken legs, sausages and kebabs on a very impressive steel gas barbecue. She presumed it was one of the hotel staff.

'What are you all drinking?' Matteo asked, handing Alex a bottle of lager without waiting for him to reply.

'Just a lemonade for me, please,' Casey said. 'I'm tonight's designated driver.'

Matteo frowned. 'Can't you leave the car here overnight? I can arrange taxis to take you home and then bring you back to collect it in the morning if you want me to.'

Casey could tell he was trying to be as helpful as possible but she didn't want to drink too much and feel ghastly in the morning, especially when she had so much still to arrange for the shoot and Vicki's wedding. 'Thanks, but I'll stick to lemonade tonight.'

'No problem.' He smiled at the others. 'How about you?'

'Pimm's for me, please,' Tara said.

'That's a great idea,' Piper agreed. 'I'll have the same as Tara, please.'

He ordered their drinks and turned back to Piper, who rested a hand on Casey's shoulder. 'This all looks amazing, Matteo. Doesn't it, Casey?'

Before Casey could answer, Martha bellowed from the living room doorway. 'Matteo!'

He looked over to her and gave a wave. 'Sorry, Martha's calling me. I'd better go. She's a little wound up at the moment. Not that I blame her. It's been intense these past few days.'

Casey heard laughter and noticed Piper tense. She wondered what had bothered her friend.

'Fliss?' Alex asked. 'What are you doing here?'

'I heard about the party and asked Matteo for an invite for me and Phoebe.'

'But I didn't even know you were on the island,' he said, looking hurt. 'When did you get here?'

'She's staying with me,' Phoebe said, gazing at Alex through her long and, Casey suspected, false eyelashes. At least she imagined they were false. Surely no one had natural lashes that long.

'Hi Phoebe. Good to see you again,' Alex said, giving her a kiss on the cheek.

'It's great to be here,' she replied.

'Yes, I'm staying with Phoebe,' Fliss said. 'So there's no need for you to worry about me, or,' she said, pulling a face, 'start thinking you can boss me around while I'm here.'

Casey imagined that Alex was only looking out for his little sister and by the tense look on Piper's face she was trying not to voice the same sentiment.

Piper seemed to sense Casey watching her and put her arm around her shoulders leading her a few steps away. 'Are you all right?'

Casey frowned. 'Yes, of course. Why?' Piper gave a pointed glance in Matteo's direction. 'Ah, I admit I'm a little smitten by him.' She looked over to where he was laughing with a group of guests and her breath caught in her throat when he unexpectedly turned to look at her. He shot a quick smile in Casey's direction.

'I think the feeling might be mutual,' Piper whispered.

'Do you really think so?' Casey asked, daring to hope he might.

'I think it's obvious that there's a spark between you.'

'I like to think there is.'

'Unmistakable.'

Casey took a few sips from her drink, watching Matteo over the rim of the tall glass. 'He is pretty amazing, don't you think?'

'I suppose he is.'

Casey noticed Alex smiling at Piper and her friend grinned back at him. He was such a lovely man and after all Piper had gone through being jilted by Rick, Casey was happy to see her friend finally enjoying the happiness she deserved.

'Food's ready,' Matteo bellowed, waving for his guests to make their way over to the barbecue area. 'Grab a plate and whatever you need from there,' he said pointing to a table set up with the cutlery, crockery and various napkins and cruets and dishes containing dressings and sauces neatly arranged next to several bowls of rolls, baguettes, salads and potatoes, chips and other side dishes.

'Look at that feast,' Tara said. 'I don't know where to begin.'

'Just don't fill your plate too much,' Casey teased. 'Try to leave room for the meat and veg they're serving from the barbecue.'

Alex arrived next to Piper and stood in front of Casey and Tara. 'Having fun?'

'I am. I didn't realise how hungry I was until I saw this lot.' Tara giggled.

Alex draped his arm around Piper's shoulders and kissed her forehead. 'I'm told the food here is always top-notch.'

'I've heard that too,' Piper said, reaching the table and picking up a plate and handing it to him before taking one for herself and trying to decide what to serve herself first. 'I've just never been here to sample it before tonight.'

Casey listened in happy contentment to her friend chatting with Alex as she placed a couple of pieces of sliced baguette on hers and Tara's plates next to some mixed salad before walking over to the barbecue to be served. She settled on some chicken and Tara asked for a steak. They found two chairs near to where Piper and Alex were already sitting eating their food.

'Enjoying yourselves?' Matteo asked as he waited for a member of staff to place a chair around the same table that they were occupying. 'I hope you don't mind me joining you.'

'Don't be silly, mate,' Alex said, moving his chair over slightly to give his friend more room between his and Casey's chairs. 'This is your party. And anyway it's good to have you to ourselves for a bit.'

'Thanks,' Matteo said, stabbing a piece of potato and popping it into his mouth. Having eaten it, he lowered his knife and fork onto the plate and Casey saw he wasn't as calm as he had been making out.

'Is everything all right?' she asked, concerned.

Before he had a chance to reply, Fliss appeared with Phoebe next to her.

'Matteo,' she said, her voice flirtatious and sweeter than Casey had heard it before. 'Phoebe and I were wondering if you wanted to come out with us tomorrow. She can show you around the island a bit.' Fliss shot Casey a triumphant look.

Casey's stomach clenched but, aware that Fliss was wanting to cause a reaction, looked down at her plate and continued eating in silence. She had no right to feel jealous of anyone spending time with Matteo. It wasn't as if there actually was anything between them. All he had done was invite her out for a meal the day before to thank her for her help. That didn't give her carte blanche to presume any attachment to him. Still, she thought as she ate some of her salad, it didn't stop her from feeling as if she was being elbowed aside by Fliss.

'That's very kind of you both,' she heard Matteo say. 'But I have far too much on while I'm here I'm afraid.'

Surprised by his immediate decline of their invitation, Casey looked up and caught his eye. She noticed then that Fliss and Phoebe had also seen the look that had passed between them and received Matteo's message, loud and clear. And by the look of fury on Fliss's face she was not done with Casey yet.

Someone turned up the music and Casey was relieved when Jax arrived, looking slightly uncomfortable. She went to wave to get his attention but then spotted Piper rushing off to greet him and lead him back to their table.

'Look who's here,' she announced. They all welcomed him and within a few seconds Alex had introduced him to Matteo and pressed a bottle of beer in Jax's hand before sitting on Piper's chair, pulling her gently to sit on his lap.

Casey watched her friend's delight as she slipped her arm around Alex's neck and kissed his cheek.

Casey looked around at the smiling faces, beautiful scenery of palm trees and colourful flowerbeds, and closed her eyes, breathing in the warm evening air. She opened her eyes and saw Matteo watching her. He raised his drink in a silent salute to her. She mirrored his action and he mouthed, 'All right?'

Casey nodded. 'Yes, thank you,' she replied quietly.

Tara nudged her gently. 'I'm going to go and chat with that good-looking bloke over there,' she said out of the side of her mouth. 'I think he's a cameraman, or sound man or something.'

Casey grinned. 'Enjoy yourself.'

As she turned to gaze at the pool, which looked rather

inviting on such a hot evening, she heard a voice ask, 'Fancy a swim?'

She turned to see Matteo standing at her shoulder. He took Tara's place in the chair next to her. 'It does look rather inviting,' she said. 'But I'm hardly dressed for a dip. Anyway,' she added, 'I don't have a costume and I think that if I went in then it might get a bit raucous here if your other guests followed suit.'

'Good point.' He stared at her and she wished she knew what he was thinking. 'Why not come for a swim in the morning? First thing.'

'Well, I...' She trailed off, feeling awkward. 'I'm not sure. There's a lot still to organise for the shoot and the wedding,' she said, aware how feeble her excuse sounded.

He leaned closer to her. 'I swim every morning and it's never as much fun by yourself.' He studied her for a moment. 'I tell you what, if you agree to come and join me for a swim I'll cook you breakfast afterwards.'

Casey relaxed slightly. She liked this idea. Very much. Matteo was lovely, as far as she could tell. If he wasn't famous she wouldn't feel awkward around him, or at least she thought she wouldn't.

'I'm not sure what you're thinking about,' Matteo said quietly. 'But I hope it's that you're going to take me up on my invitation.'

'On one condition,' she said, smiling at him. After all it wasn't every day she met a man she was so attracted to and this one seemed to like her rather a lot.

'Anything.'

She laughed. 'You don't know what I'm going to say yet.'

His dark eyes twinkled in amusement. 'I don't care. I'll agree to anything if it means you'll come and see me tomorrow morning.'

'You cook the breakfast. Not the chef.'

He threw his head back and roared with laughter. 'How do you know I won't end up poisoning you?'

'You'd better not,' she said, pretending to be cross. 'Otherwise you'll have to find your own candles and mirrors.'

He put his hand out for her to take and they shook hands. 'It's a deal. Seven a.m. sharp.'

'Seven!' *Was he mad?* 'That's incredibly early.'

He winked at her. 'If I'm cooking you breakfast you'll need to swim with me beforehand. Seven is the perfect time. It'll be peaceful and the best time of the day.'

She smiled at him, liking the idea the more she considered it. She liked him more each minute too. 'All right then. Seven it is.'

11

Matteo heard a car and went outside to see if it was Casey arriving. She was a little early but he couldn't wait to see her. The weather was humid and it was already almost twenty-six degrees. He was glad she had agreed to his offer of a swim and some breakfast. As he walked closer to her car he saw her checking her watch and presumed she was worried about arriving too early.

'Stop over-thinking this,' he heard her say as he reached her car.

'Sorry, what was that?' Matteo asked, mortified when she jumped in shock. 'I didn't mean to give you a fright.' He grimaced, opening her car door for her and waiting for her to grab her bag off the passenger seat and step out.

'It's fine, really,' she said, blushing. 'I was just going over the list of what I need to do today so I was lost in thought. Also, I hadn't wanted to be too early and didn't realise you were there.'

He reached out to take her arm. 'I really should have made my presence known before surprising you like that.' How could he have been so thoughtless, he mused, irritated with himself.

They hadn't reached the cottage yet and he had already embarrassed them both.

'It's fine,' Casey insisted, her large eyes filled with sympathy for his mortification.

He led her around the house. 'Please, take a seat.' He indicated the table on the terrace and left her for a moment before going inside to fetch the single yellow rose he had cut for her just before her arrival. Carrying the crystal vase with the rose in it outside.

'That's beautiful,' she said.

He saw her looking at the rose. 'For our breakfast table. I thought it would brighten up the place.'

Casey gazed around them. 'From that rose bush, right?'

'It is,' he said. 'Well spotted.'

'It's lovely. Very sunny looking.'

'I suppose it is.' He was glad he had thought to cut the rose.

'This is beautifully set.'

Matteo looked at the neatly placed cutlery and crisp linen napkins and placed the vase onto the table.

'Did you do all this?' she asked.

'I did. I hope you like it.' He hadn't wanted their privacy invaded by any staff that morning and had enjoyed setting the table and getting everything ready for Casey's arrival.

'I do,' she replied, looking impressed. 'Very much.'

His heart raced at her reaction and it occurred to him for the first time how much her opinion of him mattered. He smiled at her. 'Thank you for agreeing to come here this morning. I've been looking forward to spending a little time alone with you again.'

'You have?'

He studied her expression, hoping she was happy to hear what he had just said rather than alarmed. Relieved, he decided she seemed pleased. 'Yes. We always seem to have so many people around when we're in the same place.'

'I suppose we do.'

He took a deep breath. 'Well. Shall we swim?'

Casey nodded.

'You can change inside,' he said, indicating the way through the French doors. 'There's a downstairs bedroom if you go through the living room and turn left in the hallway. I'll see you out here when you're ready.'

He watched her go and hoped she noticed the large towel he had left folded for her in the bedroom. Then, already in his swimming shorts, Matteo fetched another two towels, one for himself and another should Casey want it, and set them down on one of the loungers. Not sure what to do with himself while she changed he quickly went into the kitchen to double-check he had all the ingredients he needed for their full English breakfast after they had finished in the pool.

Hearing her footsteps pass the kitchen and go to the living room, he followed her outside desperate to feel the cool water on his hot skin.

He reached the pool just as she dived into the water. Not wishing to shock her again, he waited for Casey to surface. She came up with a gasp. 'Wow, that was colder than I expected.' She laughed, treading water as she wiped her eyes.

'Feel as good as it looks?' Matteo asked, walking towards the deep end. He took off his tee shirt and dropped it onto the paving at his feet.

'Much colder,' she panted, looking, he thought, a little shocked about something. *What had he done this time?* he wondered.

'You all right?'

'Yes.' She coughed. 'I must have swallowed some water by mistake.'

She was giving him a strange look, but he couldn't decipher what it meant. 'Actually, now I'm getting acclimatised to it, it's heavenly.'

Relieved he hadn't done something to offend her, Matteo dived in, barely making a splash. Seconds later, and without thinking, he rose to the surface in front of Casey and kissed her before she had time to speak.

Casey gasped, clearly taken by surprise.

He could see she was thinking something and was about to apologise to her when she flung her arms around his neck and kissed him back, pulling them both underwater in the process.

Delighted with her response, Matteo brought them to the surface and, taking her hand, pulled her to where she could reach the bottom of the pool. Unable to think what to say, he just stared at her in silence. He wanted to kiss her again and despite her reaction to the last one thought it would be good manners to at least ask if she was happy for him to do so. 'Would you mind if I kissed you again?' he asked. 'I know I should have asked you the first time.'

'I didn't ask either, so I think we're quits.'

He felt slightly breathless, stunned at his strong feelings towards her. 'You're so beautiful, Casey.'

'You're not so bad yourself.' She grinned. 'To be honest I wasn't sure if my breath had been taken away by the cold water before or because you took off your tee shirt.'

'Really? I tan easily,' he said. 'It's my Italian heritage.'

She seemed a little shy at her unexpected boldness. Then, shrugging, added, 'You clearly work out a lot.'

'Not as much as I probably should.' He thought of Martha

and how she insisted he should go to the gym several times a week to keep fit.

'Well, your toned body says otherwise,' Casey said, smiling at him, her eyes twinkling mischievously.

She really was gorgeous and seemed to like him as much as he liked her. Matteo slipped his arms around her waist and, pulling her against him, kissed her. Casey responded with an intensity that took his breath away.

'That was nice,' he said, aware that it was probably the understatement of his entire life. He had been kissed before but never ever like this. She wrapped her arms around his neck and kissed him again. Matteo lost himself in the moment, not caring what happened next or even if there was any breakfast.

His thoughts raced. He was intensely attracted to her. He held her closer to him desperately wanting to ask her out and give himself the chance of spending more time with her, alone. Was he being foolish? Selfish? Her hands moved down to his waist and their kisses deepened. The timing couldn't have been much worse, he knew that much, but didn't want to leave the island without having spent more time with her. He decided to ask her out.

'Casey,' he asked, enjoying holding her in his arms. He vaguely became aware of someone clearing their throat and realised Casey had tensed. Matteo relaxed his arms slightly and, realising she was staring at someone, followed her gaze to see Martha striding across from the cottage. The red leather folder she carried under her right arm perfectly matched her stilettos.

Martha stopped slightly back from the side of the pool, no doubt, Matteo presumed, hoping to keep her clothes from any splashes. He caught Casey's eye for a second.

'Martha,' he said. 'You're early. Coming in to join us?'

He was teasing his manager and could see that she hadn't missed it.

Martha pursed her lips, clearly unimpressed with his question. 'No, Matteo. I've got far too much to do to waste my time playing in a pool with one of your many little friends. As do you! This shoot is turning into a fiasco.' She jutted her chin in Casey's direction. 'I'm not sure we've been properly introduced.' She narrowed her eyes and enlightenment dawning across her face. 'You're Jordi's sister, aren't you?'

Matteo felt Casey stiffen. 'Casey,' he said quietly, worried they'd have to cut their morning short. What could have gone wrong now?

'Yes, that's right,' Casey finally said, her voice clipped but steady.

'Casey's here to have breakfast with me,' Matteo said. 'I can—'

Martha picked up one of the towels from the lounger and held it open. 'I wish that were possible. Unfortunately, we have issues that take precedence over fun.'

Why did it seem that they took one step forward and two back? he thought, irritated.

'I'd better get going and leave you two to your work.' Without waiting for him to reply, Casey pushed his hand away and, ignoring his protestations, she walked up the steps and into the towel Martha was holding out for her.

'But what about breakfast?' Matteo shouted as he swam to the side of the pool and pushed himself up onto the side. Standing, he shook his head to rid his hair of excess water. Then he grabbed the other towel and quickly dried himself before wrapping the towel around his waist. 'I'm sure we've still got time, haven't we, Martha?'

'I don't think so, thanks,' Casey said, drying her feet. 'I've got a lot on today too. I should be going. Bye, Martha. Bye, Matteo.'

She gave him a doubtful look.

'Let me walk you to your car then,' he said, not ready for her to go without making things right with her.

'No, it's quite all right,' Casey said. 'I'll just fetch my things and leave you two to your work.'

'I'll see you soon?' he called as she turned and went into the house to change. 'Remember, if there's anything I or my team can do to help you must let us know.'

'Thank you,' she replied without looking at him. 'But you've probably got more than enough to be getting on with, I imagine.'

'Not too much that we can't help you if you need us to. You're doing it for us, don't forget,' he called after her. 'And your friend, Vicki, of course.'

'It's fine,' she said, clearly letting him know that their morning together was over. *What the heck just happened*? he wondered.

12

'Mum?' Casey called, looking for her mother when she couldn't find her inside the house.

'Out here, love.' Casey walked out to the backyard. 'You've been swimming,' Rowena said, looking up from sewing the hem of a new skirt. 'Your hair is still wet.' She checked her watch. 'Beach this early?'

Casey was glad she hadn't confided in her mother about Matteo's invitation to breakfast. Rowena might be her mother and the person she trusted most in the world, but the humiliation of what had just happened wasn't something she intended sharing with anyone.

Casey shook her head and sat on the small chair next to her mum's. 'No.'

'Who's got a pool that you could use before most people have got out of bed?'

Casey groaned inwardly. She might have known she couldn't keep much from her mother. 'Matteo asked me for a swim and breakfast where he's staying.'

Rowena slowly lowered her sewing, resting it on her lap, not taking her eyes off Casey. 'Say that again?'

'You heard perfectly well, Mum.' She tucked a damp strand of hair behind her ears and tried to act as if Matteo's invitation was nothing unusual.

'What time did you get to his place if you're already back at seven forty-five?' Rowena stared at Casey, making her feel as if she could see her thoughts.

'Mum, stop that. There's nothing to tell. I was there at seven but his manager, Martha, came and told him he had to deal with some work issue.'

'And?'

Casey looked up to see the windows open to make the most of the warm air. Her father could be very protective of her and Jordi if he thought someone had upset them and, unsure if he was in the house, wanted to avoid him overhearing anything she had to say to her mother.

'Where's Dad?'

'He caught the red-eye to London this morning,' Rowena said. 'He's got a couple of meetings with clients there.'

Casey was used to her father's frequent visits to the mainland and more distant locations, meeting with wealthy clients who had trusts or companies he managed for the firm where he was one of the directors.

'And breakfast was cancelled.' She shrugged as if it was no big deal. She wished it wasn't.

'Something's wrong.' Rowena narrowed her eyes. 'If that little sod...'

'Mum, stop it. Firstly, I'm in my twenties and more than capable of looking after myself. Secondly, I'm a bit disappointed, but it's fine.'

Rowena wagged her finger at Casey. 'It's not the breakfast you're upset about though, is it?'

Why did her mother know her so well? Mostly Casey liked that she didn't have to explain her feelings in too much detail to her mum but at times like these when she needed to process her thoughts before wanting to share them, she would rather her mum didn't read her emotions quite so perfectly.

'Go on,' Rowena said. 'I know there's something wrong; I can see it in your face.'

Casey sighed and got up from the chair. She lay down on nearest sunlounger and closed her eyes. 'Martha said something that made me suspect I wasn't the only person Matteo invited to breakfast.' She opened one eye and saw her mother watching her. 'I'm an idiot, I know, but I thought for a minute there that I might be a little bit special to him.'

'Firstly, my girl,' her mother said, resting a hand on Casey's ankle, 'you're not an idiot and I don't want to ever hear you refer to yourself in that way again. If anyone's an idiot it's that young man. He should be so lucky to have someone as lovely as you as a girlfriend.'

'Mum! I never mentioned anything about being a girlfriend,' she groaned, mortified. 'I just meant...'

'I know what you meant. Ooh, upstarts like him make me furious. How dare he upset a gorgeous girl like you?'

'Mum, enough. I'm fine,' she said, hoping her mother believed her but aware that she wouldn't. 'Can we change the subject please?'

'If you insist.' Her mother picked her sewing up from her lap and continued with it. 'How is it going with the scene setting?'

'Sorry?'

'You needed candles for the castle. Vicki's wedding? That singer's film thingy?'

'Ahh. Tara and I still need to work out exactly how we're going to decorate the room at the castle.'

Rowena listened, wide-eyed. 'That's because you've been gallivanting at barbecues and early morning swims.'

Casey glared at her mother and opened her mouth to give back a snappy retort when she saw the glint in her mother's eye. 'Ha ha, very funny.' She smiled, aware that her mother was trying to lighten the mood. 'We still have so many problems to sort out and the filming is tomorrow afternoon,' she said, tempted to share everything that was said at the pool with her mother. 'I told Vicki and Martha I'd do my best but I'm not really sure where to begin.'

'Firstly, you need to remember you're not on your own,' her mother said, as she always did when Casey shared her concerns about something. 'Tara is covering for you whenever you need her to at work. And she'll be there with you to set up the room at the castle.'

Casey nodded miserably. She wished she hadn't left Tara to do so much. Damn Matteo playing her for a fool, she thought, only just keeping a rein on her emotions.

'Look,' her mother said. 'Go inside and get a notepad and pen from the kitchen. We'll sit and work through what's outstanding. Maybe I'll be able to come up with something helpful.'

She liked that idea.

Her mum always seemed able to calm her and help put her mountains back into manageable molehills.

'I'm ready,' Casey said moments later, sitting with her notepad resting on her knee and biro raised ready to make her list. 'We know the location. Tara and I have been to visit the room at the castle so at least we know the size of the room now and vaguely what needs to be done to make it look perfect. Tara was speaking to one of the chaps up at The Cabbage Patch to lend us a tall candle holder to go with the ones from Paddy to give the arrangement height. If he doesn't have one then we'll need him to make one for us and Matteo's team will pay for it. We know we have enough mirrors, but we still need muslin, or lace, or something like that to drape on things.'

'I might be able to help you there,' Rowena said. 'I have a friend who's closing down her haberdashery shop in town and might have some offcuts she can let us have.'

'Don't worry if we have to pay for it,' Casey reiterated. 'Matteo is happy to pay whatever it takes to make this happen.'

'Whatever it takes?' Her mother laughed, exasperation in her voice. 'You're both going to an awful lot of effort.'

'Maybe,' Casey said, not wishing to get into an argument with her mother. 'I'm happy to do this. I wanted to help Vicki and in turn Alex's friend.' She thought over her initial feelings for Matteo. 'And to impress Matteo probably.' She closed her eyes realising how foolish she'd been.

'Hey,' Rowena said, snapping Casey out of her thoughts. 'Stop beating yourself up over this. You've been a wonderful friend to Vicki, and if all you get out of this is the knowledge that you helped that dear girl have the wedding of her dreams then I, for one, think that's payment enough.'

'Do you really though?' she asked doubtfully.

'Yes.' Her mother smiled.

She supposed they weren't doing badly. It wasn't as if she had any experience arranging weddings and certainly none where music videos were concerned, so maybe she wasn't as much of a fool as she currently felt.

Her mother thoughtfully pressed a piece of new thread between her lips before threading it through the eye of her needle and tying a knot at the end. 'Go on.'

Piper looked down at her notepad and realised she had

forgotten that Vicki still needed somewhere to hold her reception.

'We need a space big enough to hold a wedding reception.'

'That's an easy one,' Rowena said. 'Why not ask the Ecobichon sisters if you can use the smaller barn behind The Cabbage Patch. There's that lovely orchard outside, which will be perfect for photos.'

It was summer and the sun wouldn't completely set until very late. It was a possible venue, Casey decided. 'I don't think it's been used for anything other than art classes for years though. It's a bit of a mess.'

Rowena raised a hand and Casey could tell she was already working on a plan. 'You leave that to me. In fact, leave the Ecobichon sisters to me. I'll probably have to invite them to the reception but if it's not going to be very big then I'm sure Vicki won't mind.'

Casey doubted her friend would mind anything at all as long as the arrangements were in place in time for her big day.

'I'll speak to Margery. She knows everyone and will be able to rally her swimming pals and other friends. You can speak to your colleagues at The Cabbage Patch and if everyone helps clean up the place tomorrow I'm sure it would work splendidly.'

Casey thought of Piper's gran, Margery. She had lived on the pier for decades and seemed to know everyone. If she was onboard to help with the preparations then others certainly would want to be too.

'That's a brilliant idea, Mum.' She tried to picture the smaller barn as a reception area. 'I suppose we'll need some sort of decoration, but I've no idea what.'

'Nancy is a florist and Vicki's aunt, as well as her boss,' Rowena said thoughtfully. 'I'm sure she could decorate it with fresh flowers and other pretty things. She would be delighted to help make Vicki's day as perfect as possible. She's the best florist on the island, as far as I'm concerned.'

Casey hugged her mother, almost spilling her cup of tea. 'Oops, sorry,' she said, grimacing. 'That's the perfect solution though, Mum. You are clever.'

'Vicki is also going to need to feed her guests,' Rowena said, making Casey groan at the thought of yet another thing to add to her list. How did everything escalate so much? 'I'll try to come up with something for that. For now, though, you'd better help with the candle situation.'

The unmistakable roar of a motorbike could be heard coming along the lane by the house. Both of them looked up, waiting to see if it was anyone they knew.

'Casey? Rowena?'

'Out in the garden,' Casey yelled, happy to have someone take her mind off her troubles.

'Hi there,' Alex said, appearing at the doorway next to Piper.

Gosh, thought Casey, he was incredibly handsome with his golden tan contrasting against his white tee shirt and jeans. And her friend looked very loved up with him, Casey was happy to see. If only she could have that same feeling with someone. She did though, she reminded herself.

'How are you both?' Piper asked, looking happier than Casey had ever seen her before.

'We were fine,' Rowena laughed. 'Until my daughter came home and began roping us in to all the planning she's trying to sort out.'

Alex stepped outside. 'Ahh, that's my fault.'

Casey hated to think he felt guilty in any way. 'No, it isn't.'

'It is though. If I hadn't got involved then Piper wouldn't have asked you to speak to your uncle about the castle and you wouldn't have become embroiled in the wedding and end up running around trying to sort everything out.'

'Let's not argue about who's to blame,' Rowena admonished. 'I don't think it's either of your fault. You're both very kind. You,' she said to Alex, 'wanting to help this singer friend of yours, and Casey trying to help Vicki.' She frowned. 'Where is Matteo while all this is going on, if you don't mind me asking?'

Casey heard the irritation in her mother's voice and hoped Alex hadn't picked up on it.

'He's in meetings with his manager and production team trying to resolve issues with one of the crew who's been held up on the mainland.'

'Fair enough. As long as he isn't lounging about in a pool somewhere while the rest of you are working so hard on his behalf. How's your grandad getting on?' Rowena asked. 'Casey told me all about him hurting himself a few weeks ago and how he's being looked after by Vivienne from The Cabbage Patch.'

'He's doing well, thanks.' Alex smiled. 'My sister is also back on the island. She's staying with her friend Phoebe. She told me she's asked Jax to take her out sometime and show her around the island.'

Casey wasn't surprised.

'My cousin will take good care of her,' Piper said proudly.

They all knew how close Piper and Jax were and Casey wondered what it might be like to have an older brother, or a cousin like Jax, around.

'He will,' Alex agreed. 'He's a good bloke and hopefully she'll forget her woes for a while when she's out traipsing across the countryside with him.' He looked from one of them to the other. 'Sorry, we were talking about the wedding, weren't we?'

'I asked you about your grandad, so the change in subject was my fault,' Rowena said. 'We've been going over the plans,' she said glancing at Casey.

'I think most of them are coming along well,' Casey said, hoping she was right and no other dramas popped up between now and tomorrow afternoon.

Yes,' Rowena agreed. 'I'm sure we'll all band together to make it work, won't we?'

'We will,' Alex said, nodding. 'Just let me know what I can do and I'll happily do it.'

'Thank you.' Casey felt slightly better to hear his reassurance.

'I've been chatting to Mum, Gran and Nancy,' Piper said. 'My mum thought that if everyone clubs together and gives their time and some food then we'll soon have Vicki sorted for a reception.'

'Funnily enough, we've been trying to plan that too.' Casey laughed, delighted that they were all on the same page. 'We thought of asking the Ecobichon sisters if we can set up the smaller barn at The Cabbage Patch for that. What do you think?'

Piper was momentarily at a loss for words. 'I think it's perfect,' Piper cheered. 'Good thinking.'

'It was Mum's idea actually.'

Rowena shared everything she and Casey had been discussing.

Casey listened, relieved that some of the work she had imagined having to do was being delegated to others. Here she was thinking she had so much to do when her mother and other local women had been getting together behind the scenes. 'It really does feel as if it's all coming together, doesn't it?'

'Everyone loves a happy occasion,' her mother said, giving her a wink. 'And we all think the world of Vicki.'

'We do,' Piper agreed.

'I think we need to make some phone calls, don't you?' Rowena said, placing her sewing down on the table near her.

'Right,' she said, standing up. 'I'm going to make cups of tea and toast for anyone who wants it and you, Piper, can phone your mum and Nancy and tell them what we've been chatting about. Would that be all right?'

'Perfectly.' Piper grinned and pulled her mobile from her pocket. 'I'll call them both now.'

'What about me?' Casey asked.

'You stay here and add anything you can think off to your list. I won't be long.'

Ten minutes later Rowena carried a tray with mugs of tea and a plate piled with slices of buttered toast. There was a pot of jam and another of marmalade on the tray with two spoons and several knives. 'Help yourselves,' she said waiting for Casey to lift her sewing from the table before placing the tray down.

Piper came back from the other side of the garden where she had been chatting on the phone. 'Right,' she said, pushing it into her pocket. 'I spoke to Mum and then Nancy, and between us we've come up with the idea of working together to sort out the food and anything else that's needed for the reception. She said you're not to worry, Casey, and that she'll go next door now and chat to Gran. Between them they'll make sure others will join in and help with all the preparations.'

'That's so kind of them,' Casey said, relieved that some of the responsibility for the reception was being taken off her hands.

'It's not as if these sorts of things happen every day,' Piper said. 'I think that the locals from the pier will be excited to be involved.'

Casey hoped so. 'But what about the Ecobichon sisters?' she asked. 'Has anyone asked them if we can use their smaller barn?' Casey pressed her lips together trying not to laugh when her mother raised an eyebrow in disdain.

'What do you think I was doing while I was in the kitchen

waiting for the toaster to do its thing? Of course they've been asked.'

'Really?' Casey was surprised, then realised she shouldn't have been. It was just like her mother to take the opportunity of sorting things out when she had a moment to do so. 'Well done, Mum.'

'Why are you two still standing? Sit down and have something to eat and drink.' She motioned for Piper and Alex to sit on the vacant chairs.

Casey realised her mother hadn't told them what the Ecobichon sisters thought of her request. 'Were the sisters happy to let us use the barn, Mum?'

'They were,' she said picking up one of the mugs and taking a sip. 'They said they'd be delighted to think that such a happy occasion would be taking place on their property.'

Casey was so happy she thought she might cry. This was all turning out so well.

'As I was saying though, Casey,' her mother continued, 'like the rest of Vicki's close friends we'll help set up the barn at The Cabbage Patch for her, but that's it. She needs to sort her rings, licence and dress.'

'She has a dress and has sorted out the licence,' Casey recalled. 'I've no idea about a ring.'

'Good. We must remember that she has her own mother, sister, and Nancy as well as various cousins who I'm sure will be only too happy to help. We mustn't overstep the mark. You've still got to decorate the room at the castle. I think that's more than enough for you to be getting on with, don't you think?'

She did. 'You're right, Mum.' Casey sighed heavily. 'Tara and I are a bit panicky about the candles if I'm honest.'

'Don't be. I'll chat to Margery and I'm sure she'll contact her friends and ask them to spread the word that you need as many of them that have been given or bought your larger cathedral candles to give them back. I'm sure they won't mind. Not if you offer to replace them as soon as you can. If you want you can ask people to use this house as the dropping point for the candles and I'll tell the people I speak to the same thing.'

'Thanks, Rowena,' Piper said. 'We'd better get on with stuff. We'll catch up with you later.'

'Yes, thanks for all you've been doing to help Matteo,' Alex said, finishing the piece of toast he was eating then drinking more of his tea. He stood. 'He really does appreciate everything, you know.'

'Hmm,' Casey said, biting her tongue so as not to disagree with him and upset him about his friend. 'See you both soon, and thanks for all you're doing too.'

After Piper and Alex left, Casey and Rowena waited until they heard the motorbike roaring away from the house. Casey sighed. 'I must admit I feel a bit cheeky asking people to return gifts. Won't that be rude?'

'These are desperate times, Casey,' her mother said. 'And anyway, if I had a candle that I'd already half used and someone offered to replace it with a new one I can assure you I'd be delighted.'

'It might take us a few weeks to make all the replacements though,' Casey said, realising how much work she was going to have after the filming and wedding was over.

Her mother had a point though and Casey began to warm to the idea. It was a good one and she couldn't think why she hadn't come up with it herself instead of panicking.

'Yes. We could tell them that we want their candles no matter if they've been lit, or how low they've been burnt.' She shrugged. 'We're going to have to light them for filming anyway and we won't want them all to be the same height because they would look too uniform.'

'Exactly.'

'How do you always have an answer when I most need it, Mum?' Casey asked, delighted that the solution was so simple. At least she hoped it would be.

'Because I'm older than you and have more life experience. And I probably have more cheek to ask people to return gifts than you might possess.'

'That's true.' Casey giggled. 'Well, I'm grateful for your cheek.'

It would only take a few weeks to make enough to replenish their stock and those who had given back their candles would need to agree to wait until after that had taken place before theirs were replaced just so they could keep Smoke and Mirrors going. She just had to hope that no one minded having to wait.

'Don't forget I've got a few candles here,' her mother said, interrupting her thoughts. 'There's those two on the sideboard and two over by the back door in those silver glass lantern things you bought for me a couple of years ago. I think that's it though. Oh, there might be one more in my en suite.'

'Your en suite?' Casey forgot to hide her surprise.

Rowena frowned. 'Yes. What's wrong with that?'

'Er, nothing.'

'I might be your mother, young lady, but I still like a candlelit bathroom every so often thank you very much.'

Casey hadn't meant to insult her. 'Sorry, that didn't come out quite as I meant it to.'

'I'm sure it didn't.'

'Go and fetch those ones now, and we can start grouping them together to be taken up to the castle. Don't forget you need to make a note of how many people have returned candles, so you don't miss out on giving them their replacements.'

'I won't.' She ran into the house and up the stairs to her parents' bathroom and smiled as she saw the candle on the edge of the bath. There was only two-thirds of it left and it looked exactly as she had hoped it would with an accumulation of wax running in set rivulets down the sides. She picked it up carefully and carried it downstairs. She was going to need a lot more just like this one.

'Do you mind if I use one of your containers to carry these in, Mum?' It was the only way she could be certain she wouldn't knock some of the beautiful wax from the sides when she transported them in her car.

'You'll find a large Tupperware in the back of the under-sink cupboard,' Rowena shouted. 'It doesn't have a lid and I'm not really sure why I keep it any more.'

Casey crouched down and took the few cleaning packages from the Tupperware and lifted it onto the drainer. She put the candle into it and then went outside and retrieved the two from the lantern holders. Then returned to the living room and took the final two from the sideboard. 'This is brilliant. Matteo will be very grateful to you and all the others who help out.'

'I hope we get to meet him at some point.' She finished her tea. 'He's a singer of note, I gather.'

'That's right.' She held up a candle in each hand. 'Thanks so much for these.'

'It's my pleasure.' Rowena rubbed her hands together thoughtfully. 'I've had another idea.'

'What is it?' Casey was used to her mum's *ideas* and hoped it was a welcome one: not all of them were.

'You'll have to wait and see.'

13

Casey looked at her To Do list. The edges of the piece of paper were getting tatty where she had folded it to put it into her pocket and then unfolded it to keep adding to it. She ran a finger down the list, stopping at the Reception Barn point. She needed to speak to Vicki. There was no point in preparing the barn for a wedding reception if the bride didn't want them to do it. And if Vicki did like the idea, then Casey needed to ensure they were in agreement about what she was expecting. She folded the list, pushed it into her pocket and walked to Harbour Blooms.

'Hi, Nancy.' She waved, relieved to see her chatting to a customer about different blooms in buckets outside the front of her small florist's.

'Vicki's inside,' Nancy said, a little pointedly.

Casey sensed by the tone of Nancy's voice that she was becoming a little irritated by the wedding, especially if it was impacting on her working day, as Casey presumed it must be on Vicki's. Knowing Vicki, Casey thought, she would be chattering non-stop about her plans for the secret wedding to poor Nancy, desperate to share her excitement with someone close. After all it wasn't as if she could speak openly, not since Dan wasn't a party to her plans. She heard a motorbike in the distance, but aware that Alex was helping Matteo somewhere, didn't bother to look up.

Casey pushed the door open and heard the bell jangle as she entered. She closed the door behind her and waited for Vicki to appear from the small back room.

'Oh, it's you,' Vicki said cheerfully, a wide grin on her pretty face. 'I hope you've come to catch up about the wedding plans.'

'What else?' Casey said, teasing her.

Vicki walked around the counter and bent to place the bunch of dahlias and another of delphiniums into their respective buckets with other similar blooms. 'You're such a good friend, Casey,' she said standing and giving Casey a wide smile. 'I don't know what I would have done without you.'

Casey felt the heat of embarrassment rise in her face. 'I'm only doing what anyone would.'

'Rubbish,' Vicki argued. 'Most people would say they're too busy. Which—' she tilted her head to one side '—I know you are, so thanks again.'

Casey retrieved her list from her back pocket. 'No thanks needed. I can't stop long but I thought I should just go through a few things with you. I don't want either of us wasting time we don't have doing something the other might have done.'

'Good idea. Nancy said she's happy to do the flowers for the wedding.' Vicki picked up an empty bucket.

'Will she also have time to prepare some for the barn, too?' Casey wasn't sure her question was the most subtle way to mention her plans for the reception, but it was the first thing that came to her mind.

'What barn?' Vicki asked, tipping water all over Casey's feet.

Casey shrieked and leaped back.

'Argh, sorry,' Vicki cringed. 'You took me by surprise then.'

Nancy entered the shop. 'What's going on in here?'

Casey could see Vicki's aunt wasn't impressed. 'Sorry, Nancy,' she said. 'That was my fault.'

'Wedding talk again?'

Casey saw Vicki redden. 'I'll be really quick,' Casey said apologetically. 'I just wanted to run something by Vicki.'

Nancy sighed. 'Right, well hurry up about it.'

As soon as Nancy had gone into the back room, Vicki stepped forward. 'You were saying something about a barn.'

Casey explained about the smaller barn up at The Cabbage Patch. 'We have so little time to sort everything out, but it seems a shame not to have a reception of some sort.' She shrugged. 'So, what do you think?'

'I think it's a brilliant idea,' Vicki said smiling. 'And if you think it can be ready in time, then yes, please.'

'And you'll ask Nancy about flowers to decorate it?'

Vicki's smile faded slightly. 'I'll do my best.'

Casey picked up a pencil from the counter and seeing she had already ticked off the wedding and barn items pointed to *Reception Barn to Decorate*. 'What about this one? I thought we could go up there today, maybe during your lunch hour, and you could tell us how you'd like everything to look.'

'Us?' Vicki gave an anxious frown.

'Yes, a few of us up at The Cabbage Patch. They don't know who the wedding is for but I've told them it was a secret and they're excited to do what they can to help,' Casey added not wanting her friend to worry. 'I've also spoken to Jax and although he wasn't too happy to keep a secret from Dan he did promise to try his best to get him dressed up and with him at the castle in time for the wedding.'

Vicki wrung her hands for a few seconds, then stopped to

gaze at her pretty engagement ring, the small diamond chips arranged around a slightly bigger one in the shape of a daisy. It seemed appropriate to Casey that he had thought to encompass her love of flowers into such a meaningful ring.

'What's the matter?' Casey asked.

Vicki looked up and her eyes, suddenly filled with tears, caught Casey's. 'I had a dream last night that Dan was furious when he arrived and discovered what I'd done. He's such a private guy and this really isn't his sort of thing. I mean, I don't even remember when the two of us attended a wedding together,' she rambled, her voice breathless and rushed. 'Does he even like weddings?'

Casey reached out and rested her hand on Vicki's arm, aware that she would never consider doing what Vicki was planning to do to Dan but deciding that it wasn't her business to judge either way. 'Take a deep breath.' She waited for her friend to do so. 'Now another one.' She gave her friend a comforting smile. 'There. Now, you can always cancel if you really think he'll be upset. Just because you have me and a few others ready to help it doesn't mean that you should feel cornered and forced to go through with anything if you don't wish to.'

Vicki nodded slowly. 'Thank you. I appreciate that.'

'Do you want me to give you a bit of space?' Casey asked, unsure how she could in all honesty afford to do that when time was already limited. She waited for Vicki to consider her suggestion.

Eventually Vicki shook her head. 'No. I've gone this far now and if he wants to marry me, like he's always professed he does, then this takes all the stress out of him having to be involved in any planning.' She gave a stubborn nod. 'And it's not as if he'll have to pay for it either now Matteo's being so generous.' She placed her hands on her hips, clearly feeling much more confident about her decision. 'Dan should be grateful that our wedding is happening this way. I mean, when will we ever be able to afford a wedding like the one we're going to have? Never, that's when.'

Casey hoped Dan would think the same way, for Vicki's sake as well as his own. 'Then we'll carry on and hope for the best.'

'We will.'

The doorbell jangled and Vicki looked past Casey to see who had arrived. Her mouth dropped open.

Surprised to see her friend act so strangely, Casey turned to see who was behind her. 'Alex? Matteo? You're here,' she said, wishing she had thought of something less feeble to say.

Matteo stepped forward, his hand outstretched and a wide, perfect smile on his handsome face. Casey felt the effect of his charisma wash over her and wasn't surprised to see Vicki's stunned reaction to meeting him in the flesh for the first time. She still felt that way each time she saw him and she'd spent a little time with him now.

'Vicki?' Matteo asked.

Vicki stared, stupefied.

Casey realised she needed to help. She stepped forward and patted Vicki's shoulder a couple of times to try and bring her back to the present. 'Yes, this is our bride, Vicki.'

When Vicki's hand slowly moved forward Matteo took it in his and held it. 'I wanted to come and thank you for your kindness,' he said. His deep, dulcet tones made her stomach flip over several times.

'Th-thank me?' Vicki said her voice barely above a whisper.

'Yes. If it wasn't for you generously letting me and my crew take over your wedding venue before you've even used it I've no idea what we would have done.'

'I... er...'

Nancy chose that moment to return to the shop. She walked past Alex and gave him a knowing smile.

'Hi, Alex,' Nancy said. She gave a confused glance to Matteo's hand holding Vicki's and then looked up at him. 'Hi, don't I know you from somewhere?'

Matteo let go of Vicki's hand and frowned slightly. 'I'm sure I would have remembered.'

He really was a charmer, Casey thought, annoyed to think how easily his charm had worked on her.

Nancy shrugged. 'I'm sure we have,' she said tapping her lower lip. 'It'll come to me. You'll have to excuse me though, I'm rather busy at the moment.' She went to go to the back room and then stopped. 'You all right, Vicki?' she asked, looking bemused. 'Is something wrong?'

Vicki shook her head. 'No, thanks. I'm fine,' she said, her voice a high-pitched squeak.

'Right then.'

Casey watched her go and returned her attention to Vicki. 'We were just discussing wedding plans,' she explained. 'How are things coming along at your end, Matteo?' She tried to keep her voice calm. It was one thing being mortified by how he had made her feel but she didn't want to let him know how deeply he had affected her.

'Martha seems to have everything in hand. I gather the local seamstress she found began final fittings for Jordi's dress a little while ago.'

Casey was confused. 'Final fittings? That's quick, isn't it?'

'Apparently they found a dress that was almost exactly what they needed and only needed to alter it in a few places.'

'That's a relief, I'm sure.'

'I guess so.' He beamed at Vicki again. 'I want you to have everything you need to make sure your wedding is perfect,' he said. 'Anything. I really am extremely grateful to you for letting me share your venue. If you think of something you want but can't find, let me know. Will you do that?' He handed her a card and Vicki touched it with reverence, as if she were worried it might burn her hands. 'That's my manager's number. Call her any time you need something, will you?'

Vicki cleared her throat. 'I will. Thanks, M-Matteo. You've helped me as much as I've helped you,' she said, finally finding her voice. 'I wouldn't be able to afford to do this without your help. I just hope my fiancé is happy about it all.'

'You leave him to Jax,' Casey said, hoping Jax had enough influence over his friend to persuade him to turn up at the wedding venue at the right time.

'I was here to go through a few details with Vicki and to tell her about using the small barn up near The Cabbage Patch for her reception,' Casey said. 'Will you be able to come up to the barn after work?' she asked Vicki, who nodded enthusiastically.

'Yes, absolutely.'

'We'll see you up there too, then,' Matteo said, looking at Casey and holding her gaze for a little longer than was necessary.

'Fine,' she said, working hard to keep her cool around him. 'I'll see you later then too.'

'Bye then, both of you,' Matteo said. 'Until next time.'

Vicki beamed at him and Casey watched silently as both men left.

The bell jangled as the door opened and closed just as Nancy rushed back in. 'They've gone?'

'Just,' Vicki said wistfully, staring after them.

'I've just remembered where I've seen that beautiful dark-haired man. It was on the telly, wasn't it?'

'Yes,' Casey said, hoping Nancy had another chance to meet Matteo.

'He's that singer isn't he. Julio something?'

'Matteo.'

'That's the one. Buggerations,' Nancy grumbled. 'Only I would manage to not recognise someone as famous as him, and in my own shop too.'

'It happens,' Casey soothed, recalling the time she'd said hello to someone she thought she knew when she was shopping in Liberty in London. She'd thought the woman rude when she didn't say hello back, until she realised a few minutes later that it was someone she had seen on *EastEnders* a few times. 'I've done it myself.'

'I'm glad I'm not the only one.' Nancy stepped back into the back room and looked at her reflection in the mirror. 'Gah, I look such a mess too,' she said, untying the silk scarf wound in a wide band around her head to keep her hair in place and then retying it. 'Hold on a second,' she said, coming into the shop just as Casey reached the front door to leave. 'How does he know you two?'

'I'll leave you to explain everything to Nancy,' Casey said, grinning from Vicki to her boss. 'I'll meet you up at the barn later, shall I?'

'Yup, see you there.'

14

Casey walked into the busy barn and the chatter between pitch-holders and customers made her smile. She loved it here. There was a vibrancy about the place that extended beyond the colour-ful, eclectic array of items on display, from metal horse sculptures to home-spun knitted sweaters and bright pottery. It came too from the friendly atmosphere emanating from the people inside the barn.

She walked over to Tara, noticing she was on her own. 'Thanks for looking after our stall while I've been busy elsewhere. I hope you haven't been too inundated with customers.'

'It's been fairly consistent all morning but a little quieter for the past hour. Vivienne kindly stepped in to help me when I needed her to.'

Casey made a mental note to thank Vivienne. 'How is she?'

'Seems fine. How did it go?' Tara asked absent-mindedly as she packed one of their mirrors in layers of paper. She placed it in a strong paper carrier bag and indicated to a customer buying a piece of art at a nearby stall that it was ready for them to collect.

'What, my chat with Vicki?'

Tara pursed her lips together, an amused twinkle in her eyes. 'Your swim and breakfast with a certain singer.' She leaned in a little closer and lowered her voice. 'Matteo.'

'Don't ask,' she replied miserably. 'It was a disaster.'

'No, really?'

'I'm fine,' she insisted.

'As long as you're sure.'

She wasn't. 'I am.'

'Did I see Alex's bike outside?'

'I'm not sure. You could have done. Piper might be showing him the small barn to report back to Margery with more of an idea about what needs doing to get it cleaned up for the reception.' She explained about Piper phoning her mother and Nancy and that Rowena had phoned the Ecobichon sisters for permission to use the barn.

'There's so much going on at the moment,' Tara said, looking surprised.

'Yes, lots of people are starting to muck in,' Casey said, relieved. 'Thankfully, because there's little time left to do everything.'

'Oh, and Matteo,' Tara said.

Matteo? 'What about him?'

Tara grimaced. 'He's here too.'

Casey was surprised to hear that Matteo had come to The Cabbage Patch when he must have seen by all the cars parked in the car park how busy the place was. It dawned on her that Alex had probably brought him. 'Did you say Alex was with him?'

'What?' Tara typed something on her tablet. 'Sorry? Yes, he brought him up on his bike.' Tara smiled at a customer. 'I'll see to this lady. Why don't you go and find them? I'm fine here.'

Casey thanked her and then, noticing that there weren't any candles being displayed on the Smoke and Mirrors stall, pointed to the display. 'Please tell me you haven't sold all the candles we had here?'

Tara pointed to the cupboard below the counter. 'Of course not. They're all safely stored in there. I thought we should keep them back.'

'Good thinking. We're going to be too busy tomorrow to open up here,' Casey said thoughtfully. 'We can take the candles and mirrors up to the castle in the morning so we can start setting up for the recording as soon as possible.'

'Sounds good to me.'

Casey left her friend and walked around to where the smaller barn stood. The double doors were open, and Casey expected to see artists at their easels as they painted a subject given to them by their teacher. To her surprise, the place was empty. She stepped inside and gazed around the large room. It might be known as the smaller barn, she thought, but it was still a very big space.

'Alex and Piper are outside,' Matteo said as he walked up to her, his voice catching as he spoke.

'They are?' she asked, not sure what else to say as he neared her.

'Casey...'

'It's fine.' She did not wish to discuss what had happened at the pool. Not now and hopefully not ever.

'No, it isn't. You were upset and I want to put things right.'

Something in her wanted to believe that he truly liked her but she was not going to allow him to make a fool of her. 'Matteo,' she said, her voice as firm as she could make it. 'There's nothing to discuss here. I'll do what I offered for your shoot, so that my friend has a day to remember. Then you'll leave and we'll all remember how exciting it was for a few days. Nothing more.'

'Nothing more?' She saw the hurt in his eyes.

Was he really hurting, or was he just wanting her to believe that was the case? 'That's right,' she said, aware that it was her own stinging pain that was causing her to want to hurt him back.

'Please,' he said, reaching out to take her hand.

Casey snatched it away from him. 'Don't.' She turned to walk away but he rushed to stand in front of her. He might be super famous and incredibly good looking and, she thought with irritation, have an effect on her that made her want to grab him and kiss him, but she still had her pride.

'Casey, I don't know what you think happened this morning, but what Martha said about…'

'Matteo,' she snapped, furious with him for making her fall for him. 'If you're looking for someone to entertain you over the next few days then I'm not that person.'

'What are you saying?' he asked, an indignant expression on his face.

'I think it's perfectly clear.'

'But this morning. When we kissed—'

'You kissed?' Vicki's voice cut through the silence. They turned to see her there. She hesitated.

'Sorry. I didn't mean to say that out loud.' She cringed. 'Have I walked in on something I shouldn't?'

'No,' Casey replied, feeling awkward and not wanting to elaborate. She didn't want to ruin what should be a special time for her friend. 'Of course you haven't,' she said, forcing an amused laugh.

'Casey, can I just…'

'Sorry, Matteo,' Casey said. 'No time.' She turned her back on him and waved her arms in a wide arc, smiling at Vicki. 'What do you think of this place then?'

She surveyed the area quickly. They had a lot of work to do if this was going to look anything like a reception area. Casey hoped fervently that Vicki had enough vision to imagine how it might look.

'It's a brilliant space,' Vicki said thoughtfully. 'I'm sure it'll be perfect.'

'Great,' she said, aware that Matteo was still staring at her. 'I was thinking that we can ask the stallholders in The Cabbage Patch if they'd also like to volunteer to set the room up for you. If you'd like to keep the wedding a secret then we can let them know it has to be in strictest confidence.'

Vicki walked over to one end of the barn, where there was a stack of hay bales. 'It will take some doing,' she agreed. 'But I'm happy for whoever offers to come to the reception. That way I'll be able to introduce them to Dan and thank them for all they've done.' She gave Casey an apologetic smile. 'I'd like to think people won't mention anything to Dan until the wedding has taken place though, if that's possible. Then he'll have a nice surprise when he discovers what everyone has done for us up here.' She looked a little unsure.

'I'm sure they won't mind at all,' Casey said. 'Especially if we tell them that they're welcome to come along. It adds to the excitement and makes the thought of cleaning and setting up the room more of a community-spirited event.'

'And more fun,' Piper said, joining them.

'Yes,' Matteo said. 'There's a reason why I'm here,' he said focusing his attention on Vicki. 'I wanted to say something.'

Vicki frowned. 'You've done enough, offering to pay for the wedding venue.' She shot a worried glance at Casey, who noticed Matteo's eyebrows rise suddenly.

'But I really would like to do more.'

'There's no need,' Vicki assured him.

'I'd like to if you'll let me.'

Casey wished he would take the hint and leave them alone.

'What were you thinking of doing?' she asked, aware that he wouldn't leave until he had said what he had come to say.

'I thought I could arrange for a caterer to bring the food and drink for the reception.'

Vicki and Piper gasped.

'But that's so generous,' Vicki said. 'I don't think I can accept.'

'I know some of Casey's mum and my gran's friends had planned to prepare some food.' Piper looked up as Alex joined them, then turned to Casey. 'Weren't they?'

'That's right,' Casey agreed, recalling the conversation with her mother in the garden that morning.

Matteo thought for a moment. 'And of course they must if that's what's been agreed, but I thought that this way no one has to worry about food and everyone can concentrate on having fun.' Matteo gave Alex an appealing stare. 'It's up to you, Vicki, but I really would like to do this for you.'

Alex stepped forward. 'Vicki. Obviously you must have what you want for your wedding, but by the sounds of things you already have a lot to think about. Surely it makes sense to let Matteo see to the food and drink, especially when there's so little time left to prepare things.'

'I'll clear everything with you before ordering,' Matteo said. 'Well, Martha will. She's the clever one when it comes to logistics and event planning. Please say we can do this for you.'

Vicki looked at each of them in turn and Casey suspected she wanted to agree with his offer but didn't quite know how to accept so much from this relative stranger.

Casey took Vicki's hands in hers. 'If you want to accept, and I know I would,' she said, her voice gentle, 'then just say yes. It'll leave you free to focus on preparing yourself and your bridal party for your big day. What do you say?'

Matteo gave her a grateful smile that she pointedly ignored.

Vicki giggled. 'I say, thank you.' She stepped forward and kissed Casey on the cheek. Then kissed Matteo, her cheeks flaming. 'Thank you so very much. I really can't believe how incredibly kind and generous everyone is being.' Her eyes filled with tears. Casey rummaged around in her jeans pocket for a clean tissue and handed it to Vicki. 'Or that this is actually happening.'

Matteo shook his head. 'I'm just paying you back for all that you've done for me.'

'And I just want you to have the perfect wedding. I know it's going to be the best wedding the island will see for ages,' Casey said, forcing a smile.

'Me too,' Piper agreed.

'I think I should go and speak to everyone in The Cabbage Patch,' Casey said, wanting to get away from Matteo. 'We need to catch them before they make plans for this evening if we're going to ask them to stay behind and help us clean up this place.'

'Casey's right,' Piper agreed. 'Vicki, you have a think what you'd like in here so that we know what to do with the hay bales and what we need to find to hang up to decorate the barn while we go and speak to the others.'

'Will do.'

Piper took Alex's hand before turning to thank Matteo. 'You really are very generous. Thank you.'

'I'm happy to be involved in such a joyful event,' he said.

Casey realised he intended being at the reception. She hadn't expected that. Now she wouldn't be able to relax as much as she had hoped to and would be aware of his presence all night. The thought niggled at her. She wondered if he might end up using the experience for some of his future song lyrics. That would be the icing on the cake for Vicki, she thought. Then again, Vicki was living her dream right now. All that they needed to do was make sure everything was perfect for the following evening and have Dan be at the wedding and say yes.

She glanced back as she reached the large doors and caught Matteo's eye. He was frowning and looked concerned.

'What's the matter?' Alex asked just as there was a loud banging on the door.

'Let me in, quickly!'

'That's Jordi,' Casey said, pulling one of the doors open a fraction before her sister forced her way inside. 'What the...?'

'Shut it,' Jordi yelled. 'Hurry.'

Stunned, Casey did as her sister asked immediately, hearing voices outside. Excited voices. Lots of shrieks and high-pitched giggles. She had a nagging suspicion she knew what was bothering Matteo. She glanced at him again.

'It sounds like your fans have found you,' Alex said, hurrying past Casey and checking the barn door was firmly closed. 'We're going to have to leave quickly.'

'Don't they just want to take a few photos?' Piper asked.

'I think they're far too wound up for that,' Jordi said, flicking a long strand of blonde hair behind her shoulder. 'I went to The Cabbage Patch to find you after Mum suggested you might need my help,' she said, eyes wide as she addressed Casey. 'Then, realising you must be in here, I left and spotted them giggling and exchanging ideas about how to get to Matteo.'

Matteo shook his head. 'I wouldn't mind if that's all they would do if they discovered I was here. It sounds like there's already quite a few of them.'

'There are,' Jordi said. 'Maybe fifteen. I'm not really sure.'

He sighed. 'They'll be messaging their friends to tell them they think I'm here. I don't want the poor people in The Cabbage Patch having their day disrupted.'

Casey took a deep breath, aware that she couldn't not help

someone in distress. 'How can we help?' she asked, walking back to join the group.

He touched her cheek lightly with his fingertips. 'I need to leave.'

'Can I give you a lift somewhere?' It was the least she could do, she thought, and it didn't have to mean anything.

He shook his head and his rejection hurt. 'I don't want to leave you here, but I don't want them to see you with me either.'

'Oh.' That stung, she thought, taking a steadying breath.

'I don't mean I don't want to be seen with you,' he explained hurriedly. 'Just not yet.'

'Not yet?' Piper asked, looking from one of them to the other, confused.

Casey shook her head and frowned. She didn't want her friend to get any ideas about her and Matteo.

'Not until you know what you'll be dealing with,' he said, his face reddening slightly. 'If you know what I mean.'

'Sorry?' Why was he acting like they had any future together after this morning, she mused. 'I'm not sure what you think is happening here,' she said, unable to keep the irritation from her voice at his confidence that they still had something between them. 'But you need to leave and fast by the sounds of things outside.' She thought quickly. 'I seem to recall seeing a back door from the outside.'

'That'll be perfect,' Alex said, looking forlorn.

Casey tried to picture what was behind the mound of hay bales. She rarely came in here for anything other than to say hello to one of the artists and had only done that a couple of times. 'Maybe. Let's have a look.'

'I'll keep this door closed,' Alex said as Piper, Jordi, Vicki and Matteo followed Casey around the side of the bales, past sacking hanging from an area on the back wall.

'I can't see anything here,' she said feeling sorry for Matteo's situation as the noise outside increased rapidly.

'Here.' Jordi pulled the sacking back. 'There's a door. Matteo. Alex. You'd better leave this way.'

Alex and Piper came to join them. 'No. I think it's best if I go out via the main doors and bring the bike around to the back. Be ready to jump on, Matteo. I'll have you out of here before they have a chance to follow us.'

'Sounds good to me,' Matteo said, seeming to enjoy the excitement of the moment. Then he turned to Casey. 'Can we meet you for something to eat somewhere private?' He looked at Piper. 'Both of you?'

Shrieks outside the barn increased and girls began chanting his name. 'Matteo. Matteo. Matteo.'

'They're noisy, aren't they?' Vicki said.

'It's a bit scary, isn't it?' Jordi frowned.

'Casey? Please?' He stared at her.

Hearing the chanting getting louder and louder, Casey knew she didn't have time to argue. 'Fine,' she replied reluctantly. 'Piper, where do you suggest?'

Piper gave it some thought. 'I know. Jax has a beach hut on an area of land about a mile from the pier.' She frowned realising that it wouldn't be that easy to find from the road. 'If you park in the car park opposite Gorey Common then go onto the beach and turn right. Walk along the beach as if you're going towards the town and I'll take Casey in my car and make sure you see us from the beach. I'll buy us some food and we can have something to eat there.'

'Sounds very rustic,' Matteo said, looking delighted with the idea.

'Great. I'll get the bike. You lot had better try and open that door. We don't have much time.'

'It's got a key in it,' Casey said, her heart pounding.

Alex ran to the doors and Casey was glad that they were hidden from view when the sound of Matteo's fans increased massively as Alex opened the door and left.

'We need to hurry,' she said, trying not to panic. 'Better unlock the door.'

While Matteo held back the sacking, Casey stood under it and grabbed hold of the key. 'Bugger, it won't turn.'

'Try again,' Piper said.

'No. Nothing,' Casey groaned. 'I think it might be rusted in place.'

'Here, hold this,' Matteo said holding up the sacking for Piper to take. He stepped forward and took hold of the key, wiggling it slightly and trying to dislodge it.

The sound of Alex's bike roaring around the side of the building made Casey's heart flutter in panic. They had to get Matteo out somehow.

'Try again,' Casey demanded, not wanting him to get hurt when the screaming girls got to him. 'Quickly, before they follow Alex.'

Matteo tried to move it again. 'It won't budge.' He took a deep breath and tried again. The key turned. He gave them a triumphant smile, leaned forward and kissed Casey on the mouth before he turned the handle and opened the door. 'See you both soon,' he whispered before running out and stepping onto Alex's bike and taking the helmet he held out for him.

Casey was so stunned she couldn't think straight.

Vicki stared at her open-mouthed.

'Quick, let's close the door and lock it again,' Piper shouted. 'Hopefully they'll be around the back here when we're going out the front entrance.'

Her hands trembling, Casey helped the other women pull the

door closed and locked it, covering the door once again with the heavy sacking.

'Right, let's get out of here,' Piper said to Jordi, grabbing Casey's and Vicki's hands in hers. They manoeuvred past the hay bales and Casey, still shell-shocked by what Matteo had done, and unable to help seeing the funny side of their situation now that he had managed to escape, burst into laughter.

'I'll drive,' Piper said. 'I know where Jax's place is.' She pulled her keys from her shorts pocket and jangled them in front of Casey.

They pulled open the door in time to see about fifteen girls running around the corner of the barn and the shrieks and voices wending their way around to the back.

'Great, they've gone,' Casey hissed.

'I don't think we'll have long before they come back though,' Piper said. 'Let's get going. We can call Tara from the car and let her know what's happened.' A thought occurred to her. 'You don't think she'll mind us going and leaving her looking after the stalls, do you?'

Casey waited for Piper to press her fob and unlock the car doors. 'No. She's too happy spending time with Perry and gazing at him as he makes his pottery.'

'Good for her.' Jordi laughed.

'That's all right then,' Piper said. 'We'll need to stop at the shop on the way to buy food so we can get to Jax's beach hut before Matteo and Alex get there.'

'And if you wouldn't mind taking me home after dropping Vicki off that would be great,' Jordi said.

'No problem.'

Casey realised it was one thing having several of her friends and acquaintances knowing Matteo was on the island, aware they could be relied upon to react calmly to seeing him, if a little stunned in some cases, but his fans' hysteria was another thing entirely. She wasn't sure how the rest of the afternoon would pan out but after the emotional rollercoaster she had gone through so far that day, what she did know was that she was hungry and needed something to eat before facing Matteo again.

15

By the time they had dropped Vicki back at Harbour Blooms and reached the plot of land where Jax kept his beach hut, Casey had tried to call him to ask if they could eat there but hadn't received any reply.

'He's probably out working,' Piper suggested. 'Or hasn't bothered to look at his phone. It's usually on silent when he's out and about. He hates interruptions.'

'At least we've been able to pick up some food,' Casey said, holding the paper carrier bag carefully on her lap, hoping there was enough for everyone.

They parked on the scrub land near the road and left the car.

'I've never been here before,' Casey said, intrigued as she looked around at the worn path across the grassy plot overlooking Grouville beach. 'I imagine investors would snap this place up if Jax ever decided to sell it.' She doubted that would happen anytime soon. Jax had an issue with a lot of the beachfront properties being knocked down and modern homes built in their stead.

'He doesn't bring people to this place really,' Piper said. 'I love it here and have been with him many times over the years. His grandfather left the land to him and I think that the hut was probably built by his grandad too.'

'Don't you share a grandfather though?' Casey asked. They were cousins after all.

Piper shook her head. 'Not this one unfortunately.' She smiled. 'I wouldn't mind being part owner of somewhere this special.'

Casey watched her friend pass the small shabby hut, lean down and reach her arm into an overgrown flower border.

She lifted a flat pebble. 'Ta-dah,' she sang, holding up a key. 'I don't like going inside when he's not here,' she said. 'It seems like an invasion of Jax's privacy somehow, not that he'll mind.'

'Are you sure?' Casey asked, lowering the carrier bag onto the grass next to the peeling paint at the front of the hut.

'Not if it's us, he won't,' Piper reassured her. 'He'll understand. We'll put the food in the shade to keep it from getting warm.'

'I could do with sitting in the shade myself,' Casey said, carrying the bag over to a gnarled tree with branches overhanging the lawn.

'Hopefully Jax will have something we can sit on. I'm not sure we'll all fit in the beach hut, even if it was cooler in there. I'll open it up though to let some air through before Matteo gets here.'

Casey went to help.

'Here, take these, will you?' Piper asked, holding up two fold-up canvas chairs. 'He has all sorts stored in here.' She carried out two more and they set them up under the tree. 'One more thing,' Piper said, returning to the hut.

Casey watched as her friend moved an old boogie board to one side and spotted a folded tarpaulin. 'Here we are,' she cheered. 'I knew this was here somewhere.'

'I hope there aren't any spiders on it.' Casey shuddered.

'You're not the only one.' Piper grimaced. 'I'm sure if there are they'll soon run away. Open it, will you, and lay it out in front of these chairs.'

Casey did as she asked, only giving one slight shriek when something bug-like scuttled away from one corner of the blue creased tarpaulin.

'Does Jax come here often?'

Piper nodded. 'He does. In the warmer months he even sleeps here sometimes, either on the grass or on the floor of the hut. He says he likes the peace of it.'

'I don't blame him,' Casey said, turning so her back was facing the hut and she was looking out over the patchy plants to the white-gold sand and azure blue waves ahead of her. 'I think I'd be tempted to do the same thing.'

'We'd better make our way to the sea wall,' Piper said. 'I imagine Alex and Matteo would have parked the bike by now and will be walking from the car park. We need to let them know where we are because they'll never find this place if we don't.'

They crossed the grassy land and reached the narrow promenade on top of the sea wall and gazed out. Casey loved looking out over the bay; it was where she had grown up and she loved it whether it was the height of the summer or the depths of winter. She was glad Jax had this place to come to when he wanted privacy. His mum, Sheila, was kind and they all knew she adored him but everyone also knew she could be a little overbearing as far as Jax was concerned.

She turned to the left, looking out for Alex and Matteo and was surprised instead to see Jax. He wasn't alone, she noticed.

Piper leaned one foot at the edge of the top of the sea wall and groaned. 'What's he doing with her?' she grumbled. 'And why on earth is he giving her a piggyback?'

Casey peered towards Jax and saw Alex's sister, Fliss, looking very relaxed and cheerful being carried on Jax's broad back.

He looked up, saw them watching, and his smile vanished. 'What are you doing here?' he asked. 'Nothing's wrong is it?'

'No, we're fine.' Piper moved back from the promenade to make way for two elderly women coming towards them and Casey did the same.

She watched as he carried Fliss up the granite stairs, crossed the grassy area, and spotting where they had laid out the four small chairs, lowered her to sit on one of them. Leaving Fliss, he walked over to join her and Piper.

'Fliss twisted her ankle on the sand,' he explained.

Casey wondered why he felt the need to say anything and then noticed Piper's unimpressed expression.

'Really?' Piper asked. 'You don't think she might be using it as a ruse so you'd carry her and she didn't have to walk here?'

He glanced at Casey and she decided against saying anything. He seemed happy enough to have carried her, although it can't have been easy in the soft white sand.

'So, what brings you two here then?' he asked. 'I presume you're waiting for someone as you're still standing here by the sea wall and not making the most of the chairs you've set out so neatly.'

Piper explained what had happened at the barn.

'It was really noisy,' Casey said, still surprised to have found herself in that position. 'I suppose that happens to Matteo a lot, don't you think?' she asked as it dawned on her how complicated life must be for him sometimes. She wasn't really sure what she made of the whole event.

'It was pretty odd,' Piper agreed. 'Poor man. I know he was hoping to stay incognito here for the whole trip, or at least for most of it. I suppose now he's going to have to be even more careful not to be seen by anyone who might recognise him.'

'Can't he just ignore them?' Jax asked, frowning.

'He can ignore them all he likes,' Piper said. 'But he's only been here a couple of days and has already had to change the location of his filming because someone tipped off the press.'

'I remember you telling me that now.'

'And today someone must have told those girls, or one of them spotted him and told her friends that he was at the barn behind The Cabbage Patch.'

'What a horrible way to live,' Jax said. 'Why anyone would want to be famous is beyond me.' His eyebrows shot up and Piper realised he'd seen someone.

Casey's stomach clenched in, what? she wondered. Excitement? Dread? She wasn't sure what to think any more, other than that she wished he didn't have such a massive effect on her whenever he was near her. She turned as Jax peered over the sea wall.

'There are two blokes coming.' Seconds later he waved at them. 'Yup, it's Alex and Matteo.'

'That's a relief,' Piper said. 'I wasn't sure they'd find this place, it's so well hidden from everything. I suppose they couldn't miss it with you standing there waving at them though, Jax.' She giggled.

'Ahh,' he said, turning to her. 'I've just thought about what you were telling me and now I understand why you've brought them here.'

'You don't mind, do you?' Casey asked, guiltily realising it was already a fait accompli whether he minded or not. 'We had to think fast.'

Jax put an arm around hers and Piper's shoulders. 'Don't be silly. I don't mind at all. I knew it had to be something unusual because my little cuz here has never told anyone where this place was before now.'

Casey saw Piper give Fliss a pointed look. 'And you don't ordinarily bring others here either.'

Jax followed her line of vision. 'I know. I was a bit caught out too. She's lighter to carry than most girls, I imagine, but she's still heavy if you're carrying her a long way and especially in fine sand.'

As Alex and Matteo neared, Piper lowered her voice. 'I can give her a lift back to her friend's house after lunch if you like.'

'Thanks, I'd like that very much.'

Casey swapped glances with Piper. Her friend was obviously thinking the same thing as her and wondering what might have happened between Jax and Fliss to change his view of her. He was never fickle, so it must have been something that had upset him quite a bit and he certainly didn't seem at all enamoured of her now. She was intrigued but knew now was not the time to broach the sensitive subject and would either have to wait for Piper to ask him later, or speak to him herself when she had a moment alone with him.

The two men reached the stairs, both pink in the face and looking flustered.

'Phew,' Matteo said, wiping perspiration from his forehead with the back of his hand as he reached the top of the nearby stairs and joined them. 'I expected it to be cooler than this, but I forget we're closer to France than the UK here, so it's bound to be hot sometimes.'

'It was hotter work traipsing through that sand than you might think,' Alex moaned.

Casey knew only too well how much extra work it was to walk through it, especially on a day as humid as this one. 'We have cool beers and sodas waiting in the shade for you over by that beach hut.' She hoped they were still cool.

'You're a star,' Matteo said, going to rest a hand on her shoulder before thinking better of it. 'Thank you.'

'Don't worry about it,' she said non-committally.

Alex cocked his head in the direction of the hut where Fliss was sitting. 'What's my sister doing here?'

Casey wasn't sure if he was happy to see her or suspicious about what might have led her to be here but didn't want Jax to have to deal with an unhappy older brother if Alex was the protective type. 'She twisted her ankle when she was out with Jax and he carried her back here as it was the closest place he could think of,' Casey explained. 'I think she's fine though. She hasn't said otherwise.'

'I see,' Alex said, smiling at Piper before giving her a quick kiss. 'I'd better go and check up on her then.'

'You can let her know that I'll give her a lift back to Phoebe's after lunch if you like,' Piper said.

'Thank you, I'll do that.'

Piper and Jax joined the others near the tree, where they had set up the four canvas chairs.

'Take a seat if you want one,' Piper said, going to sit on the grass.

'I don't need a chair,' Matteo said sitting down on the grass. 'I'm just grateful to have some shade.'

'So am I,' Alex said.

Happy to have a chair to sit on, Casey made herself comfortable while Piper and Jax did the same.

'This looks very organised,' Alex said.

'Like reaching an oasis,' Matteo sighed, locking his fingers together and putting his hands behind his head and closing his eyes with a deep sigh.

Casey watched him as Piper busied herself organising everyone.

'I've got a couple of baguettes we can tear up and share,' Piper said. 'There's cheese in the paper bag and a pack of ham. I'm afraid I only thought to buy two wooden knives, so you'll have to do your best with everything. Oh, there's cherry tomatoes too, if you want.'

'This looks grand to me,' Alex said, indicating for Piper and Casey to help themselves first.

She sat quietly watching Matteo and thought how beautiful he was. Her heart ached to think what might have been between them if... *If what?* She was living in a fantasy world. That kiss had sent her slightly mad. It must have done, otherwise why else would she ever contemplate any kind of future, even a very short one, with a popstar. She shook her head to try and clear it of the nonsensical thoughts.

'What are you thinking?' She realised Matteo was addressing her. 'I meant what I said,' he added, gazing at Casey. She wanted desperately to go and sit next to him, be near him, but she couldn't lower herself to just be one of many others, like Martha had intimated only that morning. 'Casey.'

She caught his eye and winced. 'I think you want to believe it,' she said, needing to answer him. 'I just don't think you realise how your actions make others feel.'

'Hey, you two haven't taken any food yet,' Jax said, sitting back down on the grass near to Casey's chair, clearly oblivious to any underlying upset between her and Matteo. 'Shall I pass something to you?'

Whatever appetite she had when she was shopping had disappeared now, but she knew that if she refused the food Matteo might realise it was because of how upset she was with him. Not wishing to give him any satisfaction, she forced a smile. 'Yes please. Just a piece of the baguette and a bit of the Brie, thanks.'

Jax handed her the food and then gave out the drinks. 'Matteo, you?'

He took the beer being offered to him. 'No food for me, thanks,' he said looking briefly at Casey. 'I don't seem to have much of an appetite right now.'

'I'm not surprised after what the girls told me,' Jax said, misunderstanding Matteo's inference. Jax sat back and drank a mouthful of beer. 'Do you have to make quick escapes often?'

Matteo took a mouthful of beer and swallowed. 'It happens more often than I would like, but it goes with the territory. Most of the time things run smoothly.'

'Like how?' Fliss asked, turning her attention to them.

'For example, at my flat in London there are two exits. One through a main front door and another via the underground parking. When it's particularly bad we have two cars and I pick one to travel in. Sometimes I leave in the second car and other times in the first. Mostly, though, I like to chat to my fans.' He smiled at her. Casey watched Fliss give him a flirty smile and felt like she had been elbowed in the stomach. 'After all, without them I wouldn't be enjoying the success I am right now.'

'It must get a bit tiring though,' Piper said. 'I mean if you want to go to the cinema, or out to the park or something.'

He sighed. 'It can do. But I tell myself that my career might be short-lived and I should make the most of it while I can. I'll always be able to go to the park or cinema when I'm older.'

'You have your country home though, don't you?' Fliss asked. 'Alex told me that the grounds there are bigger than most parks.'

'That's true,' he agreed, looking a little embarrassed as he glanced at Casey and she held his gaze for a moment, desperate for him not to see how affected she was by what had happened.

'I also get to stay in amazing private homes when I go away on holiday. So as much as it can encroach on my privacy I remind myself that I get to see places others might not be lucky enough to visit.'

Casey wasn't sure what to make of this information. She listened as Jax told them about his morning with Fliss, sensing Matteo watching her every so often. One of the times he caught her eye and she saw he was frowning thoughtfully. She wished she knew what was going on in his head.

Piper sat forward and turned to Jax. 'Any news on the Dan front?'

Jax looked up from his food and frowned. 'Not much. I mentioned about accompanying me to a wedding and I think he thought I was joking.'

'Why would he think that?' Casey asked.

Jax shrugged. 'I guess because we usually only see each other out on the boat, when we're working. He's been seeing Vicki since we met and spends most of his spare time with her, so we've never really socialised outside work.' He took a bite from his piece of baguette and ate it. 'I can see why he would think me suddenly wanting him to go to a wedding with me was a little odd.'

'Ahh.' Casey hadn't realised that was the case and had presumed they saw more of each other than they did. 'Sorry about that.' It wasn't as if she could think of any alternative means to get him there so hoped Dan wasn't suspicious. 'You don't think he suspects it's for him and Vicki, do you?'

Jax laughed. 'No way. He'd never imagine she would go this far. Vicki's always been so quiet and happy to follow his ideas, as far as I'm aware.'

'Good. That's something I suppose.' Piper finished the rest of her bread and cheese.

'Don't you think it's a shame Dan's getting married?' Fliss asked, surprising Casey by her question.

'No. I think it's romantic.' Casey noticed Jax's face falling and wondered if his change of heart about Alex's sister had something to do with his business partner.

'He's very handsome, though isn't he?' Fliss asked no one in particular. 'In a rugged sort of way.'

Why was she trying to cause trouble? Casey wondered, noticing Piper's cheeks reddening as she glanced at Alex. He didn't look very impressed with his sister's comments either.

Fliss looked up from her food and studied each of them. 'What?'

Alex frowned. 'We've been talking about arrangements for his wedding and that's what occurs to you?'

Fliss laughed and waved her hand towards her brother, as if batting away a particularly irritating fly. 'Why are you always so serious? I'm allowed to have an opinion, aren't I?'

'Yes, but you could try to be a little sensitive when addressing his closest friends and those of his fiancée.' He gave her a pointed look.

'Urgh,' she said, closing her eyes and shaking her head slowly. 'You can be such a bore, Alex, do you know that?'

Casey watched silently as Alex's jaw clenched and he gave a deep sigh. 'Just don't mention anything to him if you do happen to come across him before the wedding. Please, Fliss. It would ruin everyone's plans.'

Fliss raised her hand to cover her mouth, looking shocked by his suggestion. 'Of course not.'

Casey didn't miss the unmistakable amusement in Fliss's eyes as she feigned horror and a sick sense of the damage the girl was capable of instigating coursed through her. 'You do understand how disruptive it would be if you did tip him off, don't you?' Casey asked, wanting Fliss to get the message.

She was relieved to see the amusement vanish from Fliss's

face as she slowly turned her gaze in Casey's direction. The coolness emanating from the other woman made Casey give an invol-
untary shiver. 'Please don't tell me what I should and should not
do, Casey.' Before Casey had a chance to react, Fliss looked away,
clearly dismissing her.

How rude, Casey thought, irritated by the girl's condescending
manner. She caught Matteo glaring at Fliss out of the corner of
her eye. 'I would hate for all Vicki's plans to go awry,' Casey
added, unable to help herself.

Fliss's head turned back to her. 'Are you still rambling on
about this?' she asked as if Casey had been ranting for hours
instead of mere seconds. 'Do lighten up, will you?'

Fliss looked at her brother, pulled a face and raised her
eyebrows, clearly wanting to make a fool of Casey.

Piper glared at Fliss before Casey had a chance to retaliate. 'I
think that's enough now, Fliss, don't you?' She gave Casey an
apologetic smile as if Fliss's behaviour was somehow her responsibility.

'It's fine,' Casey said quietly. It wasn't but now wasn't the time
to get into an argument with this selfish, spoilt girl. It would only
end in her being infuriated when she already had more than
enough to deal with. She doubted whether Fliss would take any
notice of her anyway.

'So, when are you going to invite me to your country pile
then?' Fliss asked Matteo, obviously bored of Casey and her
opinions.

He didn't seem to know how to answer, Casey noticed.

His index finger tapped the bottle he was holding. 'I'd love to
invite you all sometime soon,' he said eventually, looking pointedly at Casey for a couple of seconds. 'It'll have to be after my
tour or during the short break we have in the middle of it in the
autumn.'

Casey couldn't miss Fliss's annoyance that his reply included them all, and not just her, and couldn't help feeling a little soothed by his support of her.

'That would be fantastic,' Piper said. 'I'm sure we'd all love to come, wouldn't we, Casey?'

She flushed slightly. Would she? 'Yes,' she admitted. 'We would.'

Matteo's eyes widened in surprise. 'Would you really come?'

What was she doing? she wondered as the ice shard in her heart began melting. 'Yes. I'd love to,' she admitted, irritated with herself for feeling so much for him.

Piper beamed at her. Casey knew her friend wanted to see her and Matteo together and hoped desperately he wasn't playing some sort of cruel game with her emotions. She looked at Alex to see what he made of the conversation. After all he was Matteo's best friend and knew him better than the rest of them, but he was too busy glaring at his sister to have much of an opinion on anything else.

'Right, if we're all finished I'll pack away this food and drop Fliss back at Phoebe's,' Piper said, looking at Alex and clearly wanting to keep the atmosphere as light as possible.

'Do you want me to meet up with you back at the barn when I've dropped Matteo off with Martha?' Alex asked, standing and collecting the discarded wrappings and putting them into the carrier bag for disposal.

'Would you mind if I have a brief word with Casey first?' Matteo asked, giving Casey a questioning look.

'Of course not,' Piper said.

Casey wasn't sure what to expect and handed her paper plate to Piper, giving her a quick smile before standing. Not wishing to cause her friend any concern, she took Matteo's proffered hand and walked away with him towards the promenade.

16

Matteo had known he was risking Casey not taking his hand. As good as it felt to have her hand in his, he could feel how tense she was and that she didn't really want to speak to him. He suspected that if they had been alone then she would have refused to go for a walk with him.

They reached the promenade. 'Let's walk along here for a bit, shall we?' he suggested.

He felt her start to pull her hand from his but then she looked up at him before turning her head and looking in her friends' direction. Alex was smiling after them and Matteo wondered if that was why Casey had kept her hand in his.

A few seconds later, when they were hidden from everyone else by a garden fence, Casey slid her hand from his. Matteo couldn't manage to hide his hurt. He stopped and stared at her. 'Please don't be like that, Casey. I really didn't mean to offend you earlier. I promise I was busy otherwise I would have loved to have made you breakfast like I'd offered.'

She frowned and stared at him and he noticed the hurt in her eyes that was immediately replaced by annoyance.

'Did you truly think that's why I'm annoyed with you?' She shook her head and scowled at him. 'Matteo, I'm not put out because you didn't cook for me. If that's what you're thinking.'

It wasn't? 'I'm sorry, I don't understand.'

She glared at him. 'Seriously! You think I'm that petty, or—' she seemed to be struggling to come up with the right words '—or downright childish that I'd be angry with you because you didn't cook for me?'

He had no idea what he was supposed to have done. Frustrated, he held his arms outstretched. 'Then what? Please explain to me what I've done.'

She groaned and, clearly frustrated, began walking again for a few steps.

Matteo watched her, desperate to understand what had upset her. Suddenly she stopped and turned back to him. 'Matteo,' she said almost through clenched teeth.

She really was very angry, he realised. He needed to find a way to make things right with her but first he wanted to know what he had done to offend her.

'The reason I'm...' She sighed. 'Hurt? Yes, I am, and definitely embarrassed, is because of what Martha said.'

He relaxed slightly. So it hadn't been him who had upset her. Still, he thought, Martha was his manager and he needed to find out exactly what had happened so that he could make things right with Casey. 'Did she insult you?' he asked anxiously. 'Because if she did I'm sure she hadn't meant to.' Had she? He suspected Martha could be nasty when she wanted her own way. They had fallen out several times and mostly because she had been heavy-handed with her bossiness. 'Martha likes you. I'm sure she does.' He stared at her, unable to imagine there being a reason for Martha not to like Casey. 'And even if she didn't...'

'Even if she didn't?'

Damn, why did he say that? He shook his head. 'What I mean is that I'm not interested in what anyone else thinks about you, Casey. All I care about is that I like you. A lot.' He closed his eyes in frustration. Why was this going so badly? Because he cared for her, that's why, he reminded himself. 'Surely you must know that.'

She stared at him thoughtfully for a moment, hands clenched into fists at her sides. 'I don't really care whether Martha likes or approves of me. It's what she intimated that stung me,' Casey explained.

He tried to recall exactly what Martha had said but had been too irritated with her for turning up and ruining his morning with Casey to pay very much attention at the time. 'I'm sorry, you'll have to remind me.' He sensed he needed to explain why he didn't recall what had been said, determined for Casey not to think that he hadn't listened because he wasn't interested. It was time to be a bit more open about his feelings than he was used to being. 'I was too disappointed at having our morning interrupted to take in everything she said apart from the bit about us having urgent business to attend to.'

Casey frowned at him and didn't speak straight away. Matteo went to try and explain his reasons for not listening to Martha a little further when Casey opened her mouth to speak.

'It was when she commented about you not having time to waste *playing* in a pool with one of your *many little friends*.'

'She said that?' Bloody Martha. Why would she be so mean to Casey?

'For pity's sake, Matteo. Martha intimated that I am one of many women you use that line with about joining you for a swim and a cooked breakfast.'

Casey's cheeks flushed and he realised she was mortified by what had happened and now he was making her relive her embarrassment. He could have kicked himself for being so insensitive.

'That's a horrible thing for her to have done. I'm so sorry, Casey.' He reached out to take her hands in his, but she quickly moved them behind her back. If he wasn't very careful he was going to lose any chance of getting to know Casey better. Damn Martha for treating this kind girl, who was going out of her way to help resolve his filming issue, like this. It was unnecessary and unacceptable for her to have behaved in that way. 'Casey, I can't believe you thought she meant something like that.'

'You can't? How would you take it if the tables were turned?' She rested her hands on her hips and glared up at him furiously.

He needed to rescue the situation, and fast. Then he needed to have a stern word with his manager. 'I imagine I would feel the same way you do now,' he said honestly. 'But, Casey, I promise you you're the first girl I've invited back to the cottage for a swim, or breakfast. Or anything, for that matter.'

Her eyes narrowed. 'I suppose you have only been here a couple of days,' she said, flinching straight after.

Hurt by her nastiness, Matteo could feel his breathing shorten. He had never to his knowledge treated any woman badly and he was not going to stand by and be insulted by anyone, even someone he liked as much as Casey. It was Martha who had been horrible, not him, and he didn't deserve Casey's spite. 'I don't know what you think of me,' he said, his words clipped as he felt his temper rising. 'But I'm not some sort of gigolo looking for female company.'

Casey frowned and her anger seemed to vanish. 'I'm sorry. That came out wrong.'

'It did?'

Was he glad or too upset by her accusation to want to listen to anything else she had to say? He decided to at least give her a chance to explain. 'Then what did you mean exactly?'

'Hey, are you two ready to leave yet?' Alex shouted.

Matteo didn't know whether to be relieved or disappointed that his friend had interrupted their angry exchange.

'Can you give us a moment, Alex?' Matteo asked gruffly, hoping to try and at least partly resolve their conflict.

'Of course.' Alex frowned, looking from Matteo to Casey before walking for a few steps and then turned back to them. 'Everything all right, guys?'

'We're fine,' Casey said quickly.

'No. We're not,' Matteo argued.

Casey locked eyes with him and looked away. He watched her smile at Alex. 'I think it's time I went to find Piper.'

'Casey,' Matteo called, needing more time with her. But she walked away. 'Casey!'

She raised a hand over her shoulder without looking in his direction. It seemed she'd had enough.

He almost missed Alex asking him what had gone wrong between them, but couldn't take his eyes of her as she stormed off.

'You all right, mate?' Alex asked, resting a hand on Matteo's shoulders.

'I will be,' he said, not wanting his friend to worry about him. But he had no idea how he was going to sort out this mess.

17

'Er, don't I get a say in this?' Fliss asked as Casey joined them. It seemed that she and Matteo weren't the only two whose moods had taken a dive.

When no one replied, Casey watched Fliss sidle up to Jax and slip her arm around his waist. 'I thought we might take ourselves off somewhere,' she said, her voice coquettish and sugary sweet.

He looked at her as if she was speaking a language he didn't understand and Casey had to stop herself from smiling. Typical Jax not to be taken in by silly games. He moved away from her and her arm slid away from him. 'I'm going to help Casey and the others set up the barn for Vicki,' he said.

It was the first Casey had heard of this but she didn't say anything, happy to have another strong pair of hands and someone taller than most of them to be able to fix anything that they needed pinning high up in the barn. She shot him a grateful glance.

'I get to go home then and do nothing, is that it?' Fliss pouted. 'How dull.'

'You get to go and spend time at your friend's beautiful home with its gardens and pool,' Alex pointed out as he joined them. 'I don't call that being hard done by.'

'It's boring though, Alex,' Fliss snapped, marching off in Matteo's direction.

Casey followed Fliss and saw that Matteo was standing on the concrete promenade where she had left him, staring out to sea. His shoulders were hunched and he was clearly very upset by their conversation. Fliss had gone a few strides before Alex ran up to her and grabbed her left wrist. 'No, you don't,' he said. 'Leave him alone for a moment.'

Casey heard the tone in Alex's voice. It didn't leave any room for argument and even Fliss took notice of what he said and stopped walking, probably realising she had no choice but to leave Matteo to his thoughts.

Fliss sighed theatrically before turning on her heels and stomping back to the beach hut. 'Why don't you do something with this tatty dump?' she snapped at Jax, taking her temper out on him now he had made it perfectly clear he was no longer interested in spending time with her.

'I...' Jax began looking stung by her question. He loved this place more than any other, Piper had told Casey, and she suspected that hearing someone, even Fliss, speak disparagingly about the place his grandfather had adored must have been upsetting.

'I'd love somewhere like this,' Alex argued, gazing longingly at the hut and then at the view in front of it out across the beach. Casey was grateful to him for being so thoughtful. 'I think you're incredibly lucky to have this place, Jax.'

Jax brightened immediately. 'Thanks, mate. It's very special to me. In fact, Piper is the only person I've ever invited here before now.'

Piper rubbed her cousin's muscular arm. 'Technically, you didn't invite any of us here today,' she said apologetically.

'Maybe not,' Alex said. 'But I'm glad you let us stay and chill here for a bit.' He hesitated. 'Would you mind if I came here some other time?'

Jax's smile widened. 'Not at all. Why don't I bring you here at the next high tide and we can fish for mackerel off the sea wall? If you enjoy a bit of fishing that is?'

'I do,' Alex said. 'I'm not very good at it though, and I don't have a fishing rod over here, but if you let me know where I can hire one then I'll make sure I get one before coming.'

'No need for that,' Jax said walking the few steps into the hut. He took hold of three fishing rods and held them up for Alex to see. 'I've got enough here if you want to bring Matteo along with you. He might like a bit of time away from things.'

'I'd love to join you,' Matteo said, not looking in Casey's direction as he walked back to the group.

Piper smiled at her and Casey was relieved her friend had missed her altercation with Matteo. At least Piper wouldn't be asking her what had happened and she hoped that Alex wouldn't mention anything to Piper either.

'All set to go?' Piper asked.

'Yes, sure,' Casey said, looking forward to getting some space between her and Matteo for a while.

'Yes, thanks,' Matteo said. He turned to Casey. 'I'm afraid I have to go and meet my manager now but I'll see you later?'

Later? What had she missed. 'Sorry? What's happening later?'

'We're all meeting at the barn remember?' Piper laughed. 'Though with all that's been happening over the past few days I'm not surprised you've forgotten. Yes, we'll see you and Alex there,' Piper said. 'Around six to six-thirty-ish?'

'Perfect,' Matteo said, shooting a glance in Casey's direction that gave nothing away.

Casey was confused. *What was Matteo playing at?* She noticed Piper collecting their rubbish and went to help pick up some of the discarded bottles, putting them in the carrier bag her friend was holding containing other rubbish.

'Thanks,' Piper said. 'We can sort this and throw it away later.' She took her keys from her pocket and held them up. 'If everyone's ready, I think we should make a move.'

Alex slipped his arm around Piper's shoulders and moved closer to kiss her. 'You're sure you don't mind dropping my sister off at her friend's house?'

'Not at all. I'll see you later at the barn.'

'I'll like that.'

Casey watched them kiss and, without thinking, glanced at Matteo, instantly wishing she hadn't when she saw him looking at her. She couldn't tear her eyes away from his and recalled how heavenly it had felt to be kissed by him. Had it only been that morning? It seemed so long ago, she thought miserably. He was the first one to look away and she found she was staring at him, wishing she had the guts to go over to him and ask if she could take back her earlier spiteful comment. Seeing Piper and Alex so loved up exaggerated the loss she felt at not being on good terms with Matteo.

'Do you know how many people will be helping to get the place ready for Vicki and Dan's reception?' Alex asked, interrupting her thoughts.

Casey looked at her friend and pretended to give his question some thought. 'No. Why?'

'I thought I might arrange a delivery of pizzas and drinks for a bit later to keep them going when they begin to flag.'

It was a good idea. 'Thank you, that's very thoughtful. I

suppose most of them will have worked all day so they're bound to be hungry.' Those that knew Vicki, like she and Piper did, wanted to help make her day special but Casey assumed that the rest of the stallholders at The Cabbage Patch wanted to make the barn look as good as possible. They were all aware how difficult it had been for the elderly Ecobichon sisters to keep their pretty but weathered home, where they had lived their entire lives. Any prospective source of extra income was always welcome.

Who knows, Casey thought, *maybe renting out their barns for future weddings might be the next sideline they could venture into.* Another thought occurred to her. Weddings needed photographers and as far as she was aware Vicki didn't have one.

'Does Matteo have a photographer working for him?'

Alex shrugged. 'I don't know for certain, but I assume he must have someone around who takes photos. Why?'

She explained about suspecting that the other stallholders were hoping to help the sisters as well as Vicki by clearing up the barn. 'I thought that it would be a wasted opportunity if someone didn't take professional photos of the barn when the place is looking its best.' She pictured Vicki getting married. 'And maybe take photos of the bride and groom at the castle and the barn.'

She smiled at him when he looked amused. 'I know I'm being cheeky asking this, but I'm also aware that Matteo is grateful to Vicki.' When Alex didn't reply, she added, 'He said so, didn't he?'

'He did.'

'So, lending us his photographer could be another way to help make the day as perfect as possible while also helping out two elderly ladies.' She pursed her lips. 'Do you think he'll agree?'

'What?' Alex looked confused why she was asking him when Matteo was standing nearby. 'Why don't you ask him?'

'I'd rather not,' she said, keeping her voice low. 'Anyway,

you're his best friend. I thought that it might sound better coming from you.'

Alex grinned at her. 'You're rather crafty, aren't you?'

Not crafty enough, she thought, wishing she had thought first before snapping at Matteo. She tilted her head to one side, pretending to give his question some thought. 'I'm right though, don't you agree?'

He laughed.

'What are you two conspiring about?' Piper asked, grinning.

'You tell her,' Casey said, listening as Alex did as she asked.

Piper noticed Jax and Fliss watching them and nudged him with her elbow. 'Better keep our voices down. We don't want Fliss to hear any more than she already has done.'

'Good point,' Alex said. 'I know she's my sister but I don't trust her not to cause trouble, especially when she's bored, which she insists she is right now.'

'You didn't say whether or not you agreed,' Casey whispered.

He frowned and shook his head. 'To what?'

'To whether you should ask Matteo about his photographer.'

'Ah, that. Yes, I do.' His smile vanished. 'I think it would be better if you asked him yourself.'

Casey wondered if this was Alex's way of getting her and Matteo talking again. She noticed Piper staring at her.

'What's happened?' Piper asked.

'Nothing,' Alex replied before Casey had the chance to. 'Nothing that can't be sorted out anyway. Eh? Casey?'

'You'd know that better than me,' she said.

'Matteo's a good bloke,' he said quietly. 'I can vouch for him. I don't know what's happened between you but I know he's very upset.'

'Did I hear my name just then?' Matteo asked, joining them. He'd been speaking to Fliss away from the group.

Piper cleared her throat. 'Maybe.'

'Why?'

'Casey will speak to you about it later.' Piper tapped her watch. 'It's getting late and we've all got so much to do. We'd better get going now.'

'Yes, of course.' Matteo looked at Alex and then back at Casey, his face expressionless. 'I'll see you later then.'

Piper and Casey collected their things from the hut. 'How's your ankle, Fliss?'

Fliss rubbed it gently. 'Not too bad.'

'I noticed you walking about a bit, so I presume you'll be able to walk to the car,' Piper said. 'Or do you need help?'

Alex appeared beside his sister and without waiting for her to say anything, hoisted her in a fireman's lift over his left shoulder. 'Come along, little sis. Off we go.'

Casey gasped, unable to help a laugh escaping as she and Piper exchanged amused smiles.

'Put me down, right now.' Fliss slapped his back, her face red with fury.

They watched Alex carry her and then Piper must have realised she had to unlock the car to let Fliss in and pressed the fob. 'I'll see you a bit later,' Piper said to Jax, who seemed relieved that they were finally leaving him in peace and taking Fliss with them.

'Yeah, sure. See you later.'

Casey and Piper hurried over to the car and watched Fliss complaining to her brother as he marched over to the car with her slung over his shoulder like an ungainly sack of potatoes.

'You're such an oaf.'

'Thanks, sis.'

He gave Piper a wink as Fliss got into the front passenger seat. Most people would automatically get in the back seat, Casey mused. No matter, Piper would be dropping Fliss off first as she was staying furthest away from the guest house.

Casey reached the car and when Fliss didn't make any attempt to get out and let her inside the car, Piper did the honours.

18

Piper dropped Casey back at The Cabbage Patch, where she worked with Tara for a couple of hours, and then the two of them loaded up her car, filling the boot with most of the candles so that they were ready for the following morning. They carefully arranged the rest of them on the back seat and slotted the mirrors they had chosen for the filming between the back and front seats.

She drove them back to her parents' home and hadn't even turned off the ignition before shrieks of laughter reached her ears. She stepped out of the car and locked it. The voices were coming from the back garden.

'What on earth is going on there?' she asked Tara, who shrugged.

'No idea. Maybe Jordi's invited some friends round. Let's go and find out.'

Intrigued, Casey got out of the car and seeing the front door ajar pushed it open, stepped inside and followed the noisy laughter out to the garden.

'I didn't realise you were having a party?'

Jordi wasn't there but eight cheerful ladies including Piper, her mother Helen and her grandmother Margery, were drinking tea and seemed very happy with themselves. Her shock was forgotten when Casey spotted candles, many of them. They were lined up in several rows in the shade on the small patio by the back door.

'Look, ladies, young Casey's home,' Piper's gran announced.

Rowena stood and waved a hand in the direction of the candles. 'Hello, girls,' she said. 'We've been waiting for you two to arrive. What do you think of this lot then?'

Casey looked at the candles, some used, some new, and couldn't think what to say for a moment. 'I, um. Are they all for the castle?'

Rowena folded her arms across her chest, looking very pleased with herself. As well she might, Casey mused, delighted. 'They are.' She pointed to the ladies now standing behind her. 'Don't worry, Dilys here has written down each name and what candle they brought along and also their phone number.'

Casey was overwhelmed by their thoughtfulness. Collecting all these candles and being organised enough to write down names and details was incredibly helpful. Knowing who had brought what would make it much easier when it came to replacing all the candles, she realised.

'It's extremely kind of you all.' They all took seats and she realised that by working for so long she had caused them all to wait. She looked at Piper. 'You knew about this, didn't you?' She smiled gratefully.

'She did,' Margery said, beaming in Piper's direction.

'Which is why you were in a hurry to leave the beach hut.' It all made sense now, Casey thought.

'Beach hut?' Tara asked. 'Where's that?'

Not wishing to share about Jax's private place with others in earshot, Casey pointed to the candles. 'Oh, nothing. Look at these though. Aren't they wonderful?'

Tara grinned. 'I think it's these women who are wonderful,' she laughed. 'Thank you all so much. You've saved us a lot of trouble and worry by collecting these for us.'

'And thank you, Piper,' Casey said, touched by her friend's help.

'It was the least I could do,' Piper said. 'After all, you're both being so kind helping Matteo and Alex. Alex really is most grateful, as am I, that he doesn't have the worry of it.'

'We're happy to help,' Casey said, realising that she felt as if she was doing something very worthwhile. She had forgotten Alex in all of the stress of the past few days. Her focus had been so much on Vicki and Matteo that she had forgotten how worrying this must have been for him, as he had been given the job of finding the location for the recording in the first place.

'Is that cake you're all eating?' Tara asked, studying the crumbs on plates covering the small table most of the women were seated around.

'Helen brought two Victoria sponges,' Rowena said. 'I made a lemon drizzle and Dilys brought her famous walnut cake.'

Casey noticed that apart from the walnut cake only crumbs were left on the plates where the other cakes must have once been.

'Want a slice?'

She was about to decline the offer, but then saw the expectant look on Dilys's face and nodded.

'I'd love some, please.'

'So would I,' Tara said.

Casey motioned for her friend to take the last chair, near to Piper's gran, and went inside to grab one of their dining chairs and bring it outside.

She sat while her mother took a knife and cut the remainder of the walnut cake in half and placed a piece each on to two plates. Handing first Tara and then Casey a plate and cake fork, Rowena sat back and smiled. 'Isn't this fun?'

Casey pressed her fork through the end of the cake to cut a piece off and stabbed her fork into it before popping it into her mouth. It was sweet and tasty, and when she looked up from the plate and noticed eight pairs of eyes watching her, no doubt waiting for her review of the cake, she was relieved she hadn't disliked it.

'What do you think?' Dilys asked expectantly, resting her notepad and biro onto her lap. 'It's fresh. Made it this morning, I did.'

Casey swallowed the remains in her mouth. 'It's delicious,' she said honestly. Walnut cake was never her favourite, she always preferred chocolate or a plain sponge, but this was really tasty. 'Thank you.'

She ate the rest of the nutty sweet cake while they all began chatting and laughing again. She would have loved a cup of tea to wash it down with but suspected the pot was empty. She could make one for herself after everyone had left.

She looked over at the patio and the candles. There must have been almost twenty and most of them were the larger sort that she and Tara sold. How was she going to get them all to the castle? They would be heavy and although she might find a parking space along the road near the green, it was still quite a way along the pathway to the entrance and then there were all of those steps leading up to where the filming was to take place. She would worry about that a little later, she decided.

She finished her cake and placed her plate and fork on one of the others on the table. Casey sat back content and more than a little relieved that this major problem had been almost resolved.

'Bugger, the candles!' Tara exclaimed leaping to her feet.

'What?' Casey glanced at the patio but the candles seemed fine. 'What's the matter?'

'The candles in the car,' Tara said. 'We have to bring them inside before the heat melts them and they lose their gorgeous shapes.'

Rowena gasped. 'You've left candles in the car in this heat?'

Casey groaned. 'Yes. We hadn't considered the heat with all the excitement. Quickly, Tara, let's get them.'

Rowena, Piper, Helen and Dilys followed them, and as soon as the car doors and boot were opened, each grabbed as many as they could comfortably carry and took them into the cool of the kitchen.

Some of them were soft to the touch. 'Please be very careful,' Casey said, irritated at her and Tara's thoughtlessness.

Rowena took one of her older tablecloths from a drawer. 'The dining room's the coolest room in the house,' she said. 'I'm going to put this over the table to protect it. Casey fetch trays and we'll place the candles onto them so we don't keep touching them. Then we can carry them through to the dining room.'

'Good idea,' Margery said, carrying a couple in from the patio. 'We'll need to get the others inside too. The sun's moved from when we first set them out there and they'll be in the sunshine soon. We don't want them ruined either.'

Everyone worked quickly and soon the candles were set out neatly on trays on the dining room table, the mirrors stacked on the floor against each other and resting against the sideboard. The curtains had been closed and windows opened to let a breeze waft through.

'You're all amazing,' Casey said, delighted at all they had achieved together. 'Thank you so much.'

Dilys rested a hand on Casey's arm. 'I don't know about these ladies but I'm having a lovely time being involved in such an exciting event.'

'The wedding, you mean?' Tara asked.

'No, that popstar's filming at the castle.'

Word had got round, Casey mused. Then again, she wasn't sure she had ever expected it not to, but at least she presumed it was only among her fairly small and very close community. All it took was one friend to confide in another about Matteo or Vicki's wedding and soon most of them would know the secret and she assumed, keep it among themselves.

Casey smiled when Tara gave her a worried look. 'It's fine. It's also fun and with more of us involved the two events stand a far better chance of being truly successful, don't you think?'

Tara smiled. 'I suppose you're right.' She glanced over her shoulder. 'What about the material we need, the muslin for the backdrop? Shall we ask if anyone here has any while we have everyone in one place?'

'The woman I know who is closing her haberdashery store is dropping off a load of material she's happy for you to have,' Rowena said. 'She'll be bringing it here later this evening.'

Casey sighed with relief. 'This is amazing.'

'Do any of you have an amount of muslin you don't need any more?' she asked. 'I would ask to borrow it and maybe it will be fine to return to you, but we can't guarantee that's what will happen.' She pulled a face. 'That is, even if we're careful, wax from the candles might drip on it and ruin it.'

'I'm sure I have some in one of the trunks in my house,' Margery said thoughtfully.

'I can look for it for you, Gran,' Piper said. 'Save you the bother.'

'That would be very kind of you,' Casey said. 'Thank you.'

Dilys raised a hand. 'I have some fine net curtains.' She shrugged. 'I know they probably sound odd.'

Casey gave her a grateful smile. She wasn't sure if they would be able to use them but didn't like to say so. 'Thank you, Dilys, that's kind of you. Shall I collect them from your flat?'

Dilys shook her head. 'No, don't worry. I'll drop them off here later.' She gave Rowena a questioning look. 'Would that be all right, dear?'

'Of course it would, Dilys,' Rowena said. 'If you bring them at around six-ish I can give you a lift up to the barn. How about that?'

'I'd like that very much,' Dilys said, smiling widely.

Casey was grateful to her mother. They all understood how Dilys was alone since her beloved husband, Ernie, had died five years before. The couple had never had any children and had fostered for many years, eventually adopting one of the girls. Some of those children, now adults with children of their own, often came to visit if they were on the island, but the rest of the time, Dilys was alone. Although, Casey thought, she seemed to recall Piper mentioning something about Dilys being a part of her gran's wild swimming group, so maybe she was finding more things to do to keep her occupied. She hoped so.

Casey noticed the wall clock in her mother's kitchen and grimaced. She needed to get going. 'I really am grateful to all of you,' she said, standing. 'But I'm going to have to leave you all now, if you don't mind.'

'I'm sure you have a lot to be getting on with,' Rowena said as Casey bent to kiss her on her forehead. 'We'll keep these here for now until you collect them. So don't worry about taking them with you yet.'

'Thanks, Mum. I appreciate that.' She smiled at Dilys. 'Thank you for writing everything down, that'll be an enormous help. And for your delicious cake, of course. I loved that.'

'So did I,' Tara agreed. 'It was the tastiest cake I've eaten in forever.'

Dilys beamed and gave them a shy smile. 'I was happy to do it.'

Another lady, Maude, who Casey suspected might be one of Piper's gran's other swimming friends, held up a finger. 'Don't forget, girls, if there's anything else you need us to do you only have to let your mother know, or ask one of us direct.'

Casey smiled at her gratefully. 'You're all very kind. Thank you. We'll definitely keep you all in mind.' She and Tara walked to the door and it occurred to her how delighted Dilys had been. It warmed her heart to see the sweet lady so happy.

Casey had no idea how many people would still want to help from The Cabbage Patch after working all day. It wouldn't hurt to give these ladies the opportunity to join in and help decorate the smaller barn. Some of them might even be happy to do so.

Turning at the front door, Casey looked at the ladies. 'Um, I was thinking,' she said. 'And only if you want to, of course. You shouldn't feel obliged.'

'What's the matter, lovey?' Margery asked. 'Spit it out.'

Piper laughed. 'Yes, Casey. What is it?'

'Well, if you have one or two friends who might also like to come and help decorate up at the smaller barn behind The Cabbage Patch for the surprise wedding then please bring them along. They'll be very welcome to come and join us.' She pressed her palms together. 'Only if they really want to though.'

'When would you need us all there?' Maude asked, her thin pencilled eyebrows raised. 'Tonight?'

'Yes, from six o'clock onwards.' She gave them an appreciative smile. 'We'll be bringing in refreshments for those who offer their help.'

'To make sure they keep going no doubt?' Maude joked. 'Good thinking, girls.'

'Yes, pretty much.' Piper laughed. 'So, if any of you would like to pitch up there, please do so. No obligation of course, you've all been very generous already and I really am very grateful to those of you who are able to join us.'

'I'll be there,' Dilys said, her quiet voice drowned out by a couple of others volunteering their services.

'I will too, lovey,' Margery said.

'If any of you need transport, please let me know and I'll either come and collect you or arrange for someone else to do so.'

'We'll be fine,' Margery said. 'We have the bus and you're already far too busy to take on anything more.'

Hearing Piper's grandmother's determined tone, Casey nodded. 'Thank you. Well, we'd better get going and I'll maybe see some of you later on.'

'I'll see you both in a bit,' Piper called. 'Mum wants to walk home but Gran's leg is a little achy today and I've offered to take her back to her cottage. I shouldn't be very long though.' She pulled an amused faced. 'Especially now she knows she's got somewhere to be later on.'

'That's great,' Casey said. 'See you in a bit.'

Before Casey was even out of the door the lively banter had started up once more. She pressed the fob to unlock her car, smiling to herself. How grateful she was that all these people were to be able to help even though most of them hadn't known the wedding was for Vicki, although she suspected that word had got around by now. Most of them had known Vicki her entire life and all of them visited Harbour Blooms at some point throughout the year.

* * *

The florist's bell jangled as Casey entered the shop. She waited for Nancy to finish serving her customer before speaking to her.

'Hello there,' Nancy said, tidying away cerise-pink tissue paper and string from the counter and giving it a wipe down with a cloth. 'What can I do for you?' She tapped the side of her nose with a manicured finger. 'Or are you here about the wedding flowers.'

'Reception flowers actually.' Casey noticed for the first time that the photos on the wall included wedding bouquets. She'd never taken much notice of the photos before now.

Nancy stepped out from behind the counter and pointed up at one nearest the end. 'You see that one? Or the garland?' Casey nodded. 'I've done two similar to it.'

'Really?' Casey moved closer to get a better look. It seemed very elaborate and incredibly beautiful. 'It's gorgeous.'

'I'm glad you think so,' Nancy said, motioning for Casey to follow her. 'Come out the back with me and I'll show you.'

Casey walked after her, feeling a little guilty to be disturbing Nancy's work. She gave a sharp intake of breath when the florist stepped to one side, revealing a long worktable on which lay two garlands. She gauged they must be at least three metres each in length.

'You're so clever' she said. 'Vicki must be over the moon with them.'

'She hasn't got any idea I've done them yet,' Nancy said, looking very pleased with herself.

'But how?' Casey wasn't sure how someone could keep creations as large as these a secret from an assistant who worked with her all day.

'I've kept this locked and told Vicki that it's out of bounds to her today,' Nancy said, as if knowing what she was thinking. 'I said that I have a little surprise for her that I don't want her to see yet.' She gave Casey a satisfied nod. 'Knowing Vicki, she'll assume I have a couple of arrangements but she'll never imagine anything like these two. I've been working on them since five o'clock this morning.' She pointed to the pink and cream flowers entwined in the ivy. 'Most of it is ivy, of course, with some eucalyptus. And as you can see here I've included some pink and a few cream roses, a couple of peonies in each one. Do you think she'll like them?'

'How can she not like them,' Casey said. 'I think they're stunning.'

'Good, I'm pleased.' She tidied up a bit of loose ivy at one end. 'I don't think I've ever been to the smaller barn where the reception is to take place so wasn't sure what to do for the best decoration. I thought that one of them could be positioned on a back wall if that's where the bridal party, or food is to be set. If the wall is wide then we could fix the two garlands together. Or they could be hung one at each end of the barn. I won't know until I get up there with them.'

'I'm not sure it'll matter too much,' Casey said trying to picture where best to hang them. 'They're so beautiful that they could be hung anywhere and they'll be perfect.'

'It's sweet of you to say so.' She closed the door behind them and followed Casey back through to the shop. 'I've also got a couple of stands for the castle. They can hold an ornament each with the same flowers arranged in them. I thought they could be moved to the barn once the wedding has been conducted while everyone is chatting outside and photos are being taken.'

Casey was delighted to hear Nancy's ideas. 'It all sounds perfect.'

'Great. When would you like me to come up to the barn with the garlands then?'

Casey explained about the plans she had made for cleaning the barn. 'We don't want any dust to fall on your beautiful garlands, so maybe bring them up a little later if that's all right?' She tried to judge when best to suggest. 'We're having food delivered and I should think that will be at around eight this evening. So why not join us for that. I'll make sure the barn is ready for you by then.'

Casey almost wished it would help if she crossed her fingers behind her back. She had no idea how long it was going to take them to make the barn ready, but now that so many people had volunteered their help she doubted it would take them too long. Anyway, she thought, most of them had been working all day and she couldn't imagine they would want to stay on too late.

'That's fine by me.' Nancy smiled at a customer as they walked into the florist's. 'And as far as the stands and arrangements are concerned, I'll take them up to the castle tomorrow late afternoon. Will that be all right?'

'Perfect,' Casey said, mouthing another thank you to the florist before leaving her to get on with serving her customer.

Things did seem to be coming together. She still had a lot to do though and if she was going to have everything ready for eight that evening, like she had told Nancy, then she really needed to get up to the barn to start on the cleaning as soon as possible. She wasn't going to be able to relax until everything was done anyway so there was no point in hanging around at home.

She drove back to her parents' house and collected a floor mop, two buckets and a couple of brooms, together with as many cloths and sponges her mother could spare. 'I'll replace anything I use up or ruin next week, if that's OK, Mum,' she said.

'Don't worry about it,' Rowena said. 'I'll be up there very soon anyway with some of the others. I think we're all quietly enjoying the excitement of this secret wedding,' she said. 'And everyone's talking about meeting Matteo.'

The mention of his name caused her stomach to tighten painfully. He was so handsome. Casey pictured his dark eyes and perfect white teeth. If only she was seeing him as the others were, she thought, placing cleaning sprays into one of the buckets and dusters and cloths into the other. Life would be much easier if that was the case.

'Are you all right, darling?' her mum asked, giving her a concerned look.

'Yes, just thinking about all there is still to do,' Casey fibbed. 'I'd better dash. See you up there in a bit.'

'Yes, see you there.'

Casey packed her car with all the cleaning materials and drove up to Trinity. She wished Matteo wasn't going to be there but he had said he would be and she could hardly ask him not to turn up, especially as he was paying for so much and, she reminded herself, everyone else would be delighted to see him there, including Vicki.

19

Casey carried the two buckets, brushes and mop towards the barn, hearing cheerful voices as she neared. Good, at least she wasn't alone despite it still being early. It was a relief. She pushed the door open with her knee and dropped the mop, almost tripping over it as she entered the barn.

Tara rushed forward to help her, having made her way there to close up their stall while Casey visited Nancy at Harbour Blooms.

'Let me get that for you,' she said, bending to pick it up. 'Is there anything else in your car?'

'A few bits. The car isn't locked.'

Tara propped the mop handle against the nearest wall and went outside.

Casey spotted the extra light coming in from the high windows at the far end of the barn. 'Blimey! Where have all the hay bales gone?'

'Most of it is stacked outside the back.' Alex appeared behind her, a piece of hay sticking out of his hair making her smile. 'We've done quite a bit don't you think?'

'You've done an enormous amount,' Casey agreed. The hay bales that were left had been placed in small groups at the corners of the room.

'We thought those could have trays of food or drink, or something,' Alex explained. 'And if they're not needed then we can take them out the back with the others. But we thought it would be an idea to leave them there for you to see and then you could decide either way.'

'I can't get over how big it seems in here now there's all this space.' She told him about Nancy bringing up two garlands. 'I think they'll look really good attached together over there where the bales used to block that light. What do you think?'

Piper came over to join them and studied the area for a few seconds before nodding. 'I agree. It's the view people will have as they arrive and the first place that catches the eye. We need to set up a top table there, don't you think?'

'Tables.' Casey grimaced trying not to give way to the panic that coursed through her. 'I haven't arranged for any to be brought here, nor chairs.' How could she have forgotten something so important? 'What are we going to do? It's the height of summer so it's not as if we could ask businesses if we can borrow some.'

'I'm sure we'll come up with something between all of us.' Alex called everyone over to join them.

Casey tried not to let her embarrassment get the better of her as she counted nine people, including Helen, Maude, Margery, who despite her aching leg must have decided she didn't want to be left out, and Dilys, Tara, Vivienne and Colin and listened as Alex explained their problem.

'If any of you can think of how we can sort this out.' He checked his watch. 'In the next hour, preferably, then that would be perfect.'

Casey leaned against the wall and crossed her arms. Her mother would have lent them their tables and chairs from the dining room but it wouldn't be enough. She didn't even know exactly how many people were coming to the reception.

'This is terrible,' she moaned, not meaning to say the words out loud.

'I could ask Maude's son to bring up my dining table,' Dilys offered. 'It's not very big but it'll sit six at a push.'

'I have a trestle table in my garage,' Maude said. 'You're welcome to use that if you want.'

Casey appreciated their offers but how would it look having mismatched tables and chairs at a wedding reception? No, she thought miserably, unless they could find enough seating for all the guests then they would have to come up with another solution. But how on earth was that going to happen at this late stage? She wished the floor would swallow her up so she didn't have to face Vicki and admit forgetting such vital necessities.

Casey stared at the dusty wooden floor in front of her. They were pushing it, trying to even get the place clean before Nancy's arrival with the garlands, let alone trying to source places for the guests to sit.

'Use what you've already got here,' Piper's gran insisted.

Confused, Casey looked across the room at her. 'What do you mean, Margery?'

The older lady stepped forward in front of the group of volunteers and pointed to the four piles of bales at each corner of the room. Casey wasn't sure what she was getting at but didn't dare interrupt Margery, hoping that whatever was on her mind would be something that might resolve their issue.

'I presume the reception tomorrow night isn't going to be a sit down dinner.'

Piper shook her head. 'No, Gran, but Casey's right: we need places to sit.'

Her grandmother raised her hand. 'We do but all we need is a couple of trestle tables at the side of the room where the food can be displayed.'

Casey listened, still unsure how this plan was going to pan out. 'Go on.'

'Well then,' Margery continued. 'Maude, please ask your son to bring your trestle table here. Maybe he can collect another one, if someone else has one on offer.'

'We do, don't we, Mum?' Piper called out.

Helen looked up from where she was sweeping pieces of hay and dust and nodded enthusiastically. 'We do. I used to use it when I sold bits and pieces at the car boot sales years ago.'

Piper clapped her hands together, clearly happy to be able to help. 'Maude, your son will find it in the small storage room in our backyard.'

'Good,' Gran said, placing her hands firmly on her hips. 'Now we're getting somewhere.'

Casey listened intently and watched as Margery indicated exactly where she thought these tables would be set. 'Then, over at the top end there, we could have one larger table with the bride and groom and either their parents, or best man and maid of honour, or whatever sitting next to them. I'm sure we have someone who can provide that table.' She turned back to face Piper. 'Those tables don't need to match but we will need tablecloths and I know for a fact that you'll have enough of those at the guest house.'

Casey watched Margery in full flow and marvelled at how easily she rustled everyone up to help.

'Maude, ask that son of yours to bring Dilys's table after all. We'll work out which ones to use where when he brings everything here. Tell him to bring tablecloths from the large cupboard in the guest house dining room. White ones only. He shouldn't have too much trouble finding them. The front door is unlocked —' she checked her watch '—because guests will be around, so there should be no problem getting inside the place.'

'Marvellous,' Dilys said. 'Maude?'

'Yes, I heard. I'll ask him to fetch those too.'

Dilys gave Margery a beaming smile and Casey didn't think she had seen her looking so happy for a very long time. It warmed her heart to see the hustle and bustle of the locals working hard to make the following day special for one of their own.

The barn door opened and Irene and Paddy, two of the other sellers, hurried inside, stopping suddenly when Casey stared at them.

'Sorry, we're later than we hoped to be.'

Casey shook her head. 'No problem. We're just grateful to anyone who's able to offer any help at all.'

Piper opened her mouth to explain their predicament but her gran spoke before she had a chance to do so. 'We're sorting out seating arrangements for tomorrow night. Do you know where we might find a decent enough table to go at the end of the room the for the bridal party?'

'Um, I think so,' one of them replied.

'Well? Tell us more?' Margery said, waving for her to hurry.

'I remember seeing rather a large dining room table in the main house.'

'Main house?' Gran cheered. 'What the one here?'

'Yes,' Casey said recalling the well-polished ornate table she had seen. She didn't know why she hadn't thought of it herself. 'I don't think the Ecobichon sisters have cause to use it much any more, but I had to take a mirror of theirs from the dining room a year or so ago to repair it for them. I noticed it then.'

'Good,' Margery said, nodding. 'Then can we leave you to go and ask them if we can borrow it, and several of the chairs?'

Casey looked a little anxious. 'What? Now?' She had a lot of respect for the elderly sisters and was very fond of them, as the others probably were, but they were rather eccentric and could be difficult if caught in the wrong mood.

Rowena walked over, frowning. 'What's the matter?'

Piper, no doubt aware what Casey was thinking, pressed her lips together but didn't manage to hide her amusement.

'Yes, of course now,' Margery snapped. 'Tara, you go with her. We don't have any time to waste.'

Piper pulled an apologetic face at her before Casey and Tara rushed out of the barn.

'Margery is ever so bossy when she gets going, isn't she?' Tara said, giggling as they ran across the yard towards the back door of the large house.

'I just hope they're in a good mood,' Casey said. 'I don't fancy getting on the wrong side of them. Who knows where it might lead.'

They all knew of one stallholder who had upset the sisters by not giving a friend of theirs the discount they felt should be theirs. The woman had been given notice to remove her stall soon afterwards and since then everyone had been very careful not to upset them.

'Here goes,' Casey said, reaching up to knock at the door. Before her hand connected with the peeling black paint, Matteo called out to them.

'What does he want,' Casey groaned, wondering where he had appeared from.

She saw the look of shock at her tone on Tara's face but didn't have time to explain what had happened between her and Matteo to cause her mood.

'Casey, wait a second will you?'

She turned and saw him running up to them. Reaching them, he stopped. 'Do you want me to ask for you?'

'Why would I need you to do that?' she asked, irritated with him for thinking she might agree to his help.

'Um, because I heard you talking to Margery back in the smaller barn just after I arrived, and, well, you didn't sound as if you felt comfortable asking them.' His voice quietened as he reached the end of the sentence. 'Sorry, if I misunderstood.'

He might be used to acting as other people's knight in shining armour, she thought, scowling at him, but she didn't need his help talking to the Ecobichon sisters. 'No thank you,' she said firmly. 'I'm perfectly capable of asking for a favour.'

He flinched and she saw that she had hurt him. 'Sorry,' he said, his eyes darkening. 'I only meant to help.'

Casey went to give him a snappy retort but Tara spoke before she had a chance to do so. 'Thanks, Matteo,' Tara said, giving her a quick frown. 'That's very thoughtful of you, but I think Casey has this in hand.'

'Right. No problem.' He turned away from them but not before shooting Casey an annoyed look. 'I'll leave you both to it then.'

Casey knocked on the door, feeling slightly shaken by her outburst. Why was he rubbing her up the wrong way?

She tensed, hearing shuffled feet on the old stone hallway behind the door, and braced herself for one of the sisters to answer.

It was Amy who answered the door. She was the sweeter of the two and Casey was relieved to see her.

'Hello, girls,' Amy said. 'What's brought you here?' She looked past them to the barn where The Cabbage Patch stalls were and then back again. 'Nothing wrong in the barn, is there?'

'Oh no,' Tara replied quickly. 'Everything's fine. Preparations for the reception are coming along well.'

'Glad to hear it.' She raised a grey eyebrow. 'Why are you here then?'

Tara looked at Casey and she could see her friend was waiting for her to broach the subject of borrowing their table.

'We were wondering if you wouldn't mind allowing us to borrow your dining room table.'

Amy frowned briefly. 'No, I don't mind. You may borrow it, but you'll need to clear anything from it neatly and be extremely careful with it. It's very old and heavy and I'd hate for it to be damaged.'

'We'll take the very best care of it,' Casey assured her.

'And you'll need to be out of the house by the time tonight's episode of *Coronation Street* begins in—' she checked her small wristwatch '—twenty-eight minutes.'

Moments later, the two friends beamed at each other as they hurried back to join the others in the barn. 'I can't believe they are happy for us to borrow it,' Casey said gleefully. 'It does look heavy though so we're going to need all the muscle we can get to help us get it out of the house and to the barn.'

Why is it, she thought, that when she imagined muscles she pictured Matteo's taut, tanned torso glistening wet as he stood in the shallow end of the pool that morning. She took a steadying breath.

'What's the matter?' Tara said, interrupting her thoughts.

'Matteo. We've had a falling out and I don't know what to do about it,' she said, sighing heavily. 'I wouldn't mind but I think I really like him, Tara.'

'Then you're going to have to find a way to make things right

with him. And soon,' Tara said, stroking Casey's arm. 'You have
the filming tomorrow and he leaves a couple of days after that on
that tour for however many months.'

Casey groaned. 'I know. I'm just not sure whether I'd be doing
the right thing for me by trying to sort it out though.'

Tara stopped walking and grabbed Casey's wrist to stop her
and turned her to face her. 'What do you mean?'

'Have you seen how he lives his life, Tara?'

'Yes I have. Fancy hotels, great food, everyone fawning over
him wherever he goes.'

It wasn't quite what Casey had meant but hearing Margery's
booming voice coming from the smaller barn she knew she didn't
have the time or energy to waste explaining. 'Can you imagine me
in that sort of life?'

Tara frowned thoughtfully. 'I've no idea.'

'That's the problem, neither have I.' She began walking with
Tara accompanying her. 'And there's an even bigger issue I need
to consider.'

'What's that?'

'I like him very much but I'm worried that if I do anything to
take things further I'll be opening myself up for all sorts of
heartache.'

'Then you'll need to decide if he's worth taking that chance,
won't you?'

Tara was right. 'I'm not sure if I'm that brave.'

'Life is short, Casey. Sometimes we need to step out of our
comfort zones and take a chance. But it's up to you. I know which
choice I'd make.' She winked at her.

'Hmm, I don't know.'

'He's not said anything to you?' Tara looked at her, bewilder-
ment on her face.

'He has, sort of. But now I'm not sure. I've been pretty mean to him today.'

Tara sighed. She pointed to the smaller barn. 'Well, let me know if you need to talk things through. Right now though I think that if we don't get back to Margery and sort out a few people to collect the table we're both going to have a lot more to deal with than Matteo Stanford and whether he does or does not want you in his life.'

20

Casey and Tara arrived back in the smaller barn intending to round up a few of the stronger volunteers to help carry the heavy mahogany table from the farmhouse to the barn. As they walked inside though they saw Margery pace in a large circle, one hand on her hip and the other tapping her chin. She stopped suddenly. 'Yes. I'm sure it'll work.'

'What will,' Maude asked, shooting a confused look at Dilys, who shrugged in response.

'Hay bales.'

'Hay bales?' Casey whispered to Tara. 'I thought we'd decided on what to do with them, hadn't we?'

'Don't ask me,' Tara said, frowning. 'I'm just doing what I'm told and looking forward to the food arriving later.'

At that moment Casey's stomach rumbled. She realised that she hadn't eaten anything apart from the slice of walnut cake since lunch. 'Yes, I'm looking forward to eating something, too.'

'Look,' Tara said pointing discreetly at a girl with glossy dark hair and a broom in her hand. 'Isn't that Fliss's friend, Phoebe?'

Casey noticed the girl and nodded. 'Yes, it is.'

'I wonder what she's doing here?'

'Probably just wants to help like the rest of us.' Casey noticed the girl glance up as Jax passed her and her face redden slightly. 'I think she might have a bit of a crush on Jax,' she whispered.

'Ah, I think you could be right.'

Margery cleared her throat and placed both hands on her ample hips. 'Listen up everyone,' she bellowed. Seeing Alex, Matteo and Fliss's friend Phoebe who had been sweeping stop, she shook her head. 'Not you lot over there. You keep sweeping.'

'What you on about, Margery love?' Colin asked.

'If you listen, I'll tell you,' Margery glowered in response and Casey had to stifle a giggle. 'As I was trying to explain,' Margery continued. 'We can set up areas around the room with bales of hay. Each bale can fit two bottoms, so we don't need to have too many I shouldn't think.'

Casey tried to picture what Piper's gran meant. It did make sense and would also save an enormous amount of panic and fuss trying to locate and bring smaller tables and chairs to the venue. 'I think it's an inspired idea, Margery,' she said. 'Piper, your gran is a genius.'

'I wouldn't go that far, lovey.' Margery laughed. 'But this is a rustic barn after all so why not make the most of that. People will be helping themselves to the buffet and can bring their plate and glass to come and sit on the bales. I think it might even add to the atmosphere, don't you?'

'I agree,' Piper said patting her gran on the back.

'So do I,' Casey said.

Piper shook her head. 'I wouldn't tell her that too often, she's bossy enough already and always thinks she's right.'

Alex put his arm around Piper. 'I think it's a great idea.'

'So do I,' Colin said. 'Come on, lad, I'll help you fetch some of those bales back inside.'

'No, Grandad, your leg still isn't fully healed. You stay here and help with the cleaning. I can manage to bring in the bales.'

'I'll help you,' Piper offered.

'So will I,' Matteo said, following Alex and Piper.

'Wait for me!' Jax hurried out after them.

'Hang on a second,' Casey said. 'I need to tell you all about the table.'

'I'm sure this won't take long,' Jax said. 'I'll just follow to help Alex. We'll be back in here in no time.'

'Is something wrong?' Piper asked.

'We've found the perfect table,' Tara said.

Casey clapped her hands together just as Alex, Jax and Matteo walked in carrying the first hay bales.

'Everyone,' Casey shouted. 'If I could have your attention for a moment. 'Tara and I have been to see Amy and Meg, and...'

'Who?' Colin asked.

'The Ecobichon sisters,' Tara explained. 'They're the elderly ladies who own the farmhouse and these barns.'

'Oh, right. Sorry.'

Casey took a deep breath. 'They have given us permission to borrow their large dining room table.'

'That's wonderful news,' Margery said as others agreed noisily.

Casey raised her hands to indicate that she still had more to say. 'The thing is we need to fetch it straight away because they don't want to be disturbed later.'

'They don't want to miss any of tonight's episode of *Coronation Street*,' Tara said. 'So we need some of you stronger ones to help us carry it over here.'

Casey looked over at the three men who were on their way outside to fetch more bales and they all stopped. 'Guys, would you come and help us before finishing that? The table is mahogany so it's heavy.'

'Blimey,' Jax said. 'This is going to be fun.'

'Stop moaning, Jax,' Margery scolded. 'You're the strongest one here, I imagine.'

Casey didn't know if Margery actually thought that or if she was hoping that the compliment would encourage him to hurry and help.

'Sure. I'm happy to help,' he said, grinning from ear to ear.

'Typical boy,' Piper whispered, coming up to stand between Casey and Tara. 'It works every time.'

Several more men and a couple of the younger, stronger-looking women joined them.

'Great,' Casey said. 'Let's get this done.'

The table was heavier than any of them had imagined and after twenty minutes trying to turn it enough to get it out of the dining room the easiest part was carrying it across the yard from the farmhouse to the smaller barn. Finally, when it was in place under the back wall, where Casey thought the two garlands would look spectacular, she was happy.

'I can't wait to see this finished,' she said to Tara as they stood back and watched others carrying hay bales inside and setting them up in groups for people to use as seats.

'Hi there,' shouted a voice Casey recognised from the door. 'Can I have a couple of helpers to carry in two garlands please.'

She waved at Nancy and ran over to join her, with Tara and Piper close behind.

Nancy noticed the table and pointed. 'Is that where we're going to hang both of them?'

'I thought so,' Casey said. 'Do you agree?'

'Absolutely. It's the first thing you see when you walk in the barn and I'm sure Vicki's going to love it. It'll look great in photos too. Clever you,' she said resting a hand on Casey's shoulder. 'This is looking fab already. Well done.'

'Thank you,' Casey said feeling slightly embarrassed to hear such kind comments. 'But it's very much been a joint effort.' She stopped to let Nancy take in the scene with around ten to twelve people sweeping, wiping windowsills and organising the bales of hay.

'It's going to be perfect,' Nancy said, a tear in her eye.

They helped Nancy carry in the two garlands.

'Bring over one of those stepladders, Jax lad,' Colin shouted, pointing where he thought it should be placed. 'You fetch the other one, Matteo. Alex, we need a hammer and some nails and string.'

'I have those in my van,' Nancy said, giving him a self-satisfied nod. 'Piper will you fetch them for me?'

Casey watched as her friend ran off to do as she had been asked.

A few minutes later they stood back and admired the pink, cream and green luscious garlands covering the back of the wall above the top table. Before they had time to congratulate Nancy, Maude's son arrived, carrying one of the trestle tables and asking for someone to fetch the other and the tablecloths.

'This is all going perfectly,' Tara said. 'You must be so relieved, Casey.'

'I am,' she said stunned at how swimmingly it all seemed to be happening. 'I can't quite believe it.'

'You've done Vicki proud,' Nancy said. Then, pointing at one end of the table, she said. 'Is that where the wedding cake will be displayed?'

Wedding cake? Everything stilled and went quiet and Casey felt like she had been enveloped in a huge bubble. 'Wedding cake?' she gasped. 'I presumed Vicki must have arranged that.'

She crossed her fingers behind her back and willed Nancy to laugh and tell her that Vicki was bringing it up to the barn or having it delivered sometime.

'No,' Nancy said. 'She thought you were sorting it out.'

'Me? Why would I do that as well as everything else?'

Nancy shrugged. 'I've no idea.'

'Now hang on a second, Nancy,' Rowena grumbled crossing her arms across her chest. 'I think my daughter has been more than good enough to young Vicki, don't you?'

'That's not what I mean,' Nancy said shaking her head and looking surprised. 'I'm happy to try and sort something out, if you like?'

'At this late stage?' Casey groaned. *How could there be a wedding reception without a cake?* Casey thought, walking over to the nearest hay bale and sitting down heavily on it.

Her mother marched over, sat next to her and put her arm around Casey's shoulders.

'I can't believe I forgot the damn cake,' she hissed. 'I presumed Vicki was sorting it out.'

'And as it's her wedding she should be,' Rowena said. 'Don't worry. This isn't your problem.'

'But, Mum, we must have a cake!'

'And we will have one,' her mother said, standing. 'Don't worry. Leave this with me. Right, everyone,' she bellowed. 'It seems that Vicki didn't think to order her wedding cake, so we need one. Suggestions please.'

'The wedding is tomorrow though,' Vivienne said unhelpfully.

'I think we're all fully aware of that fact, thank you,' Rowena snapped. 'Come on, I need some ideas.'

Casey felt her panic rise. She tapped her feet on the floor and tried to come up with a solution. She had no baking skills whatsoever, so would be little help. She scanned the room, seeing concerned faces watching her mother.

Eventually, Dilys raised a hand. 'Does it have to be one cake?'

Margery and Piper exchanged glances. 'How about we have several cakes,' Margery suggested, her face breaking into a wide smile. 'Dilys could make her walnut one. Piper and I can make cakes. I can do a Victoria sponge and I'll ask Helen to bake a chocolate and butter icing one when she has some free time.' She looked at Rowena. 'How about you make a lemon one?'

Rowena clapped her hands together gleefully. 'Perfect. We either need to make them exactly the same size and shape or have them graduating in size. Then they can have dowel rods inserted to each one and be stacked artistically on top of each other.'

Casey was too relieved that a quick and simple solution had been found to worry about which shape or style they chose. 'Thank you all so much. I really appreciate you coming to mine and, er, Vicki's cake rescue.'

'We're more than happy to help where we can, lovey,' Dilys assured her.

She decided to leave the women to their plans and spotted Matteo reach for his phone and then say something to Alex before the two of them hurried outside. Moments later they returned carrying cool boxes and covered trays, followed by two other men carrying in more of the same.

'Trestle table there,' Margery shouted indicating the one on the left side of the door. 'Leave all the food and drink there. We can help ourselves.'

Casey thought she had better go and offer her help when the delivery people left smiling broadly and chatting quietly to each other. She presumed Alex had paid them well.

'Everyone,' Alex called. 'The food and drink has arrived.

There are plates and cutlery there,' he said indicating a pile of each, the cutlery wrapped in linen napkins. *No paper napkins here*, Piper thought, impressed. 'Help yourself to food. There's a couple of salads including potato salad, couscous, rice and burgers with buns, oh and several pizzas for those who'd prefer them.'

A couple of thanks rang through the air for Alex but he surprised Casey by shaking his head and putting his arm around Matteo, drawing him nearer to him. 'Don't thank me. I know I was the one to suggest doing this but my friend Matteo here arranged this fantastic spread.'

So Matteo had paid for this evening's food too, she mused. He was smiling at Alex but looking, Casey thought, a little embarrassed. For someone who made a living being in the spotlight he didn't seem to like it so much when he wasn't working.

'No need to thank me,' he said. 'I'm the one who's grateful to all of you for helping here this evening. It's thanks to all of you that Vicki's wedding is coming along so well. Mostly, though, it's thanks to Casey.' *What?* She hadn't expected that and blanched when everyone turned to her and cheered. 'If it wasn't for Casey Norman offering to help arrange Vicki's wedding and set up the castle with her business partner, Tara—' Tara took a theatrical bow, obviously enjoying every moment as much as Casey was hating it '—then I would be in a deep hole. I am enormously grateful to them and, as I said, to you all for your assistance with everything.'

People clapped and cheered around her and Casey wished the floor would magically open up and swallow her. She stifled a groan and clenched her teeth together, hoping that she was displaying a smile and not the grimace she suspected she had on her face. She went to move towards the table when Matteo spoke again. *Would he never finish talking?* she thought, irritated.

'As you all know, tomorrow is the wedding and then the reception. I'm sure you're all aware that Vicki has invited all the volunteers here tonight to the reception tomorrow evening.'

Another loud cheer filled the room. 'For now though, please tuck in.'

Casey stepped back out of the way of the charging volunteers.

'Anyone would think they hadn't eaten for days,' Tara said, coming to stand next to her and shaking her head.

'We should take a photo,' Margery announced. 'Does anyone know how to use the timer on their phone?'

'I do,' Alex said. 'Right, everyone move a bit closer over there.' He pointed to a space opposite the top table where he was busily setting up his phone ready to take the photo.

'Come along, Casey,' Rowena shouted. 'I know you must be shattered, love, but this will be a good keepsake from today.'

Casey walked to stand in the group, but her mother pulled her to the front and positioned her between Matteo and Alex. 'Stand there,' she said just before Alex returned to the table to check his phone was ready.

'Everyone ready?'

She felt the heat of Matteo's arm through his shirt and felt his stare as he looked down at her.

'You've been amazing,' he said quietly.

'Thank you.' She hadn't intended speaking to him but couldn't help being polite. It was some sort of reflex in her after a lifetime of her mother's upbringing. 'You've certainly done your fair share.'

'I hope to see you at the castle tomorrow.'

Urgh, she thought. Tomorrow. Today had been a little chaotic but she had so much still to do tomorrow.

'I've been speaking to your mother and I promised her that I would cover any earnings lost by you and Tara for all the work you've been doing for these few days and the costs of making new candles. You mustn't be out of pocket.'

'Thank you.'

Alex rushed back to stand next to her. 'Smile.'

Casey instinctively smiled in the camera's direction.

'One more for luck,' Alex shouted, setting the camera up again.

'I need to speak to you, Casey,' Matteo said quietly.

'You do?' She wondered what was on his mind.

'Ready?' Alex bellowed, rushing back to stand between Casey and Piper. 'Say cheers.'

A chorus of 'Cheers' rent through the air and Casey joined in.

As soon as the photo was taken people moved away and returned to the table to serve themselves more of the food and drink on offer. Casey went to follow but Matteo took her hand in his.

'What is it?' she asked, surprised that he was singling her out.

He hesitated for a moment. 'Alex mentioned that you needed a photographer. Is that right?'

So that's why he had wanted to speak to her. Not to discuss the two of them, but to offer her the services of a photographer.

'That's right,' she said trying not to show her disappointment.

* * *

'It was so embarrassing,' she confided in Tara when everyone had left and they were driving home. 'Honestly, I get so cross with myself at times. When he led me away I presumed for a second that he wanted to speak to me alone to resolve what had happened to make me so upset with him.'

'Forget it,' Tara said. 'You don't know what he was intending to talk to you about really, do you?'

'What do you mean?' Casey slowed the car ready for the sharp bend ahead.

'Maybe he meant to discuss what had happened between you but wasn't sure if you'd want to listen. So he came up with the bit about the photographer knowing you needed his help and that you wouldn't refuse to talk to him about that.'

Casey wasn't sure Tara was right, but liked to think that she might be. She hated the idea that she might come across as judgemental in his, or anyone else's, eyes.

'Maybe,' she said.

'Good. So hopefully he'll let you have the use of his photographer and then everything will be sorted. Won't it?' She gave Casey a pleading look, as if she had any power to magically make everything sorted.

'I certainly hope so,' Casey said, indicating to turn left. 'I'm fed up with all this planning, cleaning and arranging stuff. Remind me never to agree to anything like this again. Will you?'

'You didn't agree,' Tara reminded her, grinning. 'You were the one to offer your services in the first place.'

Urgh. So she was.

Tara didn't get out of the car immediately like she usually did and Casey noticed she was looking at her. 'What?'

Tara shook her head before resting her hand on the door ready to open it.

'What?' Casey asked again, unsure what to make of the glare she was getting from her cousin.

'As far as I see it, Matteo has found a reason to seek you out and talk to you without making it about anything personal.'

Casey thought about what she said and nodded. It made sense. 'Yes, so?'

'He's said he'll sort something out for you. You don't think that's his way of trying to show you he cares about you?'

Casey would like to think so but after the way she had rebuffed him she wasn't so sure. 'I think it's got more to do with the fact that he feels grateful to me for helping sort out this filming issue and the wedding rather than anything else.'

'You really do think that, don't you?'

Casey nodded. 'I really do. Yes.'

Tara groaned and opened the car door. 'I'll see you in the morning. Don't worry about picking me up. I'll make my way to your house and we'll take the candles and stuff up to the castle and get on with setting up that room. I can see by the look on your face that you're looking forward to this all being over with.'

'I am a bit,' she admitted. 'See you in the morning.'

She watched Tara get out of the car and walk up the pathway to her home before driving off, replaying her conversation with Matteo for the five-minute drive home.

21

Casey woke after a restless night's sleep and sat up. Seeing the dark rings under her eyes and mussed-up hair she was glad no one else could see her right now. 'Gah,' she moaned, rubbing her face and getting out of bed. She walked over to the window and saw that at least it wasn't raining for Vicki's big day.

Showered and dressed in a pair of cut-off dungarees and an old striped Breton tee shirt, she tied her hair back in a scarf, picked up her design from where she had left it on her dressing table and went downstairs for a bite to eat.

'Morning, lovey,' Rowena said, laughing when she stopped buttering toast to look at Casey's face. 'Someone got out of the wrong side of the bed this morning I see.'

'I didn't sleep very well,' Casey said, sitting at the table and waiting for her mother to finish making her own breakfast before attempting to do any for herself.

Rowena took a jar of homemade raspberry jam from the cupboard and placed it on the kitchen table with the plate of buttered toast. 'Here you go.'

'No, Mum,' Casey said. 'That's yours. I can make my own.'

'Nonsense. Eat it.'

'Jordi not here?' Casey asked, hoping to ask her sister how she was feeling about the recording and wish her luck.

'She left a short while ago to meet Martha, I gather,' Rowena said. 'I'm surprised you didn't hear her singing in the shower earlier.' She sighed. 'She's so happy about being in the video you know.' She rubbed Casey's right arm. 'It was so kind of you to think of your sister and put her name forward to Matteo.'

'It was my pleasure, Mum. I think she'll be brilliant and if it helps get her some attention for future work, then even better.'

'You're a good girl, Casey. You should have seen your sister this morning: she was positively glowing. She's so happy.'

'Thanks, Mum, that makes me very happy.'

Rowena bent to kiss Casey's cheek. 'Would you rather I cook you a couple of fried eggs instead?' she asked, resting one hand on the table and peering at Casey.

'I'm fine, Mum. Thanks.' She didn't want to put her mother to any trouble and wasn't that hungry. She pulled the jar towards her and unscrewed the lid, aware she should eat something. It was going to be a long day. 'Toast is great.'

'Good. I'll make you a cup of tea to go with it.'

'Thanks, Mum.' Casey smiled up at her mother, aware she was concerned about her. She didn't like it when Casey was stressed and right now that's exactly what she was. She would try to hide it from her mother if she thought for a second that Rowena wouldn't see through her pretence.

Rowena made them both a cup of tea and brought them to the table as Casey ate the delicious toast and jam. She sat down next to Casey. 'Now, how can I help today?'

'It's fine, Mum. But thanks. This is great.'

'No. I want to do something.' She thought while Casey finished a mouthful of toast. 'I can help bring the candles to the castle for you. Or at least help carry them from the car to the Medieval Great Hall.'

Knowing when her mother was in one of her determined moods, Casey acquiesced. It was the easiest thing to do. 'That would be a great help,' she admitted. 'Tara should be here sometime soon and we'll get going then, if that's all right with you?'

'I'm free to help you anytime.' She sighed. 'Your dad said that he's sorry he's away at meetings in London otherwise he would be insisting on helping you with all this.'

Casey thought of her dad and his busy life in finance. She had no idea why, but he seemed to love what he did. He was so different to her mother, who wanted nothing more than to bring up her children and, since she and Jordi were grown up, spend time working on her crafts and occasionally helping knit items for one of the stallholders at The Cabbage Patch. It wasn't what she imagined for herself in a marriage but it was fairly traditional, she supposed, and certainly seemed to work for her parents. Maybe it was their differences that helped make it work, she mused. There was no competition between them. One earned more money, the other was a homebird and loved what they did. Or at least that's what she had always imagined.

Her thoughts stubbornly went to Matteo and she wondered if, in a parallel life, they might have worked out well as a couple. There certainly wouldn't be any competitiveness between them. She had no interest in being famous, performing or even being very sociable. Whereas he was surrounded by people all the time, it seemed. Did he love all that? she wondered. Or was it that all the people who seemed to constantly surround him – his management, production teams, recording people and fans – were simply something he had to accept as being part of a popstar's life. Maybe his lifestyle was something that came with the territory and he had no choice but to accept it? If she were on better terms with him maybe she would have asked him. He seemed to like being quiet on the odd times they had been with friends. Maybe it was the joy of writing his songs, or performing them, that he loved the most? Well, she was hardly likely to find out now.

There was a noisy banging on the front door.

'Who the hell is that?' Rowena said standing up so fast her chair would have toppled over if Casey hadn't reached out to grab it.

She watched her mother and decided to follow her to the front door.

'Jax? What are you doing here so early?'

Casey reached the hall and saw her friend's usually tanned face was now ashen. 'Jax, what's the matter?' she asked as Rowena took his arm and pulled him inside.

'Come in, lovey, and take a seat,' Rowena said, pushing him ahead of her and shaking her head at Casey.

Something was clearly wrong, Casey realised. But what? She followed her mother and Jax into the kitchen and, too nervous to sit, leaned against the worktop. 'What's happened, Jax?' she asked. 'It's not Sheila, is it?'

He shook his head. 'No. Mum's fine. It's nothing like that. In fact, I was supposed to let you know last night that she's offered to do Vicki's hair for her big day, but I forgot.'

'Then what is the matter?' Rowena asked. When Jax struggled to reply, she groaned. 'For pity's sake, lovey, tell us before we imagine all sorts of terrible things.' Rowena stood next to where she had made him sit and rested a hand on his shoulder. 'What's happened?'

Jax looked up at Rowena and then slowly turned his head to Casey. She knew in that second that the wedding was off. Dread filled her stomach and she clenched her teeth.

'I don't know how to tell you this, Casey,' he said.

'Please don't tell me what I think you're about to.'

Rowena looked at her, confused. 'What? Tell you what, Casey?'

Casey closed her eyes to try and steady herself. 'The wedding's off, isn't it, Jax?' Her voice was calm but inside her head she heard screaming. Poor Vicki. Poor, poor Vicki. 'What happened?'

'Fliss...' he began.

'Fliss?'

He nodded. 'She told Dan that he was being tricked into marrying Vicki. That everyone knew and, basically, from what he told me...' He rubbed his face and for the first time Casey realised that she wasn't the only one who had suffered a sleepless night.

'Go on, Jax,' Casey said as calmly as she could manage through gritted teeth.

'He thinks we're all laughing at him behind his back.'

'What? But we're not doing anything of the sort.'

'I know that, but he won't listen to me. She told him it's common knowledge that Vicki's arranged this wedding,' he said, his voice weary. He looked from Casey to Rowena. 'He's furious with her and feels humiliated.'

'Oh hell,' Casey murmured. 'How furious exactly?' She didn't like to ask but needed to know to be able to comfort Vicki and, she thought miserably, deal with damage control.

'He's finished with her.'

'What!' Rowena grabbed Jax's shoulder. 'Why didn't you stop him from doing something so rash?'

He looked up at her, hurt. 'I tried to talk him out of it, Rowena,' he said. 'I really did but there was no reasoning with him. He's incandescent with rage. I've never seen him like this. Never.'

'For pity's sake,' Rowena shouted. 'Sorry, Jax.' She rubbed his back lightly. 'I didn't mean to take that out on you. I know you would have done all that you possibly could.'

'What are we going to do?' Casey asked. 'Whether this wedding goes ahead or not I am still committed to setting up the room for the filming.' She pictured Vicki, bereft. 'But I can't leave Vicki alone to deal with this.' Fury coursed through her. 'Bloody Fliss! How dare she? The conniving...'

Rowena pulled out a chair and sat next to Jax. She rested a hand on his arm. 'Firstly, Jax, well done for coming to tell us so soon.'

'But...'

'You did the right thing. I can go and speak to Nancy. She's close to Vicki and will know how best to deal with the dear girl.' She looked at Casey. 'You need to remain calm and carry on doing what you have to do today. You and Tara.' She tapped the table with her fingernails thoughtfully. 'Jax, where is Dan now?'

Jax shrugged. 'I've no idea. I tried to reason with him well into the early hours and then we had a row.' He looked down at his hands miserably. 'He blames me for dragging him into this.'

'Oh, no,' Casey said. 'I'm so sorry, Jax. You never wanted to be involved, did you? I shouldn't have forced you to do it.'

'It's fine,' he said, trying to smile but failing. 'You were only trying to help Vicki and Matteo and we've all been happy to do our bit to help.'

'But Dan's your friend. You shouldn't be fighting with him.'

'It's not your fault.'

'No, it isn't.' Rowena narrowed her eyes and Casey hoped her mother didn't find Fliss before she did. Fliss might think she was above the rest of them for some reason but Casey knew her mother would give the spoilt girl a piece of her mind she wouldn't forget in a hurry should she get hold of her. 'It's that little bag's fault. How dare she?' She raised her hands and looked at Casey. 'Who does something this mean and for fun?'

Jax groaned. 'I think maybe she likes Dan.'

'Dan?' Casey was confused. 'I thought it was you she liked.' She pictured Jax giving Fliss a piggyback on the beach the previous day.

'She did, but when I woke up to see her for who she really is I backed off.' He sighed. 'She came to find me late yesterday with her friend Phoebe when I was with Dan. It was a bit odd seeing her being flirtatious with him when she had been doing the same thing with me earlier,' he added thoughtfully.

'What a rotten mess. I am sorry.' Casey leaned forward and gave him a hug. 'This really is not your doing. But we must try and find Dan and find a way to make him listen to us. We have to get him to understand what Vicki was trying to do. He needs to know how much we all loved the idea of the secret wedding and that we were only helping them both because we liked them and wanted to see them together, not because we were trying to make a fool out of him.'

'I agree,' Jax said. 'But how on earth are we going to do that when the wedding is this evening?'

'I have no idea,' she admitted. 'Yet. We will come up with something though and soon. The most important thing is not to panic.'

'Cooee,' Tara called from the hallway. 'How excited are we all this morning?' She hummed a tune Casey didn't recognise as she entered the kitchen and stood still. Frowning, Tara looked from one to the other of them. 'Oh hell. What's happened now?'

Casey rose to her feet. 'I'll tell you everything on the way to the castle but first we all need to load the car. Once we've finished at the castle we can join Mum and Jax to look for Dan.'

'Why do we need to look for Dan?' Tara closed her eyes and

groaned. 'I have a feeling I'm not going to like what you're going to tell me.'

'You won't,' Jax said.

'Never mind that.' Rowena stood. 'First we need to get these things to the castle. Come along, you lot. Everything is still in the dining room.'

The car was packed a few minutes later and Casey gave Jax a sympathetic hug, told him not to worry and drove Tara to the castle.

'Mum was going to follow us,' Casey explained after telling Tara about what Fliss had done. 'But I think she'll be focusing on helping resolve this wedding issue now so it's going to take us a few trips to the car and back.'

'I don't care what we need to do,' Tara grumbled. 'I just hope your mum doesn't come across Fliss before everything is resolved.'

'Me too.'

22

'Paddy said he'll deliver the candlestick holders to us in the next hour or so,' Tara said as she, Casey and Matteo stopped to catch their breath. It was more than a hundred and fifty steps up to the Medieval Great Hall, and they had to carry the candles up every one of them. 'He showed them to me yesterday and I think you're going to be pleasantly surprised, Matteo.'

'I'm sure I'll be happy with whatever you've both arranged for me.' He felt humbled thinking how many people had stepped in with little notice to make this shoot of his happen. 'Everyone's been incredibly kind offering their help at the last minute,' he said, leaning against a wall and adjusting his hold on the heavy box. Why had he shown off when he had come across them as they unloaded their car and insisted that he could carry this box as well as several bags containing mirrors and other bits?

Wanting to get up to the room and see what Casey had in mind for it, he stepped forward. 'Come along, better keep going.'

They pressed on and eventually reached the large hall high up in the castle above the battlements.

Casey put her box on one of the windowsills and ran back,

taking two of the bags from Matteo's hands. 'Put the box down on the table if you like.'

He lowered the box, realising that all these items would need to be taken back down from the castle the following day once the wedding and shoot was finished.

She opened the bags and took out the smaller candlestick holders, muslin for the backdrop, and mirrors. Then, going over to inspect the last boxes of candles that he and Tara had just delivered, nodded. 'These are going to look brilliant when we have everything in place.'

He wished he could see the design in order to imagine what Casey had planned. He'd meant to ask, but he'd been so caught up in her that he forgot.

He watched Casey take her folded design from her dungarees pocket and, as if she had been reading his mind, she opened it, flattening it out on one of the windowsills.

'I've just realised I haven't shown this to you yet, Matteo.' She looked over her shoulder at him and gave him a nervous smile.

He went to look at what she had planned for him. It was incredible. There were grouped areas of candles on smaller and larger pedestals and candlestick holders with wax artistically dripped down the candles and ivy intertwined between them down to the ground. Mirrors were placed in several areas and muslin draped delicately behind each area.

'It's incredible,' he said, taken aback by her beautiful design.

'You really think so?'

'I told you he'd like it.' Tara grinned.

He turned to her. 'How could I not like it,' Matteo asked. 'I just can't believe you've come up with this concept and made all these arrangements in such a short time, it's... well, it's astounding.'

Casey's shoulders lowered and her mouth drew back in a

smile and for the first time he realised guiltily how tense she had been.

'I'm so relieved you approve.'

He shrugged. 'Only an idiot wouldn't. This is truly beautiful,' he reassured her. 'And perfect for what I need.'

'And for the wedding, too,' Tara added.

'Yes, and for that.'

Casey stared into his eyes for a few seconds and Matteo felt the urge to take her in his arms and kiss her, show her how much he admired her and all that she had achieved.

She cleared her throat. 'I suppose we should start arranging everything.' She turned away from him. 'And I think we should keep as close to this as we possibly can and only alter something if we really think we need to.'

'Whatever you say,' Matteo said, happy to do as she suggested.

'I agree,' Tara said, still slightly out of breath. 'The most important thing we need to remember is that this room has to be perfect for two very different occasions but I think this should suit both of them well enough.' She pointed to Casey's drawing.

He caught Casey staring at him and realised she was still angry about what had happened. He was going to have to speak to her about it, but it would have to wait until the hall had been set up.

He helped unpack everything onto the table and turned to see Casey and Tara talking at the other end of the room. Stopping to try and hear if there was anything he could help with, he heard Casey's say, 'What if the shoot goes wrong like the wedding has?' He saw her rub her face with her hands and close her eyes.

'What's the matter?' he asked, going to join them.

Casey's looked shocked to discover that he had heard them. She wiped away a stray tear, clearly hoping to hide her distress from him. 'Nothing,' she said.

'Casey? Please tell me. Maybe I can help with whatever it is.'

She opened her eyes and turned to face him.

Tara walked over to the windowsill and stared down at the design in her hands. Probably, he thought, to give them a moment alone.

Matteo went up to Casey and stood in front of her. 'What's the matter?' he asked as tenderly as he could manage. She looked so tired and miserable that he desperately wanted to take her in his arms and soothe her.

'I'm just overtired, that's all,' she said.

'Are you certain it's just that?'

'My calves ache from all the steps.' She forced a smile. 'And my arms from carrying so many candles.'

'And you're sure that's all?' He wasn't convinced.

'I'm a little stressed from a chat I had with Jax,' she said after a moment's hesitation.

He suspected she was battling to keep her composure and wished she would let him comfort her. 'Can I ask what Jax said to upset you?'

'It isn't anything Jax has done,' she explained.

'Then what is it?'

'The wedding's off,' she said, explaining about Jax's visit and what Fliss had done.

Anger welled up inside him. What was wrong with Fliss to make her do something so unkind? He clenched his teeth not wishing to say what was on his mind and offend Casey and Tara.

'It's stressed me out rather a lot,' she admitted.

'Typical Fliss.' Matteo frowned, furious. 'She's an old hand at troublemaking,' he said miserably. 'Told an ex of mine that I had come on to her when I hadn't.'

'What happened?' Tara asked, walking back to stand next to Casey.

'She didn't believe me. Girl Code, or something. Broke up with me. I was heartbroken for a while.'

He noticed Casey's expression change but wasn't sure why. 'That's awful,' she said eventually.

He shrugged. 'I thought so at the time, but after a while it dawned on me that we weren't that well suited anyway. But it still doesn't excuse Fliss's behaviour.'

'Why did she do it do you think?' Tara asked, picking up a candle, inspecting it and then placing it behind one of the shorter ones on the flagstone floor.

'She seemed to get it into her head that I liked her,' he explained. 'We danced at a friend's wedding. I was a groomsman and she was a bridesmaid and I had been told that's what I should do. I was happy to dance with her but it didn't mean anything. Unfortunately, Fliss decided it did and then was furious with me when I told her I didn't think it a good idea that I dated my best friend's little sister.' He sighed, recalling the drama she had made about it all. 'It was an excuse of course and she saw through it, which didn't help much.'

'We should speak to Alex,' Tara suggested. 'He's probably the only one who can force his sister to tell Dan that she had been making things up.'

'That's a good idea,' Matteo agreed. 'Although it'll take some doing. She's not easily persuaded, even by Alex.' He looked at all the boxes of candles. 'Can I help move these to wherever they're supposed to be?'

'Don't you have other things to be getting on with?' Casey asked. 'Like practising for the recording?'

'No. It's all pretty organised.' He smiled at her. 'Let me help you both with this and then we can go and see if we can find Alex.'

Casey went quiet and swayed slightly, shocking him into silence.

'I don't know if I can do this,' she murmured, looking a little light-headed. 'I can't bear to think of Vicki heartbroken and it's so close to the wedding too. She'll be suffering so badly right now.' She gave a strangled sob and covered her mouth.

Matteo stepped forward to take hold of her by the arms as she stepped back and leaned against the wall. Then, a moment later, her legs seemed to give way and he held her as she slowly sank to her haunches, her back against the stone wall.

'Casey? Are you all right?' Matteo asked quietly before crouching down in front of her, horrified to see her in such a delicate state. He took her face in his hands, feeling the heat of her cheeks against his palms and fingers. 'You look washed out,' he whispered.

Casey's hands reached up to cover his and she closed her eyes.

Hating to see her so distressed, he knew he had to reassure her as best he could. 'Take a long, slow, deep breath.' He watched her do as he said. 'I want you to know that I'll do whatever you need me to.'

'I think it's all the pressure of having to arrange so much in such a short time,' Tara said, bending to study her friend's face. 'Let alone carrying all these boxes up so many steps in this heat.'

'I wished you had called me earlier. I could have come and helped you when you first got here.' He frowned. 'I would have asked Alex to help too. You shouldn't have brought all this up here by yourselves, it's far too much for two people to do.'

'You can help bring up the rest of them,' Casey said, gradually looking a little better.

'Casey's determined to do all she can to ensure Vicki's day is perfect,' Tara said. 'And yours too.' Tara looked at Casey briefly and seemed to be making up her mind about something. He watched Tara take a deep breath and realised she was about to say something.

Casey glared at her.

'She's worried everything will be a disaster and that she'll let Vicki and you down.'

'Tara! Why did you have to say that?' Casey snapped.

Matteo lowered his face closer to Casey's. 'Now, you listen to me. This room is going to look outstandingly beautiful.'

Casey looked up at him, seeming slightly less wobbly. 'You're sure you think so?'

He took her hands in his and waited for her to look him in the eye before speaking. 'What I think is that you're a marvel.'

Casey stared at him, looking as if she was trying to read his thoughts and deciding if he was just trying to pacify her. 'You do?'

He nodded. 'Yes.' He raised her hands and kissed the back of each in turn. 'My biggest concern right now is you. Are you feeling any better?'

'Sorry, I felt a little dizzy but I'm much better now. Can we stand?' she asked. 'My legs are beginning to ache from crouching.'

He stood, pulling her up with him as he got to his feet. 'That better?' Casey nodded. 'Good. Now, I know you're worried about Vicki, but we'll do all we can to sort that out. You know that I love your design, so what else is worrying you?'

She went quiet for a moment and Matteo's stomach clenched anxiously.

'I meant to ask you to approve my design but then... well...'

It took him a moment to realise that she was referring to what Martha had said to her. 'I know,' he said apologetically. 'Let's not dwell on that now. We can talk about it another time. We have too much to do here first.'

'We do. Look, I'm fine now. I promise.' She tucked her hair

behind her ears and took a deep breath. 'You have a music video to prepare for. Shouldn't you be getting ready somewhere?'

He shook his head, not wanting to leave her until he felt certain she really was all right. 'There's plenty of time for that. I've been rehearsing with your sister and we're as ready as we can be.'

'You have?'

'It didn't take very long really.'

Casey frowned. 'I never thought to wish her good luck,' she murmured. 'I've been so wrapped up in everything else these past few days.'

Matteo let go of her hands and took her by the shoulders. 'We both have,' he said. 'I think we need to focus on one thing at a time, don't you?'

She nodded. 'We do.'

'Then, when today is over, you and I can go somewhere and talk,' he suggested, hoping she would agree. 'If you want to, that is.'

She seemed happy with his suggestion. 'Yes, that would be lovely.'

'I'm glad,' he said, letting his hands fall from her shoulders. 'There's a lot to be getting on with here, as far as I can see. If you tell me what you need me to do, I'll help in any way I can.'

'Brilliant,' Tara said. 'You can start by coming back down to the car and helping me fetch the rest of the stuff.'

'Hang on a sec,' Casey said. 'I'll come with you.'

'You stay here,' Matteo said. 'I'm sure Tara and I can manage, can't we?'

Tara nodded. 'We can.'

'Fine,' Casey said. 'I'll start organising everything up here then.'

He turned to leave through one of the doors leading to the stone staircase. Passing one of the windows, he couldn't help stopping to stare down at the turquoise blue of the sea, where two sailing boats were slowly passing the island. The light from outside poured into the cool room; the effect was quite magical. Casey had chosen well when she had suggested they use this room.

'Let's go,' Tara said, interrupting his thoughts.

'Lead the way.' He smiled at Casey as he went to follow her friend out of the room. At least now she had agreed to speak to him. It was a massive relief.

23

They were halfway through the staging when Paddy arrived. 'This room is going to look great,' he said, carrying in two large metal candlesticks and placing them either side of one of the larger windows. 'Bring those in will you, Dad?'

Casey watched as Paddy's father carried in three smaller ones and placed them out of the way in a corner.

'Those do you?' he asked.

The girls went to look at them and Casey grinned, impressed with his work. 'These are amazing,' she said, delighted. 'Completely perfect for what I had in mind. Thank you so much for doing them so quickly.'

'My pleasure,' he said, the colour in his cheeks heightening slightly when he noticed Matteo standing there.

Matteo walked over and shook his hand. 'They are spectacular. I'm very grateful to you and to you,' he said, shaking Paddy's father's hand, 'for helping deliver them. They'll finish off Casey's wonderful design perfectly.'

Casey was relieved he thought so and delighted to hear him

say as much. 'Yes, thank you both so much for bringing them here.'

'No worries. I'm happy to have my sculptures involved in something so massive,' he said.

Matteo took the sculptor's phone number and promised to send him some photos of his candlestick holders in the video. 'Don't forget to forward your invoice straight away to my manager.'

'Will do it as soon as I get home,' Paddy assured him, grinning from ear to ear.

The three of them continued to set everything up under Casey's direction and slowly the design took shape.

'I forgot there's something else,' Matteo said, carrying the last candle over to where Casey was pointing it should go.

'Yes, what is it?''

A man walked up to the open door and knocked a few times on the door. 'Matteo Stanford?'

'That's me.' He smiled at the man. 'Peter? I presume?'

'That's right. Martha said I'd find you here.'

Martha? Casey looked from one to the other of them trying to work out what was going on. When this was over she was going to have to catch up on some sleep, she decided, finding it hard to keep track of everything that was happening.

'Casey, Tara?' They both nodded. 'Martha sent Pete to take a few pictures here of you two setting this up, if that's all right.'

'Sure,' Tara said.

'No problem,' Casey said wishing she had thought to bring a hairbrush and put on a little make-up.

'Great, thanks.' He smiled at them. 'He'll also take some of the room when it's ready but before the filming begins. Then after we've finished shooting the video he'll stay behind to take photos of the wedding ceremony then follow on to the barn for the reception.'

Casey thought of Vicki's delight and gave him a grateful smile. 'Thank you, that's very kind of you, and Martha. I appreciate it and I'm sure Vicki will be too. If everything gets sorted in time and the wedding goes ahead.'

'We'll do everything we can to make sure it happens,' Matteo reassured her.

'I know you will,' she said honestly.

Casey got back to work, ensuring she kept to her original plan and only vaguely aware of the click of a camera as she continued to make subtle changes to the candles, material and angles of the mirrors. Finally satisfied, she stood back, hands on her hips, and studied her and Tara's hard work.

'Happy?' Tara asked.

'I think so,' she answered thoughtfully, stepping first one way and then the other to check her work from all directions. 'I could keep moving things but I might make things worse instead of better.' She looked around to try and find Matteo. Seeing him ending a call, she waited for him to come back inside the room.

'What do you think?'

He studied her work. Then pulled her into a tight hug and kissed her forehead. 'I think you've got a great eye for design. I wouldn't mind having someone like you on my team for future shoots.'

Casey smiled to cover her surprise. Was he joking about wanting her for future work? She had no idea. For now though she was delighted that he was satisfied with what she had created for today's event.

'I'm so relieved you think it's good enough.'

'I think it's spectacular,' he said. 'You should have more confidence in yourself.'

'That's what I keep telling her,' Tara said.

'Then you should listen to us.' He smiled. 'You're extremely talented and this is perfect.'

'That's very kind of you, Matteo. I appreciate your confidence in me.' She tried to picture the bride and groom standing with the lit candles behind them. 'I'm hoping it's not too gothic for the wedding, but it will have to do because we won't have time to change much.'

'Don't forget,' Tara said, 'Nancy was going to bring up some floral arrangements to go in the taller candleholders. So that will make it a little more bridal.'

'Yes, true. I wonder where she's got to?' Casey asked before realising that Nancy would no doubt be comforting Vicki. 'Maybe we should go down to Harbour Blooms and offer to collect them ourselves. It will be one less thing for her to think about now she's got to look after Vicki.'

Tara nodded. 'Good idea.'

'We'd better be off now, Matteo. Unless there's anything else you need us for, we'll see you back here later to light the candles before the shoot.'

'How are you going to light all of these?' he asked, scanning the intricate display.

'We'll bring up a few long lighters and I'm sure Tara and I can get all of them lit in a few minutes. We're going to have to time it well though so the candles aren't burnt down too low for the wedding ceremony.'

Matteo nodded sagely, arms folded. 'Good point. I'll tell Martha we need to keep an eye on that so it doesn't happen.'

They left him there and went back to the car. 'You keep the engine running outside the florist's,' Tara said as they drove down the hill the short way to the pier. 'And I'll run in and fetch the arrangements.'

Ordinarily Casey would have insisted on walking on such a glorious day but today they simply didn't have the time. 'Will do. Once we've dropped these off at the castle, we can go and try to find out what's been happening while we've been busy.'

'Yes,' Tara agreed. 'I'm crossing everything that Jax has tracked down Dan and persuaded him to go ahead with the wedding.'

'So am I.'

'I wonder where Alex has got to?' Tara asked as Casey stopped the car in front of the shop.

'I've no idea but I hope he's been told what Fliss has done and is doing something to rectify the damage.'

'Let's hope you're right.'

Casey waited outside the florist's, hoping the drama had been resolved. Although she didn't know Dan that well, she had heard enough from Vicki to assume that although he was likeable he was also determined and proud. How typical of Fliss to have worked that out and used it to cause trouble.

'Any news?' Casey asked as Tara came back out, followed by Nancy.

'Nothing, unfortunately,' Nancy said. 'Vicki's in a hell of a state, understandably. If I get my hands on that little swine, Dan, I'll give him what for.'

'Fliss is the one who should be sorted out,' Tara said as she carefully placed the decorations on the back seat. 'Tell Vicki to keep the faith.'

'Yes, we're all doing what we can to sort this out, Nancy,' Casey said. 'The castle is ready for the wedding.'

'If it goes ahead.' Nancy cleared her throat and Casey noticed that her eyes were swollen from crying.

'Try not to fret, Nancy,' Casey said. 'We need to stay positive, as does Vicki.' She took a calming breath. 'We'll do our best to calm things down and make this wedding happen. Anyway, there's hours yet.'

'There are.'

Casey didn't want to show how nervous she was feeling about the whole thing falling apart. 'Someone needs to speak to Vicki. To reassure her that there's still time to sort this mess out and calm her. We must tell her to relax in case it does go ahead.'

'Yes,' Tara agreed. 'We don't want her to spend the day in tears and end up with puffy eyes for her wedding photographs.'

'There's a photographer now?'

'Yes,' Casey said, doing her best to look cheerful. 'Matteo arranged one for her.' She gave Nancy a sympathetic smile. 'We need to drop these off. As soon as we have we'll help find Dan. We need to persuade him that he's making a mistake by taking Fliss's word over Vicki's and not taking advantage of all these plans.'

'Thanks, girls,' Nancy said, looking, Casey thought, a little cheerier.

She just hoped they were able to find Dan. She would put off worrying about everything else until after they had done that.

24

Back at the castle they found Matteo waiting for them with Martha looking very satisfied with what she and Tara had done with the room.

'I must say you girls have come up trumps here.' She glanced up quickly before looking back at her phone screen and typing something. 'Matteo, you need to come back with me, rest up and have something to eat before we do hair and make-up for you and Jordi. We'll have to return in a couple of hours to film.'

'One second, Martha.' He turned to Casey. 'Would you mind dropping me off somewhere first?'

Martha scowled at Casey as if daring her to agree to his request. 'I can take you anywhere you need to go, Matteo,' Casey said defiantly.

'You don't have time to go wandering off with friends right now, Matteo.'

'Martha,' he said, his voice calm but commanding. 'I will meet you back at the hotel cottage as soon as I can. I shouldn't be late but if I am please focus on making sure Jordi's hair and make-up has been done and that she feels ready for later. I'll be as quick as

I can, but there's something I need to do.' He looked at Casey. 'All right with you?'

Even if it hadn't been, Casey was irritated by Martha's condescending attitude towards her and would have agreed simply to irritate the woman. She knew it was childish but she had done a lot for their production and believed she was allowed a little bit of a rebellion.

'Whatever you like.'

His eyebrows shot up and she could see he was surprised at her ready agreement. He smiled, his dark eyes twinkling mischievously, and Casey suspected he knew exactly what she was doing. 'Great. Let's go.'

They closed up behind them after one last look at the room.

'No need to drop me off anywhere,' Tara said.

Casey drove off, suspecting Tara also needed a moment away from the drama of the day. She didn't blame her; she wouldn't mind a little time out herself.

'So where are we going?' she asked as they drove down the hill.

'Alex messaged me to say that Jax thinks he knows where Dan might be. We're going there now.'

'And that's where?' she asked, needing to know in which direction she should drive.

'Sorry. It's somewhere called Sorel Point? Do you know it?'

'I do,' she said, thinking that they needed to head to St John's Parish Church and then down La Route du Nord to get there.

'Do you know the way?'

'I do.'

'Have you any idea why he might have gone there?' Matteo asked as she indicated right and turned up the hill.

'Maybe. He's from around there,' she suggested. 'I've no idea apart from the fact that it's a little remote.' She puffed out her cheeks. 'Well, for Jersey, that is. It'll only take us a few minutes and we'll be there.'

They drove in silence for a while.

'Casey,' Matteo said, sounding unsure whether or not to broach whatever subject he was about to. 'About what Martha said at the pool.'

She wasn't in the mood to hear it but they were alone, for once, and maybe this was the best time to get this problem between them sorted. If it ever could be.

'Yes?'

'I'm sorry. I know you don't want to talk about it and I understand that. I'm pretty embarrassed to speak about it myself, if I'm honest.'

She felt him watching her and looked at him quickly. 'Go on.'

'Well, she was right about me having friends. There have been other women when we've stayed in different countries.' Casey's stomach dipped. Now she really didn't want to hear what he had to say. She kept silent and let him continue. 'Touring is lonely. It probably wouldn't be as bad if I was in a group.'

'I thought a band travelled with you.'

'They do, but the guys in it change a lot, so it's not as if I have any close friends. And as for female company, well, it's not the sort of life I've ever thought about asking anyone to take part in.'

'Like a girlfriend, you mean?'

'That's right.'

What was she supposed to say to that? 'I'm not sure what you expect me to say, Matteo,' she said, confused.

'I'm just trying to help you understand how things are, I think. I've had a couple of serious girlfriends but I've never asked them to tour with me. It's probably what caused a lot of my break-ups.'

'You don't say,' she said, unable to keep the sarcasm from her voice.

'I know I sound like a fool. I thought that I should keep my public and private lives separate but there's always the inevitable photo with fans or women who work at the hotels, and some of these have caused upsets with girlfriends when the tour is over and I return home. Sometimes women I'd met found ways to contact my girlfriends and lie about being with me.'

Casey frowned at him. 'Surely, then, if you're lonely and your girlfriends suspect that there's more to the photos than you tell them, the answer must be to invite your girlfriend on tour with you. Don't you think?'

He sighed. 'Yes.'

Casey slowed the car, realising they were about to reach Sorel. 'It's along here,' she said, unsure how to continue her conversation with him. When he didn't speak again, she pulled up and parked the car. Alex's bike was there and she pointed to it. 'It seems that your friend is here, so maybe they've located Dan after all.'

'Casey.'

She turned in her seat to face him. 'What, Matteo? I've no idea what you're trying to tell me, or why, but we don't have much time and I think you need to say what's bothering you quickly so that we can find Dan.'

'It's just that...'

Someone banged loudly on the roof of Casey's car, making them both jump. 'Matteo!'

'For pity's sake,' Casey gasped, seeing Jax standing by her door waiting for them to speak to him. She opened the car door and got out. 'What the hell are you doing, Jax? You nearly gave us a heart attack.'

'Sorry. I didn't mean to frighten you.' He gave them both an apologetic smile. 'It's just that we've found Dan.'

'You have?' Matteo asked. 'Where is he?'

'Follow me.' Jax began to walk away. Casey locked her car and followed, with Matteo close on her heels.

'Did Alex bring Fliss with him?'

'He did,' Jax said. 'She's a piece of work that one. I've no idea how he copes with her.'

'She can be a law unto herself,' Matteo said. 'It's why I thought I might be able to help. She listens to me sometimes.'

'Not always, though,' Casey said recalling how he had rebuffed Fliss's advances and she had caused trouble with one of his girlfriends. His girlfriends. *How many exactly had there been?* She doubted she wanted to know. She looked sideways at him. He was handsome, successful and extremely charismatic and if he had the same effect on others that he had on her then she wasn't surprised there were available women wherever he went. Why couldn't she have fallen for an ordinary man with a dull job who no one else was interested in?

They reached the pretty white lighthouse and found Dan sitting with Alex and Fliss. Alex was glaring at his sister, hands on his knees as he faced her, his expression stony. Fliss looked sullen and as they neared Casey could hear her trying to apologise and explain why she had said what she had.

'I just couldn't stand it,' Fliss groaned. 'She's like Anne of Green Gables with all those aunts, cousins and neighbours running around prettying things up for her.'

Casey realised Fliss was describing Vicki and struggled to keep hold of her temper.

'Is this your idea of an apology?' Alex asked, glaring at her. 'Stop snivelling and tell Dan what you're here to say. Then you're going back to Phoebe's place and arranging to go home on the first available flight. Your behaviour is sickening and I'm ashamed of you, Fliss. I really am.'

Alex looked as if he could do with a hug, she thought. Dan, on the other hand, seemed very thoughtful.

'Everyone all right?' Matteo asked, sounding more cheerful than Casey suspected he felt.

'My sister here,' Alex said, almost spitting the words, 'was supposed to explain to Dan that this entire mess is her doing, and that she didn't tell him about the wedding because she was concerned about him.' He gave Matteo a pointed look.

Matteo stepped forward. 'That's right, Dan,' he said, his voice much more controlled than Alex's. 'I can assure you, as can Casey here, that no one has been laughing behind your back. In fact, I think I can speak for us all when I tell you that we are unanimously stunned to discover how nasty Fliss can be.'

Dan looked at Matteo and then at Fliss. 'But why would you do something this cruel, Fliss? Is it because you dislike Vicki?' He shrugged. 'Or me?'

Fliss stood with her arms folded and scowled down at the ground in silence like a petulant child who has had their favourite toy confiscated.

'She's probably just jealous of your fiancée,' Matteo said. 'At least Vicki has the courage to try and arrange such a momentous event and did it because she loves you.'

Dan looked at Matteo aghast. 'You think she's courageous?'

'I do. Why? Don't you?' Without waiting for Dan to reply, he added, 'In fact, rather than laughing at you, I think most of us are envious that you have someone in your life willing to arrange something like this simply because they're trying to find a way to spend the rest of their life with you.'

Casey's heart leaped to her throat. Did he mean what he was saying? She studied his face and saw a sadness in his eyes she hadn't noticed before. He glanced at her, seeming surprised to find her scrutinising him.

'Envious?' Dan's chest seemed to puff out slightly.

'That's what I said and I meant it.' Matteo moved closer to Dan. 'I, for one, would be touched if the woman in my life loved me so much she found a way for us to be married even if I believed we couldn't afford it.' He took a deep breath, and smiled. 'Think about it. You're engaged so I presume your intention was to marry her, wasn't it?'

Casey noticed Piper walking towards them, and was relieved that her friend had arrived.

'Of course it was.' Dan looked insulted by the question, giving Casey hope that maybe the wedding might not have to be cancelled after all.

'Why, then, would you be upset to discover that your wife-to-be had arranged everything so that all you had to do was turn up, make your vows to her in front of your loved ones, and then spend the rest of the evening basking in her love?' He shook his head and, raising an eyebrow, gave Dan a mischievous smile. 'Because although I've never been married, or even close to it, I do know from friends who are that they would have been relieved not to spend months having conversations about who to invite to the wedding, where to hold the reception, and all that.' He seemed not to know what to say next and looked at Alex and then Casey for help. 'I can't think what else there is to arrange but I know it's a lot?'

Casey tried to think. Then recalling what Vicki needed to arrange and continuing Matteo's attempt at persuasion, said, 'Matteo's right. It seems to be the cause of most of the arguments before a wedding. Having to decide on things like who's going to apply for the marriage licence, what flowers to choose, what food to have at the reception.' She relaxed slightly when Dan's expression softened. 'Where people should sit.'

'Yes,' Piper added. 'What everyone should wear. That's another thing, isn't it?'

Dan raised his hands and grinned at them. 'All right, all right. I get it. My fiancée is a dream woman. So, what do I do now?'

'What do you mean?' Jax asked, looking baffled.

'She knows I was upset by what Fliss said.' He groaned. 'I was horrible to her about everything.'

Casey knew Vicki would simply be happy to know the wedding was back on and he was no longer furious with her. 'Look, there's still time to go ahead with the wedding. You haven't left it too late to change your mind, if that's what you're worried about.'

'She's right,' Matteo said. 'One of us will contact Vicki and let her know the wedding's on again.'

'I'll do that,' Casey said, delighted to be able to give her friend such fantastic news.

'Thanks.' Matteo smiled.

Jax patted Dan on the back. 'You've made the right decision, mate,' he said, smiling. 'I guess all you need to do is what Vicki wanted from you in the first place. Go home, get dressed in a suit and then go with me to the castle at the right time.'

Dan looked from one to the other of them, smiling happily, Casey was relieved to see. 'I will. Thanks, guys. I really appreciate all you've done for me and Vicki today, and all that I imagine you've been doing behind the scenes.'

'It was our pleasure,' Alex said. 'Now, I'm going to take my sister back to her friend's house and have a few choice words with her.'

'Oh, sod off, Alex,' Fliss snapped.

Alex ignored her. 'And I want you to go and get ready for your wedding. Enjoy every moment. You only do this once.'

'Theoretically,' Fliss said, turning her back on Dan and stomping away.

Casey watched Alex whisper something to Piper and then march off after his sister. She turned to Matteo and looked at him thoughtfully. She hoped he had meant everything he said to Dan. He certainly seemed to be speaking from the heart. But she didn't know him, not really. Could he just be playing a part to ensure Dan believed him? Maybe he was doing this so that the wedding could go ahead and the girl who had changed the time of her wedding to accommodate his filming could marry the man of her dreams. Who knew?

Maybe, though, he had been honest in her car and was lonely and truly admired Vicki and what she had done. She hoped so, because if he really did feel that way then Matteo would be the man of her dreams.

25

Casey took her phone from her pocket and when Vicki's phone went to voicemail, she knew she would have to drive to Harbour Blooms to give Nancy the latest news for her to pass on. She wanted to get there as soon as possible to put Vicki out of her misery.

'Matteo?' she called. He turned to her and she waved him over. 'I'm going to have to go straight away. I can't get through to Vicki and don't have Nancy's number, so am going to drive there. Do you want me to give you a lift?'

He nodded. 'Yes, please. I should be getting back myself,' he added. 'Martha's going to go nuts if I'm much longer.' He waved to Jax and Dan before giving Piper a smile. 'I'll see you guys later.'

Casey unlocked her car and watched him run the short distance over to her. As soon as they were making their way along the road, she realised he didn't have much time.

'I know you're in a rush,' she said, torn between speaking to Nancy as soon as she could and knowing Matteo needed to get to the filming of his video. 'If you want to let Martha know I'll drop you at the castle then at least we'll be headed in the right direction for both you and Vicki.'

'Good idea. I'll call her immediately.'

Casey listened to him speaking to Martha and couldn't help being grateful to him for his intervention with Dan. She was sure his words had been behind Dan's change of heart. Reassuring Dan like he had was the best thing Matteo could have done because it was clear when they arrived that Jax and Alex weren't getting anywhere. And as for Fliss, she thought, unable to imagine how anyone could get satisfaction from trying to cause such heartache to others. 'Nasty piece of work,' she said, almost to herself.

Matteo ended his call. 'Sorry, what was that?'

'I was just thinking about Fliss and how horrible she's been.' She slowed the car behind a row of cyclists, willing them to turn off down a lane so that they could speed up and get to the pier as quickly as possible. 'I mean, who gets joy from being that spiteful?'

He shook his head. 'I've no idea. I've known her a long time and she's always been a bit...' He thought for a moment. 'Spoilt, I guess. I've known her to have a few tantrums when she couldn't get her own way but this is on another level.'

'Tantrums? Poor Alex. His character seems so different to hers.'

'It is, thankfully. Alex is a great bloke. He'd do anything for anyone and has always had my back.'

Casey liked hearing as much. 'That's good to know,' she said. 'Especially as it looks like he and one of my best friends are getting closer each day.' She looked at Matteo briefly and saw him smile fondly.

'I'm really pleased for him,' he said. 'They seem well suited and it's good to see they're as into each other as the other one.'

'It is.' Feeling a little awkward discussing feelings, especially when she wasn't sure about how Matteo truly saw her, she decided to change the subject. 'Are you nervous at all?'

'About what?'

She glanced at him and he seemed genuinely confused by her question. 'About filming this afternoon.'

'Oh that. No, not at all. I'm only lip-syncing and I've practised with your sister so I'm pretty relaxed about the whole thing.' He laughed. 'Martha worries enough for all of us. There's no point in two of us getting into a state.'

She supposed not. The mention of her sister reminded her that Jordi would surely be anxious about her first filming. She groaned.

'What's the matter?'

'Poor Jordi. I've been so focused on Vicki's problems that it had completely slipped my mind that my little sister has a momentous day herself. I feel really guilty now that I haven't been there to wish her luck or listen to her if she does have any concerns.' Which she must have, Casey thought.

'Don't feel bad,' he soothed. 'As soon as you've passed on the message to Vicki, or Nancy, then you'll be dropping me off and can come in and be there for Jordi.'

He was right. She had to be there to help move any of the scenery should it be necessary and, she reminded herself, help Tara light the many candles they had spent hours arranging that morning.

'You're right. I can see my sister then.' She exhaled sharply. 'What a few days this has been?'

'More for you than for me,' he replied quietly. 'I've had to make decisions but mostly I've been approving things rather than running around like you've been having to do.'

She thought of all that he had contributed to Vicki's wedding.

'Nonsense. You helped us clean the barn, held a party and had to audition my sister, apart from have meetings with Martha and all that.'

He nodded thoughtfully. 'I suppose so. But most of that is in my usual day's work, whereas you've had to fit all this in with your job.'

'Hmm, not really. I've mostly left poor Tara to look after the work side of things.' She realised she needed to speak to her mother about the cakes. She handed her phone to Matteo. 'Please, find my mum's number and give her a call for me?'

He did as she asked and held the phone up, putting it on loudspeaker for Casey to speak when Rowena answered. 'Hi, Mum,' she said and explained briefly what had happened when they found Jax and Dan. 'I'm on my way to let Nancy know that the wedding is still on because Vicki isn't answering her calls.'

'I'm with her now,' Rowena said. 'So, no need to worry.'

Casey heard cheers in the background. 'Are there a few of you there?'

'Yes. Leave Vicki to us. You'd better go to the castle and meet up with Tara. I want you to be there for Jordi too, she's rather nervous about this afternoon.'

'She has no need to worry, Mrs Norman,' Matteo said. 'It'll be fun and I'll make sure she's all right.'

'Thank you, sweetheart,' Rowena said, sounding relieved. 'Was there anything else?'

'Yes,' Casey said. 'Please make sure Dilys, Helen and Piper's gran keep baking for the wedding cake, will you? We don't want to have a reception without them.'

'Will do. I'll see you later.'

Matteo ended the call as they neared Gorey.

'No need to stop at the pier now,' Casey said, relieved to be able to go directly to the castle to see her sister. She smiled at

Matteo. 'I'm glad you refused to cancel the food order for the reception.'

'It wouldn't have gone to waste,' he said. 'If the wedding had been cancelled then the people who had helped clean the barn and get everything ready would have still needed to be thanked and I would have used the food for a small party for them. If not that, then I'd have found somewhere to donate it.'

'That's so kind.'

He shrugged. 'I couldn't make such a big order to a local business and then cancel, it would be unfair.'

He really was thoughtful, Casey mused. 'That's true.'

She slowed the car as they neared the castle, looking for a space to park along the road.

'There.' He pointed. 'Someone is getting into their car. I think they're about to leave.'

They were. Casey parked, relieved to finally be there. 'We'd better hurry,' she said, wanting to speak to her sister as soon as she could. 'You don't want Martha stressing any longer than she has been already.'

'No,' he agreed. 'I don't.'

Casey locked her car, surprised to feel Matteo's hand taking hers. His skin connecting with hers sent shivers through her. She liked the feeling.

'Come along,' he said, smiling. 'We'd better make a run for it otherwise my manager and your sister and business partner are going to have a few things to say to us.'

'Agreed,' she said, breaking into a run. As they ran, Casey couldn't help hoping that maybe it was an excuse so that Matteo could hold her hand. She hoped so.

'Where the hell have you been?' Martha yelled as Casey and Matteo entered the room out of breath and laughing. Her eyes dropped to his hand holding Casey's and Casey saw the woman tense. She expected Matteo to let go but he didn't. For the first time it occurred to her that maybe Martha had feelings for Matteo. *Could she?* Or, Casey wondered, might it simply be that his manager was so used to being in charge of him that the thought of anyone else stepping in and taking his attention from his work unnerved her?

'I told you where I was, Martha,' he replied, his voice calm, although Casey heard a hint of tension in his tone and suspected he was angry. He pulled Casey closer to him and kissed her on the cheek. 'Your sister is over there,' he said quietly. 'I'll leave you to go and speak to her.' He let go of her hand and Casey, warmed by his affection, left him to go to Jordi, hearing him telling Martha he wanted a word with her in private.

They left the room and Casey looked around to find her sister. 'Wow,' she murmured, seeing Jordi standing by the deep-set arched window, its leaded panes of glass the perfect backdrop for the candles, the pewter trays they were standing on neatly camouflaged by strategically placed ivy and eucalyptus plants. Her sister looked ethereal, like a true medieval woman, her long, wavy fair hair cascading down the back of her pale cream dress.

'What do you think?' Jordi asked, noticing Casey for the first time and giving her a twirl. 'I think I look the part, at least.'

Casey shook her head slowly, mesmerised by her sister's beauty. 'You look incredible,' she said impressed. 'How do you feel?'

Jordi grimaced. 'Nervous. I know I don't have to say anything, just be in the background, mostly, looking sad and heartsore.'

'Really?' Casey tried to picture the scene then decided to simply wait to see it played out in front of her when the time came to record it.

'Yes, then Matteo makes me feel better and that's about it.'

It sounded simple enough. 'I'm sure you'll be fine. Every time I've seen you in anything you always look completely in the moment and I'm sure you'll be brilliant today.' She went to hug her sister then realised that maybe it wasn't the best idea. 'I'll blow you a good luck kiss,' Casey said, doing so. 'I daren't risk messing up your gorgeous hair, or make-up.'

'Thank you.' Jordi took a deep breath and exhaled slowly. 'Will you be watching?'

'If I'm allowed to,' she said. 'And if you don't mind.'

Jordi smiled. 'Of course I don't. You can tell me what you thought of my acting afterwards.'

Casey nodded. 'I will,' she said willing her sister to be perfect. She noticed Tara appear at the doorway and walk in, eyes wide as she suspected hers now were noticing for the first time that there were several cameras set up around the room and people, who she presumed must be the director, cameramen and sound person talking quietly in the furthest corner from her.

'Phew, this is pretty impressive, isn't it?' Tara said, reaching Casey. 'I suppose they must be happy with what we've done.'

Casey hadn't thought of that. 'Too late now if they're not.'

'True.' Tara gave Jordi a wave with her fingers before crossing her arms. 'I wonder when we start lighting the candles?'

Casey sensed her friend was even more nervous than her. She was only relatively calm because she had had so much going on all day that she barely had a second to think. Which was a good thing, she now realised. 'No idea. We don't know how long it's going to take for them to do the actual recording so we won't want to start too early.' She noticed Tara wasn't carrying anything. 'Did you forget to bring the lighters?'

'No. I dropped them off earlier,' she said pointing to a bag in one corner. 'They're in there. I brought six of them in case we ran out of gas, and a huge box of matches just as a backup.'

'Well done.'

They stood silently as Martha and Matteo re-entered the room. Casey's stomach flipped when she saw him and her breath caught in her throat. His dark hair had been damped down, with strands of hair falling onto his forehead slightly over one eye. He was wearing black trousers and a loose white linen shirt that set his tan off to perfection. She already thought he was handsome but this was something else entirely. Her heart hammered in her chest as she stared at him. *Bloody hell!* He looked like a hero from a Jane Austen novel and Casey had to concentrate on remaining calm.

'Shit, look at him,' Tara whispered. 'He is perfection.'

Casey had forgotten what a fan of his Tara was. This must be even more exciting for her than she had realised. 'He is pretty amazing, isn't he?' she had to admit. *And what do I think I'm doing imagining a future for us?*

They watched silently as he and Martha went over to speak to the woman that Casey now realised was the director. Jordi was called over and the four of them spoke for a while before breaking apart.

'I'm Tina, for those of you who don't know and I'll be directing this video today.' She turned her attention to Casey and Tara. 'I gather we have you two to thank for this stunning backdrop.'

'Thank you,' Casey and Tara replied in unison.

'Is there anything you need changing at all?' Casey asked, hoping there wasn't.

Tina narrowed her eyes and scanned the room thoughtfully. 'There was one thing. No, two.' Casey's heart dropped. 'Ah, yes. That small nook over there.' She pointed to one of two stone nooks in the vaulted room. 'If we could just leave one large candle and a much smaller one in there with the greenery that would be better, I think.'

'No problem,' Tara said as she and Casey rushed over to remove the extra three candles and place one in the fireplace and the other in a corner among two of the larger arrangements.

'Is that all right?' Casey asked not daring to look at Matteo in case he realised how nervous she was.

'Yup. Perfect. Thanks both of you.' She smiled. 'Matteo said he's happy for you both to remain in here for the filming, so as soon as you've lit the candles I'd ask that you say nothing while the camera and sound is rolling and stand at the back there.' She indicated the furthest corner, where Martha was doing something to her phone. 'Mobile phones off please.'

Casey withdrew hers from her back pocket while Tara did the same, fumbling as she turned it off. 'Shall we light them now?'

'Yes, please.'

'Here goes,' she whispered to Tara.

Five minutes later, the candles were lit and Casey realised for the first time how lucky they were to be in a room with such high vaulted ceilings, thick walls and a beaten-earth floor. At least here the sultry heat of the summer afternoon wouldn't add to the temperature emanating from the large amount of candle flames.

Casey mouthed another good luck to her sister and willed her to be as brilliant as she knew she could be. Then she and Tara moved to the corner where they had been told to stand and waited for the filming to begin.

Four and a half hours later, Casey wished that she had turned down Matteo's invitation to watch the recording. It was such slow going and although she loved the song she was beginning to think that if she heard it too many more times she might go crazy. Jordi was doing brilliantly though and all they apparently still had to do was the final scene.

'And, action,' Tina called.

Casey watched her sister gazing sadly out of the window, looking as if her heart were breaking and Matteo walked slowly up to her, sang some of the words to her as he rested a hand on her shoulders and then turned Jordi to face him, took her in his arms and kissed her. Casey covered her mouth to silence a gasp. How would she ever be able to watch him kissing another woman again? Even when it was make-believe like this it felt like a punch to her gut.

They kissed for a few more seconds as the song ended. 'And, cut!'

'Thank heavens for that,' Tara said quietly. 'I thought I was going to melt into a puddle watching them. Lucky Jordi, that's all I can say.'

Casey watched as Matteo said something to her sister and pulled her into a hug. Casey saw that Jordi was blushing and she wasn't surprised. That kiss looked incredibly romantic and she couldn't help feeling the tiniest bit envious of her sister for having been on the receiving end of it.

Tina was watching a monitor intently. 'That looked pretty perfect to me, but I'd like to do one more take, just to be certain.'

Casey groaned inwardly. No. She did not want to stand here and watch the man she liked practically make love to her sister. It might be acting, she thought, trying to reason with her brain, but who could possibly be kissed like that and not feel anything? Certainly not her.

'The candles are getting fairly low,' Tina said in a loud voice as everyone began to chatter. 'We can't waste any time and don't want them to burn out before the wedding ceremony comes to an end. Places please, Matteo. Make-up, please check Jordi's face?'

A few minutes later, Casey watched the same scene again. It looked no different to the first apart from maybe a little more enthusiasm from her sister when Matteo kissed her. How could she blame her? Casey thought, trying not to feel jealous. 'That's a wrap,' Tina announced moments later and Casey realised she had been so lost in thought that she had probably missed the very end of the kiss. Good, she thought.

'You can put out the candles, now,' Tina said to Casey and Tara. 'I gather you need them again in a couple of hours.'

Casey cleared her throat. 'Er, yes, that's right. Come along, Tara.'

They hurriedly picked up candle snuffers that Tara had also had the sense to pack and began snuffing out the candles as quickly as they could manage.

'That was so hot, wasn't it?' Tara asked.

'I'm not surprised with the candles we've got in here.'

'No, dopey. That kiss. He is perfection,' she sighed almost to herself, her hand resting on her chest.

Casey didn't reply. She concentrated on putting out the rest of the candles and forced herself to focus on how they looked and if there were still enough for the wedding. 'We're going to have to make sure we don't light these again until Vicki is about to enter the room,' she said, determined to change the subject. 'We know how long it took us to do it the first time and so we need to leave about five minutes just before she arrives.'

'What? Oh, yes.' Tara might have reacted to her comment but Casey could tell she was transfixed by Matteo and what she had just watched. Tara gave a sharp intake of breath and grabbed Casey's wrist.

'Ouch. Let go, that hurts.' She tried to snatch away from Tara's clasp but Tara clung on. Confused by what her friend was reacting to, Casey looked up and saw that Matteo was on his way over to them. 'Will you let go of my sodding wrist,' she whispered.

'Oh, sorry. I wasn't thinking.'

That much was clear, Casey mused, rubbing her skin where it ached from her friend's vice-like grip.

'What do we say?'

'Er, maybe tell him how great you think the video will be?' Casey put the candle snuffers back into Tara's bag.

'Wasn't your sister great?' Matteo asked, giving Jordi a wave as she looked over from where Martha was speaking to her.

Casey felt a pang at the thought of them kissing. 'Um, yes. She really was very good. But I knew she would be,' she said, happy that he was pleased with what Jordi had done.

'You were pretty hot... um, good, yourself,' Tara said, her voice high-pitched and cheeks pink. 'I can't wait to see the final version.'

'Neither can I,' he said. 'Er, do you mind if I have a quick chat with Casey?'

'No, of course not.' Tara grinned at her briefly before leaving them to speak privately.

'I hope that wasn't too weird for you?' he asked. When Casey couldn't think of a how to respond, he added, 'The kiss with your sister, I mean.'

'It was a little odd watching the pair of you,' she admitted.

'I would have warned you,' he said, 'but it wasn't originally in the script that Jordi and I practised.'

'It wasn't?'

He shook his head. 'No. Tina and Martha had a chat earlier and came up with the idea. They thought it ended the scene better than me just putting an arm around her to comfort her.'

Casey recalled her thoughts about his manager a little earlier. 'Does Martha often come up with ideas like this one?'

Matteo frowned and gave her question some thought. 'Not really.' He gazed at Casey. 'I think it did add something though? Don't you?'

Casey would like to have said no, but she couldn't lie to him. She nodded. 'I do. I thought it was magical and that you and my sister were brilliant,' she said. 'In fact, you both looked breathtakingly beautiful.'

He beamed at her. 'You thought that? Really?'

'Yes.' Didn't he believe her? She locked eyes with his and spotted something she hadn't expected to see. A lack of confidence. Stunned, Casey tried to understand how someone as successful as Matteo could possibly have such an issue. 'Why? Didn't you think so?'

He folded his arms across his chest. 'Honestly, I never know what to think. It's only when other people react positively to a song or video that I'm able to relax and believe that it might be OK.'

'I'm surprised,' she admitted, quite liking that he wasn't as full of himself as she had assumed.

'Why?'

'Because it's not what I expected of someone who sells millions of records each year all around the world.'

'I guess it's because I always want to do my best for my fans. Sometimes it's difficult to know when your work is as good as you hope it is.'

'Well, I think this time you've definitely succeeded.' She thought of Tara's reaction. 'I liked it and I know Tara was bowled over.'

'She was?'

Casey laughed. 'Er, yes.' She smiled at him. 'She really was.'

'Thank you.'

'Matteo!'

Casey didn't look at Martha when she called Matteo's name and noticed that neither did he.

'I suppose I should get going,' he said eventually. 'I'll need to chat with her and Tina and see what we all think of everything we filmed today.' He hesitated and then leaned forward and kissed her cheek. 'I'll see you later at the reception?'

'Of course. I need to get home to freshen up and get ready for Vicki's wedding.'

He walked off and Casey went to her sister, who was now standing with Tara, a wide smile on her face.

'You were amazing,' Casey said, pulling Jordi into a hug. 'I saw Martha speaking with you. I presume she was happy too?'

'She was,' Jordi said, looking around her and then lowering her voice. 'In fact, she said she'd like to talk to me about possibly representing me.'

Casey and Tara gasped.

'Seriously?' Casey asked, thrilled for her sister. 'That's incredibly exciting.'

'It is, isn't it?' Jordi squealed. 'She said for me to have a think about it and she'll arrange for us to meet up and talk contracts soon, if I decided to accept that is.'

'You are so lucky,' Tara said. 'First you get to act with that gorgeous man, then you kiss him.' She giggled. 'Not once but twice, and now this. Everyone is going to be so jealous of you. I know I am.'

Jordi put her arm around Tara's shoulders. 'Unfortunately, not every job will entail kissing a man like Matteo.'

'Maybe not,' Casey said, wishing she didn't have the image whirring around in her brain. 'We're going to have to leave now. Do you want a lift home both of you?'

They nodded.

'Come along then. We'd better get a move on.'

As they left the room, Matteo reached out and briefly took Casey's hand, giving it a quick squeeze. The feel of his warm skin on hers made her smile.

'See you later,' he whispered, raising her hand and kissing the back of it.

She couldn't wait.

27

Rowena looked up when Casey and Jordi walked out to the back garden. She rested her sewing on her legs. 'Darling girl,' she said, waving for Jordi to go over to her. 'Turn around.' Jordi did as she asked and Rowena clutched her hands together on her chest. 'You look like a princess from a fairy tale. Doesn't she, Casey?'

'She does, Mum,' Casey agreed.

'Thank you.' Jordi beamed at them both. 'And it's all thanks to my wonderful big sister for suggesting me for the part in the first place. Mwah.' She grabbed Casey and, pressing her lips a little too roughly on Casey's cheek, kissed her.

'Ouch!' Casey pushed her sister away with a giggle. 'You might look like something from a fairy tale but you're still a ruffian.'

Jordi pulled her into a hug. 'I know, but I love you really.'

'Girls, stop messing about. I want to know how everything went.'

'You would have been so impressed with her, Mum. She was a natural.'

'Aww, thanks, Casey.' Jordi smiled. 'I'm so grateful for you suggesting me to Matteo. And look at all you've achieved with the recording and Vicki's wedding. You should be very proud of yourself for making everything so perfect. I know I'm proud of you.'

'Jordi's right,' Rowena said, smiling happily at Casey.

Casey bit her lower lip as emotion flooded through her. 'Thanks, Mum.'

'It's true. You're already so busy, but you managed to pull everyone together and make Matteo's video happen and Vicki's wedding will be utterly magical. You're amazing.'

Casey didn't know what to say. She shrugged and gave her mum and sister a tearful smile. 'Thank you both.' Clearing her throat and wanting to find out more about her sister's experience, Casey smiled. 'Tell us how you felt though, Jordi. I want to know more.'

Jordi clasped her hands together and gave Casey's question a little thought. 'It was scary but the most incredible experience. Matteo was lovely. He spoke to me before and reassured me that it would fine, and to try and enjoy it.'

'Did you do as he suggested?'

'Yes, as well as I could.' She clapped her hands together. 'And that's not all. I've got some super exciting news to tell you.'

'What?' Rowena clasped her hands together.

'Matteo's manager, Martha, has offered to represent me.'

Casey saw her mother's mouth open but then close again without her speaking. She smiled. 'Are you all right, Mum?'

Rowena shook her head and placing her sewing on the table next to her, stood silently before walking the few steps to Jordi and pulled her into a tight hug. 'I'm so thrilled for you.' She looked over Jordi's shoulder and caught Casey's eye. 'Both of you girls. You both work so hard at everything you do.'

'Thanks, Mum,' Jordi said. 'I should really go and change out of this dress. I have to give it back to Martha tomorrow, but I asked her if I could keep it on for a bit so you could see me wearing it.'

'That's very thoughtful of you, sweetheart. Thank you.'

Casey watched her sister go into the house. 'She really was incredibly good, Mum. I'm so pleased she's following her dreams.'

'As you are following yours,' Rowena said, patting the seat next to her for Casey to sit.

'You're both such hard-working, strong-minded and kind girls and I'm immensely proud of you. As is your dad.'

Casey hugged her mother. 'Thank you. We've been taught by the best. You and Dad have always instilled into us the enthusiasm to go for what we want.' It occurred to her how different she and her sister were with their ambitions. She supposed it was their differences that helped them get along so well. She noticed her mother was wearing an old cotton skirt and tee shirt. 'You are coming to the wedding, aren't you?'

Rowena nodded. 'I am. I wouldn't miss it for anything. I just wanted to finish a bit of sewing first and make the most of this sun for a bit longer before going inside and showering.'

Casey was glad to be sitting in one place for a short time too. 'Good idea.'

'I always wish we got more sun during the winter months but when it's the height of the summer season like now, I'm relieved we're blessed with this shade.' Rowena squinted up at the azure blue sky. 'I love these longer evenings.'

'I do, too.' Casey sighed.

'You all right, love?'

Casey's shoulders felt tight and she rotated them to try and ease them slightly. She realised her feet and back were aching.

'I'm a little tired,' she said, not wanting to tell her mother how shattered she truly felt. 'I'll be relieved when this is all over.'

Rowena rubbed Casey's back, as if knowing instinctively that it ached. 'You're nearly there now, sweetheart. Not much longer and everything will be back to normal.'

Casey forced a smile. She liked the thought of being back at work, running the stall with Tara. She was also looking forward to Vicki's wedding and being able to relax once Dan had turned up and said his vows to her friend. She wasn't looking forward to saying goodbye to Matteo. His world was so different to hers and it had been rather a whirlwind being caught up in it, but she sensed that she would miss the excitement and other-worldliness of it all when he was gone.

Rowena gave her a knowing smile. 'You'll be fine whatever happens.'

Casey was glad her mother had such confidence in her capabilities. She wished she had her mother's trust in her. 'I'm suppose I'm feeling a little overwhelmed about all this, to be honest.' She chewed the inside of her cheek and winced when it hurt.

'Stop that,' Rowena snapped. 'Look, you've done an incredible job pulling this all together in such a short space of time. Not only Matteo's video but also Vicki's wedding. Even if everything doesn't go exactly according to plan, everyone involved will still appreciate your sterling efforts.'

'It's not about being appreciated though, Mum.' She hated to think that anyone might assume that's why she had worked tirelessly to arrange everything.

'I know that.' Rowena finished her sewing and bit the thread from the edge of the hem. She folded the dress and pushed the needle into the cushioned lid of her sewing basket. 'What I mean is that whatever you achieve will have helped them.'

Casey was too tired to argue. 'Thanks, Mum.'

Rowena stood. 'Right, you'd better go and shower and wash your hair. You don't want to be late back to the castle for the wedding, now do you?'

'Don't even joke about it,' Casey said, forcing a smile as she stood. 'We still have the reception afterwards to get through before I'll relax properly.'

'You make sure you do. I want you to enjoy yourself at the barn tonight. Dance a bit. Have some fun. You're young and should enjoy these exciting occasions.'

Casey stilled.

'What's the matter?'

'Music.' She covered her mouth trying not to give in to panic. 'I've forgotten to arrange any music.'

'Can't someone take a record player,' Rowena frowned. 'Or one of those docking station things for a mobile phone. Surely someone has one of those.'

'For the barn?' Casey cried. 'I know it's a big place. Hell, what am I going to do at this short notice?'

'Can't one of your friends help?'

'Who?'

'Ask Jax. He's fairly resourceful. He must have a friend he can call on to help you out.'

Casey sighed. 'I'd agree with you ordinarily but he's the one who's making sure Dan gets to the wedding at the right time. I can't give him anything else to do, Mum.'

'How about Matteo?' Jordi bellowed.

They both looked up to where Jordi was leaning out of her bedroom window, a towel around her hair and one around her body. 'Sorry, my window was open and I heard you talking.'

Casey realised it was a great idea but she had already asked him to arrange a photographer and he was paying for the food and drink. 'No, I can't ask him for anything else.'

'Rubbish,' her mother scoffed. 'He probably won't even be the one to do the arranging. What's the harm in calling him and asking?'

Casey groaned. 'I'd really rather not. I feel like I'm taking advantage of him.'

'Nonsense,' her mother argued. 'You've helped him out and he's already said he's happy to cover any costs Vicki incurs with this wedding. All he can do is say no. What's the problem?'

'I suppose there isn't one, not really,' she admitted. Her mother was right, if Matteo didn't want to help then all he had to do was say no. 'Right, I'll go inside and call him, see what he says.'

Casey left her mother and went into the house. When she was alone she called Matteo's number and was surprised when he answered within a couple of seconds. She told him what had happened and that she needed music of some sort for the reception. 'I hate to ask you, especially after all that you've already done, but I've no idea who else might be able to help at this late stage.'

There was a short silence before he replied. 'Leave it with me,' he said confidently. 'I'll sort something out. Now promise me you won't worry.'

She sighed with relief. 'I promise.'

'Good. Now, you go to your friend's wedding and I'll see you later up at the barn.'

'Thanks, Matteo. I really appreciate you doing this for me.' She realised he hadn't mentioned going to the wedding himself. 'You're not going to the castle for the ceremony then?'

'No, I don't think I should.'

Casey stared at a fat bumblebee on its way to one of the flower borders. 'If it's because you don't know Vicki or Dan all that well please don't let that put you off. I'm sure both of them will be only too happy to have you there for their big moment.'

'It's not that I don't want to,' he said, 'but rather that I don't think I should attend.'

Now she was confused. Was this just an excuse not to go, or did he really feel he shouldn't be there? 'I see,' she said, not seeing at all.

'I really would like to go,' he said. 'It's just that I know from experience that if I did then the wedding would end up being about Matteo Stanford attending a wedding and not about the bride and groom. It's their day and the focus should be on them. Do you see what I'm saying?'

'When you say it like that, it does make sense.' Poor thing, she thought. 'You must have to miss out on quite a lot of things one way and another.'

He sighed.

'I do, but it's the downside of having a recognisable face. I can't really complain though. I have a lot of advantages too.'

'I suppose so.' She couldn't imagine having to think about people recognising her each time she wanted to go out. 'Did it come as a surprise to you?'

'What? The changes to my lifestyle, you mean?'

'Yes.'

'It did, but I'm used to it now. Mostly.' He gave a slight groan. 'The only time it bothers me is like today when I really would like to be with my friends. But mostly it bothers me when it affects the person I'm with.'

Her mood dipped. 'People like...'

'Like my mother, friends like Alex, a girl I'm out with, that sort of thing.'

'That must be difficult.'

'It can be.' He laughed. 'Anyway, I don't want you feeling sorry for me because it's not necessary. I'll sort out the music, so please don't give it another thought.'

Her heart swelled with affection for his thoughtfulness. 'Thank you, that's really sweet.'

'I have one stipulation,' he said, amusement clear in his voice.

'Go one then, what is it?'

'You have to promise to dance with me.'

Casey groaned loudly. 'I don't dance.'

'Why not?'

'Because I'm lousy at it. Is there anything else I can do instead?'

He didn't reply and it occurred to her what she had said. Mortified, she cringed. 'I didn't mean that.'

'What?'

Again, that amusement in his voice. 'You know what I meant.'

He laughed and Casey relaxed, enjoying their friendly banter. 'You just said you didn't mean it though.'

'You're becoming annoying now, Matteo Stanford,' she said, finding the funny side of their conversation.

'I know. And I don't care that you can't dance,' he laughed. 'Although I'm sure you can really, which is why I won't accept your refusal.'

'Seriously though...'

'No. Now you go and get to that wedding. I'll see you later like we agreed.'

'But, I didn't agree...' She realised he had ended the call. 'Bloody man,' she said through clenched teeth. She really didn't like dancing. Her sister was the artistic one when it came to dancing and singing and anything that might entertain people. She was always happy to be the one in the background, crafting and making something interesting with her hands. She thought of Vicki and how much the wedding was going to mean to her and closed her eyes, today wasn't about her.

She would simply have to shut up and dance with the infuriating man. It occurred to her that no one would be looking at her anyway because they would all be too focused on Matteo. The thought made her feel much better and she threw her phone onto her bed and walked to the bathroom to shower.

28

Casey arrived at the wedding in good time. Her sister had still been trying to choose what to wear when Casey was ready to leave and, not wanting to let Vicki down by being late, she left Jordi and her mum to follow along later when they were both ready.

'I can't wait to see Vicki's face, can you?' Tara asked as she and Casey entered the Medieval Great Hall.

They saw that someone had brought in benches and set them up in several rows. 'I'm glad there's somewhere for the guests to sit,' Casey said thoughtfully.

'That's a relief.' Tara nodded. 'I was assuming we'd all have to stand for the ceremony. Vicki's going to love this, don't you think?'

'I'm sure she will. I know I would,' Casey said, picturing her friend's arrival. The last few days' rollercoaster of emotions was catching up with her but she focused on what she needed to do next and determined that when everything was finished with she would give herself a day to relax, go for a long cliff-path walk and let all the feelings building up inside her go.

Tara nudged her. 'I can see you're in a world of your own right now,' she said, giving her a thoughtful look. 'Don't worry. Only four million candles to light and then snuff out before we can go to the reception and go crazy.'

Casey laughed. Tara wasn't far wrong. She looked around her at all their hard work and couldn't help thinking how beautiful the candles looked. Then a thought occurred to her. 'We'll have to come back here tomorrow and collect all these candles and mirrors though, won't we?'

'Eugh. I'd forgotten about clearing this lot away. It's going to be quite a big job, especially with all those damn steps.'

'It is.'

'I was hoping to have a chilled day tomorrow,' Tara grumbled.

'So was I,' Casey admitted. 'But we have to leave this room as we found it.'

Tara placed her hands on her hips and sighed deeply. 'We're going to have to ask Jax, Piper and Alex to help us carry them down to the car. Even with their help it's going to be exhausting.'

It was, Casey realised. 'We'll deserve a holiday after this ends.'

'Chance would be a fine thing, not with all the stock we're going to have to make now.'

They heard voices and Casey's phone vibrated. 'Piper,' she said, answering the call.

'Jax and Dan are here,' she said. 'They're having photos taken but I've told them to go right up to you. The celebrant is also on her way and should be with you before they are, so I reckon you have a few minutes before all those candles of yours need to be lit. See you soon.'

'Yup, thanks.' She pointed to the bag and Tara went to unzip it. 'We'll start lighting the candles so everything's ready. Let us know when Vicki arrives too, will you?'

'Will do. Good luck, girls.'

'Thanks.' Casey ended the call and turned to Tara. 'Action

stations. Dan and Jax are here so we'd better hurry and light these candles.'

Tara unzipped the bag and handed Casey two long lighters. Armed with two herself they began working their way through the arrangements, slowly lighting all the candles.

Tara only managed to burn her finger once and Casey twice; halfway through lighting them all, Casey's thumb ached from the repetition of pulling back the lighter key. She heard footsteps and the door opened and a woman in a smart dark grey suit entered.

'Hello, I'm Sadie,' the woman said, scanning the room. 'Crikey, this room looks beautiful. Is this your work?'

'It is,' Tara said as Casey battled with one of the lighters before realising it must be running out.

'You've done an incredible job. I've been to weddings in this room before and although they're always lovely this decoration is way beyond anything I've ever seen here.'

'Thank you,' Casey said, delighted. 'You must be the celebrant.'

'That's right.' She walked over to the dark oak table that had been set in front of the fireplace and opened her small briefcase, taking out what Casey presumed must be the register and marriage certificate.

Moments later, Casey heard muffled talking before the door opened and Dan and Jax entered. The three women watched as Dan scanned the room.

'Wow.' His eyes looked as if they were filling with tears. He cleared his throat. 'This is...' he hesitated, shaking his head '...out of this world. I've never seen anything so beautiful. I don't know how to thank you,' he said, his voice cracking with emotion. 'Vicki is going to love this.'

'We hope so,' Casey said, delighted to see his stunned reaction. Her shoulders relaxed slightly and she realised for the first time how tense they had been. Her mother was right: it was all going to be fine.

Dan went to speak to the celebrant and Jax joined Casey and Tara. 'If you have a spare one of those lighter thingies I can help you.'

'In the bag over there,' Tara said. 'Remember to start lighting from the back so you don't burn yourself.'

Casey stifled a giggle as Jax gave Tara a baffled look.

'I'm not totally hopeless.' He grinned.

Tara laughed. 'Sorry. I don't mean to insinuate that you are, I was only trying to be helpful.'

Shortly afterwards Casey heard voices coming ever closer as people made their way up towards the Medieval Great Hall. The guests were arriving and soon Vicki would too. She took a deep breath to try and remain calm.

'They're all lit,' Tara whispered, taking Jax's lighter from him. 'Thanks for your help, Jax.'

'My pleasure.'

Casey studied each arrangement.

She smiled at guests as they came in and indicated the rows of benches. She wanted them to congregate away from the fireplace and table so that the area was kept free for the wedding party and Sadie.

Her phone vibrated again. 'It's Piper,' she whispered to Tara after seeing her friend's name on the screen.

'Vicki's here,' Piper said. 'She looks so pretty, Casey.' There was a momentary silence. 'There's also a photographer coming up with her and her dad. He's been taking pictures of her and her guests arriving. We're all going to make our way up to the battlements now.'

'We're ready for her here,' Casey assured her. 'Dan and Jax are up here too and speaking with the celebrant.'

She heard Piper give an excited squeal. 'I'm so excited. Oh, and Alex is on his way up. Will you try to save a place for him and me so that I can join him when I get there?'

'Will do.'

Casey placed their bag with the lighters under one of the benches and told Tara what Piper had said. 'If you sit there and keep it free for the two of them, I'll leave a bit of space to keep it free for Mum and Jordi when they get here. Then we can all enjoy this together.'

Jordi and Rowena entered the room seconds later and looked around. Casey saw her sister whisper something to her mother, pointing at the window as she did. Casey presumed she must be describing the recording earlier. She waved. Her mother spotted her and, taking Jordi's arm, led her to sit on one of the benches.

Alex followed soon after and then Piper, a wide smile on her face. She scanned the room and, seeing Casey, joined the rest of them.

'It looks incredible in here,' Piper whispered. 'You've both done an amazing job.'

'Thank you,' Casey and Tara said in unison.

'Yes, darlings,' Rowena agreed. 'You've really pulled this off. It's like something from a film set.'

Jordi laughed. 'It is something from a film set, Mum,' she teased.

Vicki's older sister, Beth, entered the room. 'They're almost here,' she announced, clapping her hands together with excitement.

Casey saw Jax stare at Beth and for a few seconds he seemed to have been hypnotised. He couldn't look away from the beautiful woman, her strawberry blonde hair cascading over her right shoulder, who at thirty-three was a few years older than him.

Beth noticed him and gave a little wave, causing Jax's cheeks to redden under his tan.

'I can't believe it,' Casey whispered, leaning closer to Piper. 'I think your cousin has a crush on Vicki's sister, Beth.'

Piper looked at him and, just when Casey was wondering if she had imagined his stunned reaction, Piper nodded. 'I believe you're right.'

Casey leaned closer to Piper and kept her voice low. 'I haven't seen much of Beth since she came back to the island but she's always been lovely.'

'She has. It's such a shame about her husband dying so suddenly.'

'I know. Mum and I were shocked, and her little boy is only a toddler too. It's so sad.'

'It is.' She saw movement by the door. 'Ooh, look, here she comes.'

A hush descended on the room as Vicki entered on the arm of her father. Casey covered her mouth to silence a gasp. She stared at her friend, her pretty, large blue eyes wide and auburn hair loose around her bare shoulders, the sweetheart neckline of her white dress showing off her pale skin to perfection. She had a plain veil held in place with a small halo of tiny roses and greenery and Casey didn't think she had ever seen Vicki looking more beautiful or happier as her gaze fell upon Dan. Seeing his eyes fill ruined any hope Casey had of holding back her emotions. And when Dan reached out and took Vicki's hand in his and told her he loved her, Casey had to reach into her pocket for tissues.

The celebrant said something to Vicki and Dan then turned to address the guests. 'It's wonderful to see you all gathered here today to celebrate Vicki and Dan's wedding. Shall we begin the proceedings?'

The wedding passed in a beautiful haze and Casey loved every moment. Finally, her friend was married and by the looks on both the bride's and groom's faces as they kissed for the first time as a married couple, they were both extremely happy. It was an enormous relief.

As soon as the wedding party and guests had left, Jax, Alex and Piper helped Tara and Casey to extinguish all the candles. Then, satisfied that all were completely out, she followed everyone down the many steps for the group photos.

Unable to relax properly until she had checked that everything was ready for everyone's arrival at the barn, Casey went up to her mother. 'I'm going to leave now,' she told her mother and Jordi quietly as the photographer positioned Vicki in Dan's arms, making the most of Grouville Bay in the background before taking more photos. 'I need to check that everything is in order up at the barn. I don't want the bridal party arriving and finding something is amiss.'

'I'll come with you,' her mother said.

'Yes, me too,' Jordi added.

'Only if you're sure,' Casey said gratefully. 'I don't want you to miss anything here.'

'Don't be silly,' her mother said, linking arms with her. 'We can't have you doing everything by yourself. We're coming with you.'

Happy to have company and help in case something needed doing, Casey drove them the few minutes up to Trinity.

As Casey changed gears and slowed down behind a tractor she realised she didn't know what to expect when she got there. She knew the magnificent garlands were up and the seating made from hay bales had been arranged. She was happy with the top table but what about the food, the music and the general look of the place that Vicki and Dan would be greeted with when they arrived? She felt a little sick to think that she had so little time to change anything if it wasn't exactly as she hoped it to be.

'We're here,' her mother said, sounding excited. 'Ooh, look.'

Casey followed her mother's pointed finger to the large double front doors to the barn and gasped in delight. Nancy must have come back with more flowers because there was a beautiful garland that matched the two inside arranged around the doors.

'Nancy has certainly done Vicki proud,' Jordi said.

'Hasn't she just?' Casey exhaled sharply. 'Let's get inside, shall we?'

Casey got out of the car and took a calming breath. It was almost too late to change anything now, but she reminded herself of her mother's words: Vicki and Dan would be grateful for everything she had done to help. She pushed open the barn doors and walked in, bracing herself for what she was about to see.

It took Casey's mind a moment to process what was in front of her. The trestle tables were dressed in brilliant white tablecloths with crockery, glasses and white napkins wrapped around sets of cutlery. A small stage had been set up at the opposite end of the barn to the top table with a couple of amps on either side, a set of drums and microphones. Behind that there was another table with a laptop and a screen. Lanterns with small candles glowing inside them hung from various hooks around the walls and ceiling, giving the room a cosy glow. Casey thought it the most romantic reception room she had ever seen.

'The food is being kept cool in the refrigerated van outside,' Matteo said from behind her.

Casey spun around to face him. 'I didn't realise you were here,' she said, realising how much work he must have put in to find the people to do all this for the newly married couple.

'I'm not sure what to say.' She indicated the room. 'This is exquisite and I know it's all your doing.'

'Martha arranged the food,' he said.

'But I know you've been helping lay this out.'

He looked surprised and Casey indicated the lanterns he was holding in each hand.

'Ah, these. Well I could hardly stand by watching everyone else working, could I?'

He seemed embarrassed to have been caught out but she thought it the sweetest thing.

'Vicki will be so grateful to you for all you've done.'

He stared at her for a few seconds. 'I'm glad you think she'll be happy.'

Casey laughed. 'Happy? She'll be ecstatic.'

'You're so kind to do this for her.'

'I did this for you.'

'Me?' She gazed into his dark eyes, mesmerised. 'Really?' He nodded. *Why?* 'I don't know what to say,' she murmured.

'You don't need to say anything.'

'Matteo!'

They spun round at the sound of her mother's voice. Flustered, Casey tried to regain some composure as her mum and Jordi came to join them in the barn. *He did this for me?*

'Mrs Norman,' she heard Matteo say before her mother began exclaiming how beautiful the barn looked and how excited Jordi was to be offered representation.

'I'm glad everyone's happy,' he said. 'It's the least I could do for Vicki and I'm grateful to you, Jordi, for stepping in at the last minute and being so perfect in the part.' He smiled at Casey. 'And I'm extremely grateful to you for all that you've done for her and for me, Casey. I wanted to find a way to thank you and thought this might be a way to begin.'

'There's no need,' she said, embarrassed by his gratitude. 'I was happy to help in any way I could.'

'Don't be silly, sweetheart,' she heard her mother say. 'Matteo is right. He needed the venue to work out; Vicki needed to find a way for her wedding to come together and be paid for and thanks to your efforts, and of course to Tara's, that's what happened. Accept the thanks: you deserve them.'

'Thank you, Mrs Norman,' Matteo said nodding.

Her mother placed a hand on her chest, clearly flattered that he remembered her name. 'Please, call me Rowena.'

'Thank you, Rowena.' He gave her one of his bright, mesmerising smiles and Casey couldn't miss her mother's flushed reaction to him. He really did have a way with the ladies, she thought, amused. Then again, she was one of them, so maybe she shouldn't find it so amusing.

'Mum,' Casey said, feeling compelled to interrupt her mother's flow of words. 'He still has a couple of things to do.'

'What?'

'The lanterns.' Casey pointed to them and gave Matteo an apologetic smile. 'Everyone will be arriving soon.'

Jordi smiled at him coyly. 'This does all look amazing, Matteo.'

'Thank you, but it was very much a joint effort.' He looked at Casey. 'Wasn't it?'

Casey saw her mother watching her and waiting for her reaction. 'It was.' She smiled. 'We had a lot of helpers from The Cabbage Patch who helped clean this barn out and Nancy has done all the beautiful flowers.'

'Who's the band?' Jordi asked.

Matteo looked towards the stage. 'Martha found a local band she's been interested in for a while and they've agreed to come and play a set. Then there's a DJ for later. Another local guy that I've heard is excellent.'

'And will you sing?' Jordi asked, surprising Casey.

She wasn't sure if her sister should have asked, especially after all that Matteo had done for the wedding and clearly was still doing.

'Tara told me that Vicki was a fan so I thought I would sing a couple of songs at some point.'

'Oh, my days,' Jordi shrieked seemingly forgetting her shyness as she clapped her hands together and jumped up and down a couple of times, surprising Casey with her enthusiasm.

'I take it you think she might like that?' He seemed amused.

'Er, yes!'

'Good, then that's what I'll do.' He took Casey's hand in his. 'So, if you're happy with everything I'll go and tell the staff they can bring the rest into the barn and set it all up.'

'Is there anything you need us to do?' she asked him.

'Um, you could make sure the waiting staff start pouring the champagne so they're ready with trays to serve people if you like.'

'Will do.' Casey smiled at him, hoping he understood how much his thoughtfulness meant to her. 'You've been a star, Matteo. You really have.' Relieved, she looked around the room one more time. 'It does look pretty amazing, doesn't it?'

'So do you,' he said, a husky tone to his voice.

29

'How are you doing?' Matteo asked, walking over to Casey with two plates of food in his hands. 'I thought you could do with this.'

She looked at the plate of delicious food in front of her and took it. 'Thank you,' she said. At least now the speeches had been done and everyone was relaxed and seemed to be having fun. She lifted a mini quiche to her mouth and popped it in, closing her eyes as the delicious flavours reached her taste buds. 'This really is the most incredible food.'

'Is that the first thing you've eaten this evening?' he asked, narrowing his eyes thoughtfully.

Casey tried to think of the last thing she had eaten. 'Yes. Since breakfast, actually.' She shrugged. 'I hadn't realised I was hungry until now.'

He made himself comfortable next to her on the hay bale. 'I suppose you'll be glad to see the back of my lot when we go?'

She wouldn't and decided to say so. 'Actually, I'll miss you.'

'Even Martha?' He winked.

Casey giggled. 'Maybe not her so much. Although now my sister will more than likely be signing with her I might end up having to see her occasionally when I visit Jordi in London. She's moving there now.'

'What about me?'

She looked into his dark eyes, unable to miss the intensity of his question. She rarely let a man into her thoughts but this time was different. Everyone knew Matteo was about to leave Jersey and then the United Kingdom on a massive world tour. It wasn't as if she had much hope of ever seeing him again, however much she might dream of doing so.

'I'll especially miss you,' she admitted, unable to tear her gaze from his.

'Even after all the chaos of the past few days?' His eyes bored into hers.

She sighed. 'It has been a little chaotic and certainly exhausting but I'll always remember how it felt to step into your world, if only for a moment.'

'Fondly?'

'Sorry?' She wasn't sure what he meant.

'You said you'll always remember it, but I was wondering in what context.' He looked away from her finally and she realised he was unsure of her reaction. The revelation surprised her. Here he was, Matteo Stanford, with the world at his beck and call and he was concerned about how the last few days had made her feel.

'It's mostly been fascinating, also exciting at times.' She smiled in an effort to soften the words she was about to add. 'And sometimes upsetting.'

He turned to her. 'I want to apologise again about what Martha said that day in the pool.'

Casey didn't want him to feel badly. 'It's fine. You've already apologised. Anyway, it happened and was probably for the best if you think about it.'

Matteo frowned. 'Why would you think that?'

Did he not realise what it felt like to have a taste of his world, of him, only for it to be snatched away? 'Because there's no future for us, is there. Not really.' She took a deep breath, not relishing having such a conversation when others were nearby. 'Not when you're about to leave on a massive world tour. After I've cleared up at the castle and helped in here tomorrow, I'll be going back to work and carrying on as if all of this was a dream.'

'I... I don't know what to say.' He looked crestfallen, then, distracted for a moment, leaned forward and kissed her on the cheek. 'I can see a couple of the guys warming up over on the stage. I'd better go and do my set.'

She watched in stunned silence as he picked up his plate and walked away. Casey stared after him for a few seconds, crushed. She hadn't meant to upset him, but what was the point of lying? *Maybe I should have kept my mouth shut.* Her mother probably would have encouraged her to keep her thoughts to herself about the past few days, smile sweetly and say goodbye when the time came for Matteo and his entourage to leave. She wished she had said nothing, but she had done and now it was too late to take those words back.

She looked down at her plate, feeling slightly sick. Probably, she realised, because she hadn't eaten enough all day. Deciding not to waste the tasty food in front of her, Casey picked up a tiny fish goujon and ate it. Another delicious triumph.

Cheers filled the room, followed by enthusiastic shrieks from a couple of the younger guests. Casey looked up to see Matteo standing on the stage, a wide smile on his handsome face as he held the microphone with one hand.

'I would like to congratulate our hosts tonight, Vicki and Dan, and wish them both a very happy, healthy and fun future together.' A chorus of cheers rang out once again. 'I'd also like to dedicate my first song to them.'

Casey lowered her plate and watched enthralled as he began to sing his most recent hit, his deep voice sending thrills through her. He really deserved his superstar status, she decided, her heart aching for what would never be hers. She glanced at her plate and, as much as she hated to waste anything, knew she would be unable to swallow another morsel.

Hugging herself, she watched Matteo, her throat constricted by emotion. He was so gorgeous, and she now knew how thoughtful and kind he was too. Why wasn't he an ordinary man with an ordinary job like any one of her friends? It was such a cruel twist of fate to fall for a man who could never be hers. She watched him. He was so at ease on the stage, commanding the attention of everyone in the room, even older guests she assumed had probably never heard him sing before.

Casey noticed the Ecobichon sisters swaying to his song and smiled. Bless them, she thought. In their eighties at least and as enthralled by Matteo as she was. She sighed. Why was life so unfair sometimes?

His song finished and everyone clapped and cheered.

'More,' Tara bellowed.

'Yes, give us another one,' Piper yelled, clapping frantically and nudging Alex, who put his hands up either side of his mouth and cheered for his friend.

Matteo beamed at them all. 'Thank you all.' He put out his hands slowly lowering them to quieten the noise. 'We've brought in a brilliant local band for you, so I don't want to take up any of their time. After they've finished their set, DJ Silver will be playing any requests for the next few hours.'

'Sing another song,' Margery yelled.

'Yes, sing,' Dilys insisted.

Casey couldn't help giggling at their excitement and listened as Tara called for him to sing one more song.

'Just one more,' Matteo said. 'This song is my new Christmas record.' He cocked his head to one side and grinned. 'Not really the right theme for a summer wedding, but this will be the first time I sing it to a live audience, so an exclusive especially for you.' Guests cheered and once they had quietened, he continued, 'Some of you may know that we recorded the video for this song at Mont Orgueil Castle earlier today, thanks to Vicki's kindness.' Casey saw Vicki's cheeks redden and Dan bend to kiss her, his arm around her waist. 'When the video comes out you'll be able to see how incredible my leading lady, Jordi Norman, was in it.'

'Young Jordi?' Meg Ecobichon asked.

'Yes, dear,' Casey heard her mother reply. 'My daughter was splendid, I'm told.'

'She's certainly pretty,' Amy Ecobichon said.

'I'd like to dedicate this song to the woman who made today and this evening possible. Many of you here have helped prepare the barn as well as the castle, especially Tara, who I can see standing just here.' He gave Tara a slight bow and she gave a theatrical sigh, putting the back of her hand against her forehead making everyone laugh. 'But there's one woman especially who has made the past few days not only possible, but enjoyable and I want to dedicate this song to her. This is for Casey.'

The room fell silent for a few seconds and Casey felt at least fifty pairs of eyes turn to stare at her, before Tara and Jordi cheered and the rest of them turned back to watch Matteo, clapping and cheering. Casey stared at him, stunned. Had he just singled her out? Her eyes locked with his and a frisson of electricity passed between them. She had no idea what to do, or say, or even think.

Someone patted her on the back and another gave her hand a squeeze and she could hear people saying things to her from a distance as if she was in a plastic bubble.

He began to sing and the audience fell silent. Casey watched him transfixed for a few seconds until Jax led Beth to the middle of the dance floor, interrupting Casey's line of vision. She had rarely seen Jax dancing and it surprised her to see how good he was, if a little awkward. Lack of practice probably, she decided. Beth was gazing up at him through her eyelashes and Casey realised that the attraction between them was mutual. She spotted Phoebe walking to the barn door, stop and stare miserably at Jax and Beth for a moment then leave. Poor girl, Casey thought hating to see anyone looking so sad.

She heard Jax laughing and turned her attention back to him excited to see he seemed happy. Although Casey felt sorry for Phoebe, she was happy that Jax was having fun with someone. Beth was a lovely woman and although Casey didn't know her nearly as well as she did Vicki, she recalled Beth as being fun-loving and kind-hearted. She hoped this was the beginning of something happy for them both.

Matteo's deep voice continued with his song. She gazed at him, watching him singing. She had heard the song enough times that afternoon to almost know it by heart but she listened as he sang, his eyes never leaving her.

The song ended and Matteo bowed as everyone cheered and called out his name. Casey wasn't sure what to do. He had sung to her in front of most of the people she knew and it was a little too much to process. Casey heard him introduce the band and decided she needed time to think. She'd go outside, where she could be alone to make the most of the quiet summer evening.

As soon as Casey was outside, she leaned back against the wooden building and took a deep breath. The warm air filled with the scents of nearby nicotiana, night phlox and honeysuckle calmed her slightly and she closed her eyes to try and block out some of the music, chatter and laughter emanating from the barn. She was only slightly aware of the noise increasing momentarily but was distracted by the hoot of an owl in a nearby tree.

'There you are. I've been looking for you,' Matteo said quietly. 'Are you all right?'

She opened her eyes. 'Yes,' she said, attempting to sound more cheerful than she felt.

He walked over and stood in front of her, watching her. 'I'm sorry if I embarrassed you in there. I only meant to show you how much I appreciate what you've done for me.'

Is that all? He's grateful? She had hoped it might be something more, even if it could never amount to anything.

'I'm not embarrassed,' she said, fibbing. 'A little overwhelmed maybe.'

'I'm sorry.' His voice was quiet, almost a whisper.

She looked up into his eyes. 'Don't apologise. You've made a lot of people incredibly happy and I'm grateful to you for all that you've done to make this wedding so perfect.'

30

He studied her face and wondered if she had any idea how beautiful he found her. He doubted it.

'Did you want me for something?'

He leaned his shoulder against the wooden barn next to her, unable to take his gaze from her, trying to decide what to say next. 'I wanted to ask you for a dance.'

Light from the moon seemed to sparkle in Casey's eyes. 'Ah, yes... I'd almost forgotten the payment you insisted upon for sorting out the music.'

'Or maybe you'd hoped I'd be the one to forget?' he asked, enjoying their comfortable banter.

Casey placed her hands on her hips. 'You're telling me I have to go back inside to all that noisy excitement so you can have your dance?'

He pretended to think about what she had said. 'Not necessarily,' he said narrowing his eyes and smiling. 'We could dance out here instead if you'd rather.'

They both listened to the music for a couple of seconds. He

held out his hand for her and she looked at it before taking it in hers.

Happy that she had agreed to dance with him, Matteo stood upright and gently pulled her towards him, taking her in his arms and relishing being able to finally hold her close against him.

Casey smiled.

'What?' he asked, intrigued, as they moved slowly from side to side, not keeping to the beat of the music.

'I was thinking we could dance outside because we'd be able to hear the music but they're not playing a slow enough song.'

'Ah, so you noticed?'

'It's a little difficult to ignore.'

He heard the amusement in her voice and held her closer. 'Just close your eyes like I have and listen to the owls.'

She was quiet and he presumed she had done as he suggested and immediately relaxed, relishing the touch of her left hand in his right one and being able to rest his free hand lightly on her back as they swayed together.

It was a while before she rested her head against his chest. Matteo smiled to himself, happier than he had been for a very long time. He began humming a tune that had come into his head, sparked by the emotions that came from being alone with Casey. He felt her take a slow, deep breath before holding him closer to her and Matteo didn't think he could ever recall feeling as alive as he did right then. He was exactly where he was supposed to be.

His heart raced slightly and, desperate to kiss her, he lowered his head just as she lifted hers and pressed his lips against Casey's.

Casey responded to his kisses and Matteo knew that he was opening himself up to having his heart broken for the first time if this relationship didn't work out. He decided that he didn't care, that it would be worth it to fall in love with someone as amazing as Casey.

Aware that they were at a wedding reception and could be caught at any moment, he reluctantly moved away, smiling down at her, craving more but wanting to do the right thing by Casey. Her mother and sister were inside and he wouldn't want them to catch the two of them kissing.

But instead of Casey smiling back at him, she stepped closer and slipped one hand behind his neck and pulled him down for another kiss. Matteo's mouth drew back into a smile as his lips met hers.

'Wow,' he said minutes later, aware that if he hadn't already been lost then he certainly was now.

'I'm glad we decided to stay outside,' she said, smiling.

'So am I.'

They gazed at each other in silence, each lost in their own thoughts until Casey looked away.

'What's the matter?' Her eyes met his and he could see they were filled with sadness.

'I've just remembered that however incredible this evening is you'll be leaving the day after tomorrow and I've got to spend most of tomorrow clearing up at the castle, so there'll be very little time for us to see each other.' Her cheeks reddened. 'If you wanted to.'

Of course he wanted to. He stared at her, saddened to think that they had so little time left together, closing his eyes and wrapping his arms around her as she rested her head on his chest once more. He wanted to make the most of the sensation of Casey being wrapped in his arms, determined to find a way to make their mutual attraction work for both of them. He just wasn't sure how that could happen yet.

Needing to address the issue of their oncoming separation, he moved slightly away from her and, placing a finger under her chin, lifted it so she had to look at him. 'Talk to me, Casey.'

She sighed. 'I wish this evening didn't have to end.'

He hated the thought of being parted from her but was buoyed to know she was reluctant to leave him as he was to leave her. 'I know the timing isn't exactly perfect.' He kissed her again. 'But I will be back.'

She sighed heavily before looking up at him, a serious look on her face. 'I don't expect you to make any promises to return to the island.'

He was confused. 'Why ever not?'

He couldn't miss the sadness in her beautiful eyes.

'We have completely different lives, Matteo. That's something neither of us can deny. We've only spent a short time together and most of that has been surrounded by other people.' She shrugged. 'I don't think we should get ahead of ourselves because one of us will end up getting hurt.'

He took her gently by the shoulders. 'Casey, we don't know that we can't make this work,' he said, wanting to reassure her. 'I know that I'm not ready for what we have here to end so soon. Are you? Really ready for that?'

He watched her as she gave his question some thought and studied his face for a moment. Was she really going to push him away? He could tell she was mulling something over and was worried she might be about to make a decision that would devastate them both before she had given them a chance to make things work.

'Casey? Please tell me what you're thinking. We need to talk about this while we can.'

He heard voices getting louder and, unsure if some of them were going to walk out of the barn at any moment, knew he had to get her to open up to him before it was too late.

'Casey, talk to me.'

'Of course I'm not ready for that, Matteo,' she said. She grimaced and he guessed it was because she wasn't really ready to be so open with him about her feelings. 'But I can't see how someone like you with your busy life away for months at a time is even contemplating any sort of relationship with me. Unless it's a casual one and that really isn't what I'm looking for.'

Matteo winced. Her comment stung as painfully as if she'd slapped him. His arms fell from her and he stepped back, hurt. 'I'm sorry if I gave you that impression, Casey.' He folded his arms across his chest, his breath shortening at hearing her opinion of him. 'I know how the press like to report about the constant string of women in my life but I've explained how it's not like that. Not any more. I told you I'm not looking for anything casual either.'

He could tell she was struggling to continue with the conversation. 'That's good to know, but it doesn't take away the fact that our lives are completely different, does it?'

She was right, it didn't. 'I know, but that doesn't mean we can't try and find a way to sort this out.'

He noticed a flash of hope cross her face, but then disappear almost as fast. 'I just can't see how it could truly work.' She reached out and touched his forearm and Matteo looked down to where her skin connected with his. 'I'm sorry, Matteo. I didn't mean to insult you,' she said, her voice gentle. 'I suppose I see you with your management team and all your support and feel very much like the one who would be trailing behind.'

He looked her in the eye to try and gauge what she meant. 'I don't understand.'

She seemed to struggle as she decided how to reply. 'I'm just an ordinary person. I have my small artisan business and still live at home with my parents. You have this international, successful life, travelling a lot of the time. You have homes all over the place and a team of people to do your bidding.' She shrugged. 'Don't get me wrong, I'll never forget how brilliantly you worked with that team to make the wedding go so smoothly.' He opened his mouth to speak but she raised her hand to stop him. 'That's not the point I'm trying to make here though.'

Seeing she was becoming distressed and wanting to soothe her, Matteo took her hands in his. 'It's fine. I know what you mean,' he said understanding her viewpoint. 'Our lives are different but I've not had this life for so long that I've forgotten how it felt before, Casey. I know how it can seem from where you're standing but I'm no different to Alex. Not really. I want someone to spend time with, to love and to—' He exhaled sharply, frustrated when he heard voices closer to them, hoping no one left the barn until they had finished what each of them needed to say. 'I probably sound as if I'm feeling sorry for myself, which I promise you I'm not. I appreciate everything I have in my life and, to be honest with you, until I met you I thought I was content with it all.'

Casey's eyes widened. 'Seriously?'

The barn door sprang open and Matteo had to stifle a groan as singing and laughter spilled outside into the yard, closely followed by a line of merry people dancing a conga.

'Hey,' a male guest yelled, pointing at him. 'Look what we have here. Hey, there's that singer bloke you like, love!' he shouted over his shoulder to the woman gripping his waist. She was staring open-mouthed at Matteo and Casey standing together.

Matteo forced a smile and then took Casey's hand and led her around to the side of the barn. 'We can't talk here, not with all these people around.'

'I agree,' she said.

'Will you meet me tomorrow. Please, Casey.'

She frowned. 'I'd love to but I need to clear up at the castle in the morning with Tara.'

'Early then,' he suggested. 'Or later. When you've finished maybe.'

'Fine. I'll leave it to you to let me know when and where.'

Relieved, Matteo smiled. 'I think you're best placed to do that. I've no idea where a good place would be to meet.' He checked no one was around, pulled her into his arms and kissed her again.

'Fine,' she said afterwards, looking a little happier. 'I think I know just the place.'

'You do?' He grinned, happy to think he was able to see her the following day. 'Where?'

Casey tapped the side of her nose. 'You'll have to wait and see.'

'I can't persuade you to tell me now?'

She shook her head and laughed. 'No. You can kiss me again though.'

'Happily,' he replied, delighted with her response as he held her tightly and kissed her.

31

Casey woke early the following morning and immediately sent a text to Matteo.

I'll pick you up at 7 a.m. Bring your swim shorts.

She had no idea when he would wake and read her text and she was taking a chance that he might not see it until it was too late and she would need to collect Tara to go to the castle.

She left her room quietly and went to the bathroom to shower. She was stunned when she returned to her room to hear her phone ping with a text from Matteo.

I'll meet you outside the cottage. Looking forward to it. x

Casey laughed, happy to know he was as keen to spend time with her this morning as he had been at the reception the night before. She yawned, exhausted from the previous few days and her late night but had no intention of missing out on spending whatever time she could with him before he left.

She wasn't surprised to see Matteo standing waiting for her in the car park at the hotel, saving her the walk to his cottage.

'Good morning,' he said, beaming at her as he opened the passenger door and got inside her car. He leaned forward to kiss her. 'How are you after last night's reception?'

She waited for him to fasten his seatbelt trying to work out whether he meant their dancing together, what they had discussed, or the fact that they had kissed. 'I'm fine, thanks.' She turned the car and began their drive out to the south-west of the island.

'I'm looking forward to finding out where you're taking me this morning.'

Casey hoped he would like it. 'I thought we'd go somewhere away from here.'

'And where might that be?'

'We're going to Ouaisne.'

'Way Nay?'

She laughed. 'It's pronounced that way but written quite differently. We're going to the beach there so we can talk without being disturbed, hopefully.'

'Sounds interesting.'

Casey drove down the winding, narrow, tree-lined road, stopping every so often to let an oncoming car pass.

'I feel like we've gone back in time down here,' Matteo said. 'It's lovely.'

She thought so too. They passed the Smugglers Inn on their left and then drove as if to the slipway before turning right into the almost empty parking area.

They got out of the car and Casey locked it. 'Shall we go straight to the beach?'

Matteo joined her and, taking her hand in his, accompanied her to the slipway, stopping at the top to study the beach with its cliffs to the left and the open expanse of beach to their right beneath a high concrete wall. She led him onto the sand and began to walk along the beach. The tide was partially out and the sound of the breaking waves soothed her as it always did.

'What's that larger beach over there?' he asked.

'St Brelade's Bay. When the tide is out a little further you can walk around the cliffs to the other end of that beach, but it will be hours before that's possible today, I'm afraid.'

'No problem,' he said. 'I'm just happy to be here alone with you. We'll make sure to do that some time.'

'I'd like that.' She looked up at him and he gave her hand a gentle squeeze as he gazed into her eyes.

She slipped off her sandals, wanting to make the most of the sand beneath her feet.

They walked on in relaxed silence. Casey relished the warm sun on her face as they neared the rocks jutting out at the end of the bay.

'It's so peaceful down here. You're very lucky living on this island.'

'I know I am,' she said, breathing in the warm salty air. 'I'm grateful every day.'

'I would be too.'

Casey didn't like to spoil their peaceful walk but reminded herself it was the reason they had come out this way so early. She realised he must have been thinking the same thing because he gave her hand a gentle tug.

'Shall we go and sit at the bottom of the wall and have our chat?'

'Good idea.' She liked the thought of sitting still and gazing out to sea as they spoke.

Once seated on the soft warm sand, leaning back against the

warm concrete of the wall, Matteo drew up his knees and rested his hands on them.

'I don't know about you, but I feel that we have a deep connection.' He turned to her, waiting for her to answer.

'I agree,' she said honestly. There was no point in keeping her thoughts to herself, not if she truly wanted to see if there was a way forward for them as a couple. A couple. Her and Matteo. It seemed a little quick but both of them felt an intense attraction to the other and it wasn't as if there was a rule book for falling in love.

He smiled at her. 'Hearing you say that makes me so happy,' he said quietly before turning to stare back at the rolling waves. 'I want to find a way for us to be together. I know our lives are very different, but maybe that's not such a bad thing.'

'How do you work that out?' she asked, unsure that he would find a resolution to their problem.

'I know that for the next few months I'll mostly be away,' he said. 'But whenever I have a couple of days free, I could either send for you to fly out to meet me, or I'd come to London and meet you there. If I had more than a couple of days, I could come here.'

She frowned thoughtfully. 'You'd "send" for me?' She wasn't sure she liked the idea of being summoned.

She realised he was staring at her. He took her nearest hand in his and moved so he was facing her better. 'OK that probably didn't sound as I had intended it to. What I mean is that if you're not working, or Tara is able to cover for you at The Cabbage Patch—' he smiled cheekily at her '—and if you wanted to, then I'd send a jet for you.'

This sounded like something out of one of those American celebrity programmes. 'I'm not sure I'd be happy with you doing that.'

'Why not?'

It was all a little surreal trying to picture herself on a private jet. 'Because it must be incredibly expensive for one thing,' she said trying not to sound ungrateful. 'And it feels a bit alien to me.'

'What does?'

He genuinely didn't know, she thought. 'Having someone I barely know paying out a lot of money so I could travel in such a luxurious way.'

He shook his head and bent lower. 'But I would be doing it for me mostly, Casey. Don't you see that?'

She gave his words some thought. She raked the fingers of her free hand through the light sand next to her. 'Would you?'

'Yes, of course. If you fly to me then I would be able to see you even if I only have one or two free days. Obviously if I had longer I would come to you.' He pressed one hand on his chest. 'And it would only be while I was on tour.'

She could see how his suggestion made sense when he put it like that. 'I suppose that we would be able to get to know each other slowly that way.'

'Exactly.' He grinned at her. 'Although I already know how I feel about you.'

She cleared her throat. 'What about after your tour ends? What do you see us doing then?'

He was quiet for a few seconds, staring out to sea. Then he turned back to face her, his expression turned serious. 'I've asked Martha to look into applying for residential qualifications for me here.'

'What? Seriously?'

He nodded. 'I know Alex wants to move here, but he tells me that there are categories people have to fit into and there's an application process.'

'There is,' she said, aware that the qualifications to live on the island changed every so often. 'You used to have to live here twenty years to be given your qualifications, but I think it's ten years now, unless you are an essential worker, or married to a local resident.' Why did she say that? she wondered. 'Um, or a high-wealth resident, which is probably what you are, although I don't know. I was born here so it's not something I've needed to worry about.'

'It sounds very complicated.'

'It does.'

They sat in thoughtful silence for a while before he spoke again. 'Casey, I don't mind how you choose to do this, but I would love to spend time with you. I don't want to leave here tomorrow without knowing for certain that I'll be seeing you again.'

She smiled at him and reached up. She pulled his head down to her level so she could kiss him. 'I like that you feel that way,' she admitted.

'I'm so relieved. I hear myself talking to you and it doesn't even sound like me.' He cocked his head to one side. 'I mean, I've heard people say there's such a thing as love at first sight but I never believed it before I saw you for the first time.'

Casey opened her mouth to reply but couldn't think what to say she was so stunned.

'Casey? I don't mean to frighten you by telling you this,' he whispered, frowning. 'I'm sorry if I have. That really wasn't my intention.'

She eventually managed to shake her head, wanting to put him at ease but unable to find the right words. 'No. It's not that. I'm a little thrown by...' He did say he loved her, didn't he? 'That is, did you just say—'

'I love you,' he interrupted, his words rushed. 'Yes, I did. I do.' He looked downcast. 'I know it sounds a bit intense maybe? And if I wasn't leaving so soon I'm pretty sure I wouldn't be admitting how I feel, not this honestly, not after knowing you such a short time.' He shifted awkwardly. 'I hadn't meant to get this deep.'

'It's fine,' she said, realising that it was. 'How can I mind you telling me you love me, Matteo? It's lovely to hear you say such a thing, if a little unexpected.'

He sighed. 'Do you think you could ever feel the same way about me?' He gazed into her eyes and Casey knew she already felt the same way as he did about her.

It seemed strange admitting such feelings to someone she had only known for a few days, but if he had been open with her about his feelings then surely she owed him the same courtesy.

'I already do,' she said, a little elated when she saw joy in his eyes. 'And, if I'm honest, I would love to travel to see you. Although I'd only agree to go by private jet if it was absolutely necessary if we had very little time in which to see each other.' She grimaced. 'Listen to me. I sound as if I know what it's like to go on a private jet. I've never been on one, but I wouldn't mind giving it a go if it was to come and see you.'

'Thank you.' He leaned forward and took her in his arms, holding her close, and kissed her. Casey gave in to the moment, relishing every second in his arms with his perfect lips on hers. She was only vaguely aware of movement next to her and was trying to ignore it when she was nudged by something. Opening her eyes and turning, she came face to face with a damp, sandy Labrador, who seemed intent on investigating her and Matteo.

'Barney! Get here now!' a female voice bellowed.

Instead of doing what he was told, Barney prodded Matteo's neck with his wet nose.

Matteo laughed and gave the dog a hug. 'Hello there, Barney. Thanks for the kiss.' He turned to Casey and lowered his voice. 'I think you have competition.'

She smiled and reached out to stroke the happy dog's head as he wagged his tail, sending sand all about him. 'Hello, boy. Eugh.' She rubbed her hands together to rid them of the sand and noticed Matteo didn't seem to mind the dog nuzzling him again.

'I'm so sorry,' a young woman said marching up to them. 'Barney, leave that poor ma—' Casey saw the woman's mouth drop open and her eyes widen and then point to Matteo, seemingly lost for words. 'You're him.'

Casey wondered if this happened to Matteo often and presumed it must.

'Hi,' Matteo said, his voice calm as he patted Barney once again. 'Please don't worry. He's only come to say hello.'

'He's so naughty. Oh, I'm so embarrassed,' the woman eventually said. She seemed to notice Casey sitting there for the first time. 'Hi, I'm so sorry to interrupt you both.' She patted her thigh with her hand. 'Barney, here. Now!' The dog gave Matteo one last kiss and then walked back to his owner. 'Um, it was nice to meet you,' the woman said.

'Lovely to meet you too,' Matteo said. 'And Barney, of course.'

They watched the woman walk away, looking back over her shoulder a couple of times. Casey noticed she had taken her phone out of her pocket and seconds later quickly turned and took a photo before running down the beach with Barney following her.

'Maybe we should go back to Gorey and get some breakfast there,' she suggested. 'This is only a small beach and I can see more people coming down to the the slipway now and I doubt we'll have much chance of privacy.' She knew that most well-known residents were rarely bothered by the locals but his was a new face here and would probably cause some interest.

'Good idea,' he said, getting to his feet and reaching out to take her hand to help her up. 'I'm famished.'

She drove them back to the east of the island and parked her car at her parent's home. Taking his hand in hers, Casey led him to a café at the top of a slipway. 'Here's the place,' she said. 'We can grab something here and either eat it at one of the tables or take it back down to the beach.'

They ordered an egg and bacon baguette and a coffee each before walking down the slipway and sat on the beach.

'Now if I could start my day doing this every day I'd be very happy,' Matteo said before taking his first bite of his roll.

'Even I don't do that—' she smiled '—and I live across the road from here.'

He swallowed and gave her a questioning look. 'Why ever not?'

Casey thought for a moment. 'Probably because I don't give myself enough time before work to do something like this. Also, although this is a tasty treat, it's not something I would eat every day.'

He laughed. 'I suppose not. Nice to have the choice to do it though, don't you think?'

'Yes, I suppose it is.'

He laughed. 'You can tell you've always lived here. You're so used to this beautiful place with its grand castle up on the hill—' he indicated Mont Orgueil Castle standing proudly above the pier to their left '—the silvery blue expanse of the sea and this fine, white-gold sand.'

His voice had a dreamy, faraway tone and Casey realised that what he was saying was right. 'I do love living here,' she admitted, 'but I probably don't notice the beauty of it most days.'

He finished his baguette and wiped his fingers with the paper napkin they had been given.

She realised Matteo was staring at her and smiling. 'What?'

'Nothing.'

'No, tell me.'

'I was just thinking about how when I arrived I only expected to see Alex and be working the whole time, but meeting you and your friends and all the others around here has been a revelation.'

She had no idea what he was getting at. 'What do you mean?'

'Everyone is so nice.' He took a sip of his coffee.

'Nice?'

'Helpful, quick to step in and help others out. I mean, look at how everyone pulled together for Vicki's wedding. How all those people gave you back their candles so that you had enough for my shoot. There's a real sense of community here.'

'You must get that at home too?' She realised she had no idea where his home was. 'In fact, where is your home?'

He shrugged. 'I wouldn't say I really have a home right now.'

'You must live somewhere, surely?'

He drank more of his coffee. 'I have a base where I keep my things, if that's what you mean,' he answered thoughtfully. 'But I wouldn't call it a home, not really.' He went quiet and stared over at the couple who had now turned and were walking up the beach in their general direction. 'I haven't minded at all for the past few years. I've been so focused on writing songs, recording and touring that I haven't missed having somewhere I could really feel content.' He turned to her. 'Since meeting you and spending time here on this pretty island with its close-knit community it's made me aware of how much is missing from my life.' He rolled his eyes heavenward.

Casey found it difficult to hear how little contentment he enjoyed. Had she been wrong to assume he had everything? It seemed like she was. She supposed that the perfect photos of him having fun, meeting other celebrities and winning awards were all superficial and not what really mattered to someone, not deep down.

'Don't look so sad,' he said, resting his hand on hers.

'It is sad that you don't have a proper home. I suppose you haven't had much time to focus on that, have you?'

'Not really. I think I've felt so lucky to have the opportunities that have come to me in my professional life that I've let my personal life fall into the background. Now my trip here has shone a spotlight on the things I need to change about my life-style, I can focus on doing something about it.'

'I'm glad.'

'If I do manage to get my qualifications to move here, you can help me find a home. What do you think?'

She smiled. 'Now that I can help you with.'

'Good, then that's a date.' He crossed his fingers. 'If I'm lucky enough to be accepted.'

She laughed. 'By whom? Me, or the officials on the island?'

'Both.'

'You're really serious about applying to come and live here?' She studied his expression.

'One hundred per cent serious,' he said. 'You see...' He leaned forward and motioned for her to come closer. He lowered his voice. 'There's this Jersey girl I've fallen in love with.'

Casey's heart raced. He really did mean what he had said at Ouaisne, she realised.

'And I'm determined to do all I can to make her fall as much in love with me. I figure that if I live on the same island as she does then I'll have a far better chance of making her believe we should be together.'

Casey pressed her lips together, unsure how to react.

'Do you think I have a chance of persuading her?'

She stared into his eyes and knew that if she was ever going to be brave in a relationship then it should surely be with this gorgeous man. She motioned for him to move closer. 'Yes,' she said, excitement bubbling inside her. 'In fact something tells me you have a very good chance of persuading her.'

'I do?' She could see the delight in his eyes. 'How can you be so sure?'

'Because I think she's already falling in love with you.'

Before she had a chance to say anything further, Matteo pulled her into his arms and kissed her. 'Then I'm a very lucky man.'

ACKNOWLEDGMENTS

Firstly, my thanks to my son James's great friends, Casey Corrigan and Tara Henley, who kindly let me use their lovely first names for two of my characters in the Sunshine Island series. *A Secret Escape to Sunshine Island* is my Casey's story and Tara's story will be in a later book.

Also, grateful thanks to Jordi Sunier, my daughter Saskia's friend, who inspired me when I was writing the character for Casey's sister and who kindly let me use her beautiful first name for the actress in Matteo's music video.

To Tara Loder, my amazing editor, who helps make my books the best version of themselves; to copy-editor, Eleanor Leese for helping me sort out continuity issues; to Sandra Ferguson for proof-reading my book; and to the rest of the brilliant team at Boldwood Books and all the massively supportive Boldwood authors, thank you.

As always, I'd like to thank my family for their ongoing support and for making me step away from my writing occasionally to go out with them and be a bit sociable.

Finally, I'd like to thank you for choosing to read *A Secret Escape to Sunshine Island*. I hope you enjoyed spending time with Casey, Matteo and their friends.

AUTHOR LETTER

Dear Reader,

Thank you for choosing to read *A Secret Escape to Sunshine Island*. I hope you enjoyed Casey's story and fell in love with Matteo as I did when I wrote his character. As with *Finding Love on Sunshine Island*, Gorey Pier and the homes and businesses on it are real. I have used artistic licence for the Blue Haven Guest House, Nancy's Harbour Blooms where Vicki works, and Jax's mum Sheila's hair salon. Mont Orgueil Castle is high above the pier and is open for visitors to see the magnificent castle with all its fascinating history, including the Medieval Great Hall. From the castle you will have a perfect view of Gorey harbour and the golden expanse that is the Royal Bay of Grouville. Gorey Village, where Casey, Jordi and Rowena live is also real but The Cabbage Patch is imagined. Although, there are many beautiful farmhouses on the island with outbuildings that could pass for this place.

You can also visit Grantez headland which is owned by the National Trust for Jersey and see the incredible view through the pine trees over St Ouen's Bay mentioned in Chapter One. This is also the place where each year the Sunset Concerts are held over two nights and nearby you can visit one of several neolithic (4000–3250 BC) dolmens on the island, Dolmen du Monts Grantez. This was discovered in 1839 and when excavated in 1912 by the Société Jersiaise was found to contain various skeletons.

I hope you're enjoying the Sunshine Island series and visiting my home island. The next book in this series is Jax's story. I know Jax is already a firm favourite with readers of this series and I've been enjoying writing his story very much and look forward to bringing it to you after this book.

Until next time, I wish you long, sunny days and very warm wishes from Jersey.

Georgina x

MORE FROM GEORGINA TROY

We hope you enjoyed reading *A Secret Escape To Sunshine Island*. If you did, please leave a review.

If you'd like to gift a copy, this book is also available as an ebook, digital audio download and audiobook CD.

Sign up to Georgina Troy's mailing list for news, competitions and updates on future books.

https://bit.ly/GeorginaTroyNews

Explore more wonderful escapist fiction from Georgina Troy:

ABOUT THE AUTHOR

Georgina Troy writes bestselling uplifting romantic escapes and sets her novels on the island of Jersey where she was born and has lived for most of her life. She has done a twelve-book deal with Boldwood, including backlist titles, and the first book in her Sunshine Island series was published in May 2022.

Visit Georgina's website: https://deborahcarr.org/my-books/georgina-troy-books/

Follow Georgina on social media here:

facebook.com/GeorginaTroyAuthor

twitter.com/GeorginaTroy

instagram.com/ajerseywriter

bookbub.com/authors/georgina-troy

Boldw👁👁d

Boldwood Books is an award-winning fiction
publishing company seeking out the best
stories from around the world.

Find out more at www.boldwoodbooks.com

Join our reader community for brilliant books,
competitions and offers!

Follow us
@BoldwoodBooks
@BookandTonic

Sign up to our weekly
deals newsletter

https://bit.ly/BoldwoodBNewsletter

Printed in Great Britain
by Amazon

34755562R00172